THE WILLS OF JANE KANWHISTLE

Borgo Press Books by S. Fowler Wright

Arresting Delia: An Inspector Cleveland Classic Crime Novel

The Attic Murder: An Inspector Combridge and Mr. Jellipot Classic Crime Novel

The Bell Street Murders: An Inspector Combridge and Mr. Jellipot Classic Crime Novel

Black Widow: A Classic Crime Novel

The Capone Caper: Mr. Jellipot vs. the King of Crime: A Classic Crime Novel

Crime & Co.: An Inspector Cleveland Classic Crime Novel

Dawn: A Novel of Global Warming

Dead by Saturday: An Inspector Cleveland Classic Crime Novel

The End of the Mildew Gang: An Inspector Cauldron Classic Crime Novel (Mildew Gang #3)

Four Callers in Razor Street: An Inspector Combridge and Mr. Jellipot Classic Crime Novel

The Hanging of Constance Hillier: An Inspector Cleveland Classic Crime Novel

The Jordans Murder: An Inspector Combridge and Mr. Jellipot Classic Crime Novel

The King Against Anne Bickerton: A Classic Crime Novel

The Mildew Gang: An Inspector Cauldron Classic Crime Novel (Mildew Gang #1)

Murder in Bethnal Square: An Inspector Combridge and Mr. Jellipot Classic Crime Novel

The Police and the Public

Post-Mortem Evidence: An Inspector Combridge and Mr. Jellipot Classic Crime Novel

The Return of the Mildew Gang: An Inspector Cauldron Classic Crime Novel (Mildew Gang #2)

The Rissole Mystery: An Inspector Combridge and Mr. Jellipot Classic Crime Novel

The Screaming Lake: A Lost Race Novel

The Secret of the Screen: An Inspector Combridge and Mr. Jellipot Classic Crime Novel

Three Witnesses: A Classic Crime Novel

Too Much for Mr. Jellipot: An Inspector Combridge and Mr. Jellipot Classic Crime Novel

The Vengeance of Gwa: A Fantasy of Prehistory

Was Murder Done? A Classic Crime Novel

Who Murdered Reynard? A Classic Crime Novel

The Wills of Jane Kanwhistle: An Inspector Combridge and Mr. Jellipot Classic Crime Novel

With Cause Enough?: An Inspector Combridge and Mr. Jellipot Classic Crime Novel

THE WILLS OF JANE KANWHISTLE

AN INSPECTOR COMBRIDGE AND MR. JELLIPOT CLASSIC CRIME NOVEL

by

S. FOWLER WRIGHT

WRITING AS "SYDNEY FOWLER"

The Borgo Press
An Imprint of Wildside Press LLC

MMVIII

CONTENTS

CHAPTER I.

THE IMPLICATIONS OF A LAWYER'S LETTER

80A Basinghall St., E.C.2.

Dear Sir,

Re Jane Kanwhistle deceased.

In accordance with the instructions of my late client, I have to advise you that it has become my duty to communicate the terms of her will to those whom it may concern, and to request that you will attend at this office at 10:30 A.M., tomorrow, Wednesday, the 13th inst., for the above-mentioned purpose.

I am instructed to inform you that it may be of benefit to yourself to be present.

Yours faithfully,

E. E. Jellipot

Frederick Corder looked at his watch. It was now 9:35.

He looked across the breakfast table. "Addie," he said, "you might have let me have this a bit earlier."

"Yes, dear? It isn't anything serious, is it? I thought it was only about removing the typewriter, and we always get that about this time in the month."

"No, it isn't that. It's about Aunt Jane."

Adeline looked faintly interested. "She hasn't left you anything, has she? It would take more than a letter to make me believe that!"

She might have responded differently had her husband's tone sounded a more jubilant note, but his expression had not been that of a man to whom unexpected affluence had suddenly come.

"I don't know," he replied dubiously. "Perhaps it'll sound better to you than it does to me."

He handed over the letter.

She read it with brightening eyes. "I don't see," she commented, with her customary common sense, "how the terms of the will can concern you unless you benefit from it. If she's only left you an odd thousand or two, it will make a lot of difference to us."

"Yes—if! But you know what Aunt Jane was. I never had a penny from her, and when she borrowed five shillings, I don't believe her purse was any farther off than her own bag. She just did it in the hope that I hadn't got it to lend, or to make me a bit poorer. I suppose I can get that back now, if I make a fuss. I don't expect anything more."

"Well, I think there is. I think that's what the letter means. Anyway, you'll soon know. I'd better see whether your shoes are clean."

"I don't think I shall go. If she's left me anything, it will be a dose of rat poison more likely than not. You know she was about the most unpleasant joker you ever met."

"Anyway, there's a chance. Unpleasant people sometimes leave quite decent wills. You'd be silly not to find out."

"Yes, perhaps I should. But I don't want to sit there watching Percy grin. It isn't only what we know Aunt Jane was. There's something in the tone of that damned lawyer's letter I don't like."

Adeline passed this without denial. She had had a similar thought, which it had seemed inexpedient to mention. As the literary member of their marital and the value of words, and there were implications in the last paragraph which she did not like. The "may be of benefit" suggested a conditional rather than an absolute blessing, and even that the cautious lawyer did not support with his own assurance. He had been "instructed to inform." But, closely considered, this sentence did not bear directly upon the benefits accruing under the will so much as the presence of one of those "to whom it may concern," at a meeting which was due to be held in about forty minutes. It might be that Fred's absence would be fatal to the terms of the probable legacy, and that this short notice had been enjoined by the peculiar sense of humour in which Aunt Jane had specialised, as only a wealthy spinster may. Certainly Fred must be there.

She said aloud: "Well, we shall soon know. It'll be the quickest way on the tube."

She looked at the window of their fourth-floor Bloomsbury Street flat, against which the rain beat. She said: "You can't go in that old raincoat. I'll see whether Bill's taken his."

Frederick Corder made a gesture of protest, a half-articulate murmur, and he half rose from the breakfast table. But these abortive demonstrations ceased as Adeline disappeared through the door. He would much rather have gone in "that old raincoat" than borrowed on such an occasion from the flat below, but he recognised that the decision was not for him.

Ten minutes later he set out, with a black overcoat on his back (Bill Saxton's Fleet Street duties occupied him during the night hours, and it had been fine when he had left last evening), and with two minutes to spare, he arrived at Mr. Jellipot's office, and was promptly shown into the solicitor's private room.

CHAPTER II.

A Most Conditional Legacy

MR. JELLIPOT read the will. It was somewhat long, and Adeline might have criticised it for an excessive prolixity, but, having been drawn up by Mr. Jellipot himself, it was a document of legal clarity and soundness.

It was also, and perhaps unexpectedly, prosaic. But Mr. Jellipot was not a type of solicitor who would be likely to countenance a post-mortem joke. Mr. Corder, listening to it, was relieved, puzzled, disappointed of the vague hope which he had endeavoured to suppress, but which had refused to be entirely banished.

It left Miss Kanwhistle's whole estate to her dearly loved nephew, Percival Kanwhistle, subject only to the liability to pay somewhat numerous legacies and annuities under conditions set out with detailed particularity, and including some charitable bequests of liberal amount, but not such as to seriously impair a fortune which was not less than eighty thousand pounds, as Mr Jellipot's cautious estimate had allowed, even after due allowance had been made for the claims of a rapacious Government.

Mr. Percy Kanwhistle, the only other relative invited to hear the will, who had, at first, viewed his cousin's presence with a rather nervous hostility, fearing that it might portend some diminution in his own confidently anticipated inheritance, soon came to wear the complacent grin which Fred had prophesied would be on his face. Indeed, as the will proceeded to its conclusion, he looked at Fred with a puzzled wonder mingled with his customary contemptuous toleration, sharing his own speculation as to why he had been invited at all.

But Mr. Jellipot, after reading the concluding attestation with his usual punctilious respect for legal exactness, paused for no more than one impressive moment, and then said, with an added gravity of expression: "So much for the will as it was drawn up on my own advice in accordance with the instructions that I received. It has not been revoked, and its provisions stand"—the momentary blankness passed from Percy's countenance, and the grin resumed—"But there is a codicil of no legal validity, though it has the appearance of having been regularly signed and witnessed, of which I need scarcely say that I had no previous knowledge, and with which I should have declined to be associated under any circumstances. But I feel, with some hesitation, that it is best to communicate it to you two gentlemen, and to tender my advice thereon, if you should ask me to do so. The codicil is this:

I further direct that my nephew, Percival Kanwhistle aforesaid, shall pay the sum of ten thousand pounds to my nephew, Frederick Corder, now of 73A Bloomsbury Street, London, W.C.2, within thirteen calendar months of the date on which the said Percival Kanwhistle and the said Frederick Corder, having been summoned for that purpose by less than twenty-four hours' notice, shall be apprised together of the contents of this codicil; providing that the said Frederick Corder shall not fail to attend punctually to the said summons, and that he shall commit at least one legal crime, either felony or misdemeanour, on that day, and on each of the three hundred and sixty-four following days, of which crimes he shall supply a detailed list, with any evidences which may reasonably be required in confirmation thereof within seven days of the commission of the last of the said series of misdemeanours or felonies, to a solicitor to be mutually agreed between my said nephews; provided that in the event of the said Frederick Corder failing to attend the summons to the reading of this my will or either failing to regularly commit the full series of misdemeanours or felonies above provided or being convicted in any court of summary jurisdiction or committed for trial in relation to any one or more of the said series, then this codicil shall be absolutely void and of none effect; but providing also that if the said Frederick Corder shall fulfil the conditions herein set out and the said Percival Kanwhistle shall refuse or neglect for a period of two calendar months thereafter to pay over the said sum of ten thousand pounds, then the whole benefit of this will

11

shall pass to the London Institute for Physical Research of 47 Creech Street, London. N.W.7., as though their name had been substituted for that of the said Percival Kanwhistle throughout, and subject only to the same provision that they shall pay to the said Frederick Corder the said sum of ten thousand pounds. As witness, etc.

Mr. Jellipot read this lengthy codicil in an expressionless tone, and, having done so, paused silently, as though desiring to learn the reactions of the two young men most directly concerned.

Frederick Corder's face had flushed with mingled resentment and disappointment, as he realised the mockery which the dead woman had made of his reputation for somewhat timid observance of the laws of his native land. But he sat still, offering no comment upon it, while his cousin, leaning back with outstretched legs in Mr. Jellipot's most comfortable chair, broke the silence with: "And you tell us all that's bunkum, from end to end?"

"I should prefer," Mr. Jellipot replied, with his usual precision, "to put it with greater exactness, and in somewhat different phraseology, but your supposition is not materially inaccurate.

"The codicil, though not drafted with the full clarity which the law prefers, would yet be, in my opinion, of undoubted validity, but for the fact that it purports to encourage the commission of crime, and I must advise you that it is radically invalidated by that defect."

"Then we can just give it a miss?"

"You must, of course, both decide for yourselves the attitude you will adopt, and the actions, if any, which you will take upon it. It may occur to you, Mr. Kanwhistle"—Mr. Jellipot turned to the young man who was likely to be his more profitable client, and sank his voice to a pleasantly persuasive earnestness as he said this— "that the codicil, apart from its eccentric, and perhaps I may be allowed to add, reprehensible conditions, indicated with exactness the amount—the very moderate proportion—by which your late aunt desired that Mr. Corder should benefit from the estate. I am happy to be able to advise you that an unconditional and voluntary instruction to me that he should receive that sum, upon realisation, would be entirely legal, and, if I may say so, a happy method of dealing with the fantastic, if not impossible, condition which it sets out."

"Yes," Mr. Kanwhistle replied, with a suggestion of sarcasm in his voice which was not overlooked by either of his auditors, "I should say it would!"

"Do I gather," Mr. Jellipot asked, in a carefully expressionless voice, "that you approve the suggestion which I have made?"

"I should say not! I am going to do what the old lady wished, neither more nor less."

"You mean that if Mr. Corder should see his way to fulfil the condition imposed upon him—I need not say that I am neither advising nor contemplating such a possibility—you would make no difficulty about paying over the amount in due course?"

"No one ever said that Percival Kanwhistle wasn't a good sport. If Fred likes to sweat for it, there'll be the cash ready the day it's earned. He's got to commit three hundred and sixty-five crimes at the rate of one a day, and keep out of quod? That's what I understood. It ought to be worth that to watch!"

Mr. Kanwhistle's eyes, as he said this, met those of his angry cousin with a sardonic humour hard to endure. He added: "You needn't think you won't collect, if you romp in at the post. I don't mind Mr. Jellipot holding the stakes."

Mr. Jellipot, speaking with unusual emphasis, said that he must decline to undertake any such responsibility.

"Well," Percival replied, "that's for you to say. I only thought that he might make a better running if he saw that the cash was there."

Fred knew that his cousin meant what he said, in his mocking way, and that though he would not give him a single fiver of the inheritance from any sense of equity or goodwill; yet, if the condition should be fulfilled, he would no more refuse to pay because the codicil could not be legally enforced, than repudiate a betting debt on the same ground.

But the mocking tone, emphasising the previous mockery of the dead, angered him to such a point that, had the conditions been even a little less monstrous than they were, he would have accepted the challenge. As it was, it roused him, when he might otherwise have retired without further words from a place to which, apart from Adeline's urging, he would not have come, to hit back with the question: "I suppose the will's good?"

"Yes," Mr. Jellipot answered, without hesitation. "I'm afraid it is."

There was a note of finality and regret in this pronouncement which neither invited further questions nor encouraged hope that it might be upset. Mr. Corder rose. "I expect," he said, "you'll have other things to talk over, and, anyway, there's nothing more for me to hear." It was rather with the intention of leaving his cousin in a state of doubt than with any thought of undertaking a career of criminality that he added: "I don't know yet what I shall do. You can't expect me to decide without thinking it out."

"You haven't much time for that," Percival answered, with cheerful sarcasm. "You ought to be getting busy with the first crime."

CHAPTER III.

ADELINE STATES HER VIEWS

MR. FREDERICK CORDER, so shockingly incited to a life of unceasing crime, sat down to a modest tea shop lunch in Cheapside, with his thoughts still upon the mocking insult which he had received from his deceased relative, whose only grievance against him had been the inoffensive rectitude of his simple life. Was he really, he reflected, the spineless worm which he had appeared in that lady's eyes?

It was an unwelcome thought to one whose daily bread was earned by the designing of book jackets which usually depicted the lethal actions of stern-jawed men, or women with clothing missing or disarrayed, whose fingers pressed the trigger of fate, or who thrust remorseless daggers into the bodies of their would-be ravishers.

Was he really a spineless worm? Or, if not, how could he demonstrate his challenged manhood in refutation of this insult from one to whom the satisfaction of verbal reply was no longer possible?

Obviously, by fulfilling the conditions of the codicil and picking up the money. But that was not a reasonable proposition. He doubted whether there were so many as three hundred and sixty-five various offences in the whole code of criminality. He would have to repeat some distasteful crime with monotonous reiteration! Did the codicil allow that, or did it imply that he must wake each morning with the plan for a new manner of wrongdoing developed during the night?

So far as he could recollect the wording, that would not be necessary. He might steal a bun from the plate which the waitress had now deposited before him, and repeat that operation every day for the required period (unless the shop should be closed on Sundays), and so earn the reward. But without detection so many times? He thought not. Yet his mind strayed to think how much he could do with so large a sum. He might even make secret purchase of a publishing house. Without disclosing the unsuspected ownership, he could change its staff until he found men of real ability and discernment, who would prefer his book jackets on their merits, and accept Adeline's novels with judgment equally sure.

So he might dream; but what could he *really* do? His mind recurred to the thought to which he had given voice in Mr. Jellipot's office. Might it not be possible to contest the will?

He remembered that the lawyer's reception of that suggestion had been discouraging. But might that not having been owing to Percy's presence? Or even to the fact that the document had been drawn in his own office?

He recalled the proposal which Mr. Jellipot had made that the money should be paid unconditionally. That, at least, had been a gesture of kindliness in his direction. It encouraged him to the idea that he would give the solicitor a second visit. If he could state convincing reasons why it would be vain to challenge that eccentric document, well and good. If he should fail to do so, might it not be wise to take an independent opinion? He saw that, if the will could be upset, his position would be far better than if he should win the reward of a year of crime. He rose, paid his check, as law-abiding citizens are accustomed to do, and went back to Basinghall Street. He found that Mr. Jellipot was disengaged, and was shown without delay into his private office.

"I am pleased," the solicitor said at once, in his pleasantly diffident, almost apologetic manner, "that you have come back for a further talk, though I am afraid that I can do nothing which will be of material assistance to you.

"You will, I am sure, acquit me of any complicity in the codicil which may well seem to you to be evidence of an unbalanced mind; and you will perhaps believe that I only resolved to carry out the instructions of my late client, which, as I had not accepted them during her lifetime, I was under no obligation to undertake, through the hope that I might have become instrumental in arranging a happier settlement of the matter, as I have been unable to do."

"What I wanted to ask you," Mr. Corder, encouraged by this friendly reception, replied, "was whether, in your considered opinion, there is no possibility of contesting successfully a will which contains such condition. Even," he concluded shrewdly, "should there be no more than a doubtful chance, my cousin might prefer to settle for a moderate sum rather than contest an issue by which he might lose more."

"I had considered that aspect of the matter," Mr. Jellipot replied, "and was not surprised when you raised the question; but I am unable to advise you to entertain such a course of action.

"In the first place the will, which was of my own drafting, is dated two years earlier than the codicil, and even could you produce evidence that your aunt was *non compos mentis* at the date when she made the addition to which you naturally object, it would not affect the validity of the earlier document.

"I must add that I am satisfied in my own mind that she was of full testamentary capacity when the will was drawn. It is free from eccentricity of any kind, and even the codicil is evidence of a sardonic humour rather than any mental weakness. It could be argued that, as she could not have seriously supposed that you would attempt the fulfilment of its conditions, its wording should not be taken seriously, having no real intention, except to annoy one whom, from whatever reason, she did not like."

"Yes, I can see that. I dare say there aren't as many different crimes recognised by English law as there are days in the year, even though you might include murder and manslaughter, and a lot of others that no one would seriously consider in connexion with such a proposal."

Mr. Jellipot was not quick to reply. He was a respecter of English law. Emphatically, he was not going to be a party to any suggestion of fulfilling the codicil's terms. But he had a speculative, active, and ingenious mind, and he had given some idle thought to the subject. He was not merely unable to assent to Mr. Corder's proposition. He had arrived at the contrary conclusion that a total of three hundred and sixty-five separate misdemeanours would make little difference to the total of an English citizen's possible iniquities, even though he should prefer to avoid the more dangerous and repulsive, and even the more recondite crimes, such as marrying his grandmother or stealing a locomotive, for which the bylaws of the Great Western Railway Company provide an appropriate penalty, which, though relatively moderate, has proved sufficient to prevent this particular form of theft becoming widely popular.

He contented himself with a noncommittal reply that the offences recognised by a well-organised civilisation are somewhat numerous, and include delinquencies of great variety.

Mr. Corder, who was by no means a fool, recognised the restraint of the lawyer's words, and the idea came to his mind that the course of criminality which had been thrust before him might seem less impracticable to Mr. Jellipot's judgment than repellent to his moral code.

Perhaps for the first time, a doubt that the ten thousand pounds might not be utterly unattainable took shallow, uncertain root, and may explain the next enquiry which he addressed to the solicitor, with the obliquity which the subject required.

"It isn't only the absurdity of the idea in itself. It isn't easy to see how any proof would be possible. It's easy to imagine what you would say, as a law-respecting solicitor, if anyone should come to you to give your certificate, so to speak, that three hundred and sixty-five crimes had been committed with impunity, so that the amount due under the codicil could be properly claimed."

"The idea," Mr. Jellipot agreed, "is fundamentally foolish. But, approaching it as a strictly hypothetical question, if I should be informed of the wrongdoings of a client, under the customary obligations of professional secrecy, and providing that the retention of misappropriated property were not involved, and that the contingency of further delinquencies did not arise—"

He paused, leaving the sentence incomplete, and Mr. Corder, feeling that there was no further wisdom to be obtained in that office, and having no clear purpose in his own mind, remarked vaguely that it was a silly business, and that he was much obliged to Mr. Jellipot, shook hands, and departed. He remembered that he had now been several hours absent from home, and that Adeline would have some natural impatience to hear what he had to tell.

He reached Bloomsbury Street at about four, and found her laying tea for two in intelligent anticipation of his return, for it was a meal he would seldom miss. She had already decided that good news would have been more speedily brought, and a glance at his face confirmed her belief that there was none to hear. She said tactfully: "You'd better get your shoes off and return that overcoat, and then tell me while we have tea."

"Oh, it's soon told," he answered, with a sound instinct that the dramatic quality of the news would be reduced by a more gradual approach, "we're to have ten thousand pounds in a year from now, if I commit three hundred and sixty-five crimes."

"Ten thousand pounds! Well, that isn't so bad, though we could do with it a bit sooner than that. But don't stand there, dear, dropping water all over the floor. Perhaps you'd better dry the coat on the towel rail before you take it down. But be quick. Don't be ages washing; the tea's ready now."

Fred disappeared obediently into the bathroom, and Adeline turned her mind to pleasant anticipation of spending the substantial sum which was to be theirs in a year's time.

She had not taken her husband's statement literally. She supposed that Miss Kanwhistle had imposed some unpleasant condition, such as that Fred should engage in an uncongenial occupation. His aunt had always sneered at his obstinately patient efforts to make a living in the way he did. Well—poor Fred! Adeline, an affectionate and intelligent wife, knew how he would feel. He would have all the sympathy from her that the occasion required. A year of uncongenial drudgery—perhaps with the stipulation that he should not touch a pencil during that period. And every day, as he had graphically said, he would consider a crime. But, after all, a year is soon done! It did not enter her mind that Fred might be excused from fulfilling the condition which had been imposed upon him. Probably the poor dear had been wandering about in the rain all these hours trying to reconcile himself to what he would have the sense to see that he could not avoid.

She poured out the tea, tactfully took a rather burnt piece of toast for herself, put a better slice on her husband's plate, and prepared herself to give him her undivided attention as he came back into the room.

She listened with exemplary patience to his account of the morning's interview, and though realising that the proposition was not as simple as she had hoped, she still did not easily reconcile herself to resigning the substantial legacy.

"When you say crimes," she remarked, "you don't mean really serious things, not that do anyone any harm. You mean anything that's against the law."

"Yes. That's about how I understand it."

"There mayn't be quite as much in it as it sounds," she said optimistically. "I dare say most of us break a law most days, more likely than not."

"We don't do it for twelve months, without missing a day."

"No. But if you set your mind to it, you might find it would be easy enough."

"Think so? I don't. And just about the last day I might get caught, and blue the whole thing."

"You mean you might get locked up, and the crime business would have to stop? But I don't see why it should. You could break a mug, or whatever they give you there."

"I don't mean that. Though if I went on that way, I expect I should end in a straightjacket or a padded cell, and what could I do then? Probably there'd be nothing left but suicide on the last day. I believe that's a legal crime, though it always seems to me the best day's work that some people would ever be able to do. But I wasn't thinking of doing crimes in a jail. I meant that, if I get caught, it's all off. That's one of the conditions."

"You hadn't told me that before. What a dirty pig your aunt must have been."

Fred observed with some satisfaction that Adeline took this last snag very seriously. He had not liked some of her previous remarks, which had seemed to contemplate his prospective criminality with a levity which he could not share.

Indeed, up to that point, angry as she was at the obstacle which Miss Kanwhistle had erected between her nephew and the coveted legacy, she had had a certain amount of sympathy with the old lady's attitude. She did not regard her husband (of whom she was genuinely fond) as a spineless worm, but she was aware that he had a reputation for rectitude which might irritate an unholy mind.

But now her thoughts strayed to the idea which his vision of final suicide had suggested. Under such—indeed, under any circumstances—would Percival pay an amount which she saw would be impossible to recover by legal process? But on this point Fred gave her a reluctant assurance. If he should run the course, he felt that the reward was sure. But, he said what an "if"!

Adeline was beginning to feel the same. If a conviction would cancel the legacy, she saw the unpleasant possibility of much onerous amateur criminality ending in disgrace, such as, should the tale become known, would bring derision upon her husband, if not contempt, with no golden consolation to follow. "I shouldn't like," she said, "to hear Percival laugh."

"He couldn't do that if we just leave it alone, which is the only sensible thing to do."

"He wouldn't laugh if he had to pay over the cash."

"There isn't much chance of that."

"There won't be any unless we get busy before midnight. I'll tell you what, Fred. I want to think this out quietly, and while I'm doing it you'd better make a list of all the crimes you can think of. They might give us some bright ideas."

She went to the mantelpiece and lighted a cigarette, and as she did this Fred shivered with a premonition of doom, for Adeline never smoked during the day.

But he went obediently to the bureau, fetched out unused memorandum book, headed the pages methodically with the letters of the alphabet, and began to enter the crimes that came first to his particularly innocent mind.

For the next twenty minutes there was silence, broken only by an explanation from Adeline: "I wish it hadn't been the thirteenth! It seems rather like hitting below the belt."

But Fred made no reply. He was commencing the page dedicated to "T" with Treason, which he felt to have vaguely better possibilities than Stealing Locomotives, with which he had decorated the opposite page. Adeline, having made her protest against the date, lit a third cigarette from the second, and relapsed into silent thought.

She put the ashes of the third cigarette into the ashtray as she said: "I suppose it wouldn't matter if you got convicted after the year was up, so long as you keep clear for that time?"

"No, I don't know that it would. Not after I'd got the money. I suppose not. Why do you ask that?"

"Only that it sets a time limit. It's nice to feel that, if we once got our hands on it, we shouldn't have to cough it up, whatever happened afterwards. I think it may turn out to be rather fun."

"You don't really mean—?"

"I think there'll be plenty left for Percy after he's handed over what's coming to us. But let's look at your index of crimes. You ought to have got some good ideas all the time you've been writing there." Fred passed over the book. The pages consecrated to the first two letters of the alphabet lay open before her. She read *Arson— Bigamy*. She frowned over the latter word. She had not supposed that Fred had such a deplorable mind. "I don't think," she said coldly, "that you'll need that." She turned further pages. "You seem," she said, "to be thinking of going into the crime business in quite a large way."

She put the book down, and became thoughtful again. "Fred," she said surprisingly, "now the rain's stopped, I wish you'd go to the two-penny library in New Oxford Street, and get me a copy of Reggie's *Wantons Don't Starve*. I know there's one there. I saw it yesterday. But if it's out, go on to another library. I want that book particularly. It'll be three pence, being a new one."

"I thought you said Hardwick's books were all tripe."

"So they are, but I want this."

Glad that he was not being sent on a less innocent errand, he went out in the fawn raincoat which had been considered unfit for the morning ceremony, and procured the book without difficulty.

Adeline looked at it with disfavour. "You didn't," she asked anxiously, "have to pay a deposit upon it?"

"No, they know us too well for that."

"Very well. Then if you tear it up, it will be a crime. I expect they could prosecute you if they saw you do it. That ought to be good enough. But as they won't, all they'll be able to do is to sue for what it's worth, and they may never trouble to do that."

"You want me to tear it up?"

"Yes. You can't burn it. That's the worst of having nothing but gas fires. But we can always rob one of the meters if it's getting late, and we're hard up for an idea."

Overborne by a more resolute will, and feeling that the event was in better hands than his own, Fred proceeded without further words to tear up the work which his wife disliked, and to drop the fragments into the wastepaper basket.

While he did so, Adeline got out the book in which she had intended to write the later portion of the novel *More Jam for Jane* on which she was now engaged. She had resolved to put it to a more profitable, if not to a better use.

Neatly, she entered the date, and the particulars of the crime. She ruled a column for Fred to initial the entry, and another for herself as witness. She intended to have that record complete, orderly, and convincing to Mr. Jellipot's legal mind, when the year should end. Under her watchful care, Fred should not be jailed, nor Percival allowed to escape. As she did so, she heard the cover of *Wantons Don't Starve* rip. The year of crime had begun.

CHAPTER IV.

Two More from the List

HAVING completed the destruction of Reggie Hardwick's masterpiece, Fred returned to his laborious compilation of a schedule of prospective crimes. It may have been the subtle influence of the lurid book jackets on which his imagination was habitually exercised which inclined him to recollection of the major iniquities of civilised or semi-civilised men, rather than the myriad misdemeanours known to, or even created by, English law.

Yet, as the catalogue increased in length, it was inevitable that it should diminish in average seriousness, and contain a larger proportion of more feasible wrongdoings. Adeline, looking over his shoulder, observed him to enter *Sleeping-out* under the less practical suggestion of purloining a substantial item of the Great Western Railway Co.'s property.

"I think," he said hopefully, "that that might be rather a good idea for a summer night."

"You're sure that it is a crime?"

"Yes. I've read about people being sent to jail for it, though I've never understood why."

"That's when they've no visible means of support."

"So that I should have to be careful not to take a walking stick with me?"

"Don't try to joke. It's too serious. It sounds to me the kind of thing you might get caught at, and spoil everything. But, of course," she added more hopefully, "I might keep watch, and give you warning to run away. The worst objection would be that you couldn't be sure that you'd go off.

"Fancy lying awake at eleven-fifty-five, knowing that if you weren't asleep within five minutes it would cost you ten thousand pounds! Unless, of course, the law says it's sleeping-out to lie awake under a hedge."

"It probably does. It's just the sort of thing that it would. In twelve months' time, we ought to know a lot more law than we do now. I shouldn't wonder if I could get a job by then in Mr. Jellipot's office.

"I suppose it won't do for tomorrow if I lift one of Bill's ideas for a jacket for *Dead Man's Revenge*? I saw something on his desk last night that would just do."

"I shouldn't risk it. Laws don't have much concern with things that are really wrong. They're more concerned with stopping what decent people are likely to do."

Fred did not reply. He had just thought of hawking without a licence. Simple. Brief. Surely the law would be broken sufficiently by a single hawk? He scribbled in haste, lest an idea of such value should be lost, and as he did it his spirits rose. In imagination, he was surrounded by a forest of brittle laws. They snapped around him like rotten wood. With this optimistic vision, he went to bed.

Next morning, the conversation was resumed upon waking, for the lawless enterprise on which they had entered obsessed their minds. Tactful as ever, and convinced of her superior discretion, Adeline proposed that the programmes of evil-doing should be her department, and only (and inevitably) the execution his.

She did not crudely suggest her own superiority. She emphasised anxiety to help, even though, as she allowed, it could be in no more than a subordinate rôle. The firing line would be his. It would be her part to do no more than to plan, to propose, to watch. Fred accepted this allocation without demur. He was not jealous of the responsibility which she assumed. Rather, he was secretly content, both with the assistance she offered, and the support of a spirit more resolute and buoyant than he possessed.

It was not until breakfast was nearly over that he learnt, with some relief, the simple nature of his second venture upon the slippery path of dishonesty.

"You're going to the Bleech Publishing Company this morning, aren't you?" Adeline asked.

"Yes. I'm taking half a dozen rough sketches for the jacket of Hotbottle's new novel. Hotbottle's to be there himself. He always likes a voice in choosing his own jackets."

"You'd be likely to be left alone in the top office, if you get there much before time?"

"Yes. I can, anyway, if I want to. I've got a lot of drawings there. I could say I was sorting some out to bring away."

"You could pick up something in the office that isn't yours, and bring it away just as easily?"

"Yes, of course. If you could call that a crime. They wouldn't make any fuss, if they saw me do it. They'd only think it was a mistake. They've known me too long."

"It would be theft, all the same."

"Not if they saw me do it, and didn't object."

"Well, that depends. But they mustn't see you. We've got to have three hundred and sixty-five hundred percent cast-iron crimes. Have you worked out how that number goes into ten thousand?"

"Not exactly. You know how I hate figures."

"Well, I have. I did it when I waked in the night. It's either twenty-seven or twenty-eight. I couldn't quite make out which, doing it all in my head. Say twenty-seven pounds, ten shillings a day. It's worthwhile being careful for that."

It was an argument with which Fred had no disposition to disagree. His thoughts settled upon a ruler which had lain on the desk of that upper office, unused, as far as he knew, for the nine years during which the Bleech Publishing Co. had had the assistance of his facile pencil. He knew that, if the directors of the firm should see him bearing it away, they would not raise their voices to call him back.

But it must be worth at least a shilling. More probably two. He remembered vaguely having read that, in an earlier century, it had been a capital offence to steal anything of greater value than a shilling (or was it ten pence?), and though he had no fear that he would be led by this petty larceny to the hangman's noose, the memory sufficed to dismiss any remaining doubt that he would fulfil the requirements of the codicil when he should remove the ruler from the custody of its legal owners. With this purpose he set out, and opportunity became his, as he had foreseen. But he did not bear the ruler away.

When he returned home for tea, he pulled out of his pocket a fountain pen. It was of good make, with a gold nib of superior quality. It was certainly worth much more than a shilling.

He looked at it with satisfaction rather than shame.

"This," he said, "is Mr. Hotbottle's pen."

Adeline's brows contracted slightly. "He won't guess that you've got it?"

"No, how should he? I saw him drop it, going down the stairs, and waited a moment to see whether he'd come back, before picking it up."

But Adeline still looked serious. She knew that Fred disliked Mr. Hotbottle, as she disliked Reggie Hardwick. Probably more. Suppose Fred were to get out of hand?

25

She made remarks of some abstract wisdom concerning the necessity of subduing emotional impulses in business matters, to which he assented readily, but without appearing to give them the full attention which they deserved.

He was considering another difficulty. What was to be done with the pen?

"I can't carry it about," he said. "I might pull it out where Hotbottle would see it. You know what my memory is."

"No, of course not. We shall have to put things like that on one side till the year's over."

"We might get quite a lot."

"I've been thinking of that. We shall need a cache. But you'd better leave that to me. If any one gets into trouble, it will be you, and it may be just as well that you shouldn't know where everything is."

Fred made no objection to that, and Adeline went on to the subject of the next day's crime.

In the course of her researches at the British Museum necessitated by the writing of *More Jam for Jane*, she had come, that morning, upon the curious information that though it is no legal offence for a woman to parade the public streets in male attire, the law exacts a higher standard of propriety for men, and inflicts penalties upon them if they are found wandering in a woman's skirts.

Here, she had instantly seen, was a crime which could be committed easily, quickly, and safely, and would provide something of the variety which would ensure that poor Fred would not become weary of ill-doing before the total would be complete.

"You can change into some of my things, and I will go into the street first, and give a signal when I am sure that no cops are about, and you can just walk up and down a few yards, and run in again if you see anyone coming. If it's after twelve, it will do for tomorrow's crime, and you can have the day free."

"I don't see why we shouldn't do that every evening and save trouble in other ways."

"Fred, dear, I've often heard you say silly things, but never anything much sillier than that. A thing may be safe once, but if you make a practice of it, it's an absolutely different matter. That applies to almost anything, but particularly to this. If you were to take to running out every night with my things on, it would be certain to be observed before long, and very likely someone would hide and watch. If you were doing that, I'd be glad to sell the whole ten thousand for two pounds ten, and think I'd got the best of the deal."

"All right, Addie. You win."

Feeling that she had the situation well in hand, Adeline got out the book which was to be at once a warrant for the drawing of £10,000, and a record of evil courses probably unequalled for variety, persistence, and regularity in the history of the civilised world, and had the second item entered, signed, and witnessed by herself as having inspected the stolen pen.

At about twenty minutes before midnight, they went into the bedroom together, and Fred adventured what he had supposed would be the swift and easy process of putting on his wife's clothes. Half an hour later he knew more.

The ordeal was not simplified by Adeline's insistence that the change should be most thoroughly made. She said, with reason, that the law could not descend with penal force upon a man who wore no more feminine attire than a shoe, a scarf, or a glove. Probably (though here she admitted less certainly) not a hat. With the degree of completeness doubtful, there could be no absolute surety apart from an entire change.

But a woman's stockings are still articles of feminine attire, even though they may split halfway down (not to speak of the foot), as in fact they did. But the ankles remained sound, and they were (need it be said?) an old pair.

"I never noticed that you had such slim ankles," Adeline remarked sweetly to a gratified Fred, whose temper, by this time, was in a dangerously inflammable condition. "They're all right really. The suspenders will hold them up. There's no reason that you shouldn't dress as a beggar maid."

It was far past midnight when Adeline went out to an empty street, while Fred lurked behind the half-opened street door, praying that his guardian angel might not be too disgusted by his recent conduct to protect him from being seen by any occupant of the other flats.

But nothing happened. After a cautious patrol of the pavement, Adeline called him to come forth. He emerged for a few yards, and ran hastily back to cover.

Adeline followed him in. "You're sure," she asked, "that that bit was enough?"

"It's got to be," he answered, with more emphasis than he could usually command. "I felt something burst at the back."

He went to sleep that night with the pleasant consciousness that he could go through the coming day "wearing the white flower of a blameless life," and that he had surmounted the third step of the long and difficult stair which Miss Kanwhistle's malign humour had invited him to ascend.

CHAPTER V.

Adeline Studies Crime

ADELINE spent the greater part of the following morning in the reading room of the British Museum improving her knowledge of English criminal law.

It cannot be said that she had any reason for disappointment in the number or variety of offences which it recognises, and for which it imposes penalties sufficient to bring them within the conditions the codicil required. But she observed that a very large proportion of them were such as Fred was not eligible to commit, either age, or sex, or occupation shutting him out from graduation in the full chorus of English crime.

She learnt for the first time that, under the Poor Law Assessment Act of 1869, it is a criminal offence to omit a ratepayer's name from the rating list, but this is a form of wickedness only possible to rating officials; she observed other classes of turpitude which, while not impossible, would require much preliminary preparation, particularly if they were to be committed with the necessary impunity. Such, for instance, was the impersonating of seamen in the endeavour to collect their pay, for which the Admiralty Act of 1865 provides six months' hard labour for those who adventure it in a blundering manner. Fred could not desert from the Royal Navy, neither had he any facilities for refusing to weigh bread.

There was another category, almost equally large, of offences which she felt sure that Fred would not consent to perpetrate, even should she be willing to incite him thereto; for she could not fail to observe that the law, although primarily concerned in less defensible interferences with human liberty, prohibits many things which are personally degrading, and even morally wrong. A man of unvarying sobriety is naturally unwilling to be drunk in a public place, and the occupation of a "fraudulent displayer of wounds" is not one which most designers of book jackets would desire to enter.

A third category must be ruled out as too likely to lead to the prosecution which would make the cost of the enterprise so much heavier, while rendering it barren of the gain which it was intended to reach. The risk of keeping a lottery was evident even to her inexperienced judgment, while to undertake the role of a refractory pauper would be to make disaster sure.

She gave more optimistic consideration to the fact, of which she had been ignorant previously, that it is a criminal offence to be in possession of more than five counterfeit foreign coins. It had the aspect of a singularly innocent form of wrongdoing, and one which could be practised with the reticence which the occasion required. She even had a passing thought that the conditions of the codicil might be fulfilled by a continuous retention of the worthless coinage. Would it not be a fresh daily crime every twenty-four hours that Fred should walk abroad with the six lawless metal discs in a hip pocket which might be stitched up to avoid the inadvertent publicity which his absent-minded methods would otherwise be too likely to give?

But she put this speculation from her mind as she recollected that Percival would be the sole judge, with no possibility of appeal against his decision. She intended that the required conditions should be observed beyond possibility of cavil. And, besides, how could more than five counterfeit foreign coins be obtained? The difficulties in the way of a would-be criminal were not easy to overcome.

Yet, when she surveyed the sum of her morning's work, she could not complain of an empty net.

The Larceny Act of 1861 had been replete with the most useful hints, as, in less variety, had the Profane Oaths Act of the previous century. There were possibilities in unlicensed peddling. Fred might damage trees, shrubs, plants, and telegraph posts with the good hope that his nefarious activities would escape the notice of the police: he might kill hares in warrens, or pigeons under a variety of unlawful circumstances. Fishing in private waters during daytime might be arranged with a reasonable certainty that it would never come before the single magistrate who is empowered to deal with its comparatively venial guilt. Yes, for a first morning's research, it was not bad. But she had never previously realised how many days there are in a year.

Meanwhile Fred went through the innocent hours in a state of nervous anxiety, such as he had certainly never expected to feel in his wildest dreams. He was afraid lest he might be inadvertently led into some casual breach of his country's very numerous laws, and so commit a second crime in a single day. It was a waste which he could not afford.

CHAPTER VI.

ENTER THE PRESS

THE months passed, and the neatly entered record of Mr. Frederick Corder's daily crimes lengthened with the steady regularity of their setting suns.

It had been early February when he had gone through the rain in Bill Saxton's overcoat to Mr. Jellipot's office. It was now May. In the meantime he had committed ninety-two crimes, and remained a man of good repute, unconvicted, and (as far as he could observe) unsuspected of any wrong.

There had been narrow escapes, occasions when he had skirted the edge of discovery, or had found it difficult to outrun an involuntary innocence before the striking of the midnight hour. Once he had narrowly avoided the dual perils, when he decided at 11:35 P.M. that he was too near the possibility of allowing midnight to arrive without having perpetrated the selected crime. Adeline had let him loose at 8:00 P.M. with an airgun concealed in his trouser leg on what should have been a moonlit night, in a wood which (as she had gone to some trouble to ascertain) no gamekeeper controlled, but in which rabbits were said to gambol in multitudes. Fred had talked with some confidence of his airgun skill, and Adeline, waiting in a friend's car at the side of the lonely road, had expected that a few minutes would be sufficient to enable him to secure the single rabbit which the occasion required.

But the moon had been hidden by clouds. It had been densely dark under the boughs, and the rabbits, possibly shunning the discomfort of a drizzling rain, could neither be seen nor heard. Could an intention of poaching, under impossible conditions, rank as an accomplished crime? Perhaps it could, but Fred, stumbling in the dark, and waiting for moonlight which did not come, had a cold doubt. He went back to Adeline while there might yet be time to save the position, and reported his non-success.

31

"Jump in," she said hurriedly, "we'll do something else to make sure."

The street in the little country town where he smashed the Belisha beacon three minutes before midnight struck had appeared to be quite deserted, but a constable had leapt from the shadows, and blown his whistle as Fred scrambled back to the car.

Disaster, final and absolute, would have been the sequel of this intervention had not a plan, already designed for such an emergency, been put into successful operation.

Fred had not entered the car. He had mounted the running board, holding on until pursuit was outdistanced, and then, as the car slowed, dropped off and gone off by himself down a side lane. The constable, as they had feared, had taken the number of the car, and it was only five minutes later that Adeline was stopped, and the car searched for a man who was not there.

She being questioned was entirely truthful, and moderately frank. She had seen the beacon smashed. She had, at that moment, been going at a very moderate pace. A man had jumped on to the running board. She had no doubt that he was the one who had smashed the beacon. He had been wearing a dark coat. She had not seen his face. She had accelerated, perhaps foolishly. But was it not a natural action? Was it not natural to wish to shake him off, she being alone in the car? Anyway, he *had* dropped off. What more was there to be said?

It was a needless elaboration of precaution that had caused Fred to carry out the plan also agreed, by which he made a cross-country way to a local railway station, travelled some distance from London during the night, and arrived back at Euston at 8:30 A.M. as Adeline, had the enquiry proceeded to such a point, would have said that she was expecting her husband to do.

Except for one or two such narrow escapes as these, the ninety-two crimes had been safely perpetrated, and with no more than negligible harm or inconvenience to the community against whom they made lawless war.

Adeline, directing the campaign, had been careful to assort crimes in such a way as to avoid monotony and distribute degrees of risk. She was resolved that Fred should stay the course, but she was vigilant to make it as attractive as possible. Actually, it appeared, so far, to have done him good rather than harm. His physical condition had clearly improved. His eyes were brighter. His walk was more active and confident. It seemed that a new interest had come into his life. It made her afraid at times that he might err from overboldness, and bring their hopes to ruin by attracting the notice of the police.

But, on the Friday in May to which we have come, she was mentally at ease, both with the knowledge that the crime of the day (the purloining of a bottle of milk) had been committed without possibility of detection following, and that she had a safe and pleasant plan for the following morning.

He had scarcely taken his seat on the opposite side of the low fireside tea table when she began: "I thought we might go to Hampton Court tomorrow." She knew that the weekend habit made it rarely possible for him to do any business in the city on Saturday mornings. She added: "There's a train soon after eleven that we might catch."

"If you're staging the next event there, I should say you'd better move it about a hundred miles farther off. A profane oath in the middle of Salisbury Plain is about the only thing that's left for us now."

It was the tone more than the words that warned her that Fred was in a despondent mood, and her first care was to assure him of the ease with which he would be able to execute the next of the series of diurnal iniquities.

"There's a compartment at the end of that train that's reserved for ladies. It's not a full train, and nobody gets into the compartment, more often than not. Anyway, I watched, and there wasn't anyone this morning; and the guard's at the far end of the train.

"If we get in together, or rather I get in first, just as the train's going to start, we can change at the first stop, and you'll have broken the law without one chance in a million that you'd get prosecuted, and not one in a hundred that it will be noticed at all."

Fred did not fail to observe that Addie had planned with her usual careful efficiency, but his mood did not improve. He objected: "If it's only you in the compartment, and you don't object, I'm not sure that it's a crime at all, unless a railway official asked me to get out, and I wouldn't budge, and then I should get a summons for sure. I might be a short-sighted man."

"Well, so you are. But why make up your mind that I shan't object? I shall probably kick up a ghastly fuss. In fact, I object now. I think it will be a most ungentlemanly thing for you to do."

"Well," he said rather ungraciously, "I don't say it was a bad idea. A bit better than some, anyway. It isn't like impersonating a policeman, or robbing a church poor box.

"But the fact is that the game's up. They've got the whole tale in the *Talker*, and I suppose it'll be in the morning papers tomorrow, from one end of the country to the other."

"What do you mean by the whole tale?"

"I mean the codicil to the will, of course."

"They don't say that you're trying to earn the money?"

"No, even if they guessed it, they wouldn't dare. But we couldn't go on with everyone watching."

"You're not willing to give up now, after all we've done?"

"I don't see that there's anything else possible."

Adeline became silent. The publicity which was threatened must certainly increase the risks of detection, and there were still one hundred and seventy-three daily crimes to be contrived and perpetrated before the day would arrive on which Fred could claim the inheritance so hardly and wickedly to be won.

And Percival might make some excuse, even then! It was a fear which would often haunt her in the hours of too-wakeful nights, and which roused a fierce determination that they should not be foiled, if the conditions had been fulfilled. Or, if so, there should be one more than the required total! Would not murder be a fitting climax to the long and varied list of the twelve months' crimes? She did not go far enough in imagination to decide which of them should stain their hands with Percival Kanwhistle's blood, nor would it have been easy to imagine Fred murdering his cousin, or anyone else. ("Infirm of purpose!—Give me the daggers.") But she was clearly resolved that there should be no further peaceful existence for Miss Kanwhistle's heir while that ten thousand pounds, having been fairly earned, should remain in his banker's hands. Her mind swung back to the immediate trouble which threatened to make the more remote one of no more than theoretical interest, but the thought of Percival had given her resolution a harder quality, which was apparent in her next words: "We can't give up now, after all we've done. We've got to think out a way."

Fred had been thinking, too. He was not uninfluenced by the fact that Adeline had taken the news in a fighting mood; and he was as reluctant as she to surrender the hope of wealth, for which he had already steeped himself so deeply in his country's crimes. He said: "It all seems to me to depend upon whether they can guess that I've started to win the stakes."

Yes. She saw that, if those around him, or who might make enquiry, should be convinced of his past and present innocence, there could be no reason to suspect him now of beginning a criminal career which would be three months too late. But could they bluff it out, even in the midst of unceasing guilt? She had some confidence in her own power to deceive. She had the great advantage of being habitually truthful and direct in action and speech. It is an incidental asset of such characteristics that, at sufficient need, they can lie more convincingly than their weaker neighbours. She had some confidence in herself; but of Fred she was less sure. She looked at him doubtfully. "You never," she said, "could tell a really good lie."

Fred, who would have resented a charge of untruthfulness, was not pleased by this dubiously worded compliment. "I don't know," he said, "what you mean. I'm not going to let out what I've been doing, if you're hinting at that."

Adeline answered vaguely: "Well, you know what these pressmen are." Fred could be warned, but not changed. She asked "Did you bring the paper?"

"The *Talker*? No. I saw it at the Club. I tried to get a copy afterwards, but they were sold out, so they said. I expect they'd never had any to sell. It's not a paper you often see on the stalls."

"How much did they say?"

"Oh, just the facts. They've printed the codicil in full, under the heading: 'Lady's Eccentric Will. Legacy to Be Won by Crime.' That wouldn't matter so much. It's the daily papers. It's sure to get into them. "

Adeline did not dispute that. They both knew Fleet Street too well. It was that same knowledge which gave confidence to her next words: "Whatever they print, it will be forgotten in less than a week, if we can bluff them off now."

She added: "If any reporters come smelling round, you'd better leave them to me."

Fred said she could take on the lot, if she felt she could handle them better than he; but, while he spoke, Bill Saxton, with his usual grinning cheekiness, put his head in at the door, and asked: "May I come in? Or is it an awkward time?"

Adeline, cursing him in her heart, though she would have welcomed his cheerful presence under different circumstances, answered: "Yes, of course. But I'm afraid the tea's getting cold."

"I don't mind that," Mr. Saxton answered, as he advanced briskly to the offered chair. "I only thought Fred wouldn't want me prying about if he were just packing up the poisoned chocolates, or forging a cheque."

"Yes," Adeline answered, without affecting not to understand him, "I suppose it's a good joke to you; but it's a bad one to us, and a bit stale."

"Must have been rotten for you," the journalist agreed, with cheerful superficial sympathy. "But Cartwright's told me off to interview Fred, and we'll pay ten guineas. I told him Fred was too fly to give me the tale for nothing."

"Well," Adeline answered, as Fred's silence showed his willingness to leave the initial skirmish to her, "if you think anything we can tell you is worth the money! But that's your risk. You'd better finish the tea cake first, and then ask what you want to know."

CHAPTER VII.

MR. SAXTON REMEMBERS THE MILK

BILL SAXTON grinned genially at Fred, who looked at him with less friendly eyes. Fred knew that such interviews were no more than occasional parts of the journalist's duties. Normally, Bill was an inside man, and his being delegated to this interview might fairly be attributed to the fact that they were known to be neighbours, and on friendly terms. Looked at from that angle, it had an aspect of hitting below the belt, which he was disposed to resent. It was through the use—perhaps it might be said, the abuse—of that friendship that he had been able to walk in uninvited, and claim that which might have been refused to another reporter.

On the other hand, friendship counts for something. Bill had shown this when he had arranged payment for an interview which a reporter thinking only of the interests of his paper would have aimed to obtain freely. Also, if Bill would publish what Fred would wish his acquaintances, the general public, and especially the police, to believe, he might do him a service greater than, and very different from, anything that he would suppose.

But Fred knew that friendship, however real, would weigh little against the instincts of the journalist, and the interests of the *Morning News*. He asked cautiously: "What do you want me to say?"

"I want you to tell me, in your own words, what you think of your aunt's will."

"I think it's about the lousiest ever made."

As Bill's pencil rapidly jotted down this explosive opinion, Adeline interposed: "You mean, what did Fred think of it, when we heard of it three months ago? We can't keep thinking about it all the time; we've got other things to do."

"And you've given up trying to earn the money?"

"Oh, no, he hasn't."

"You mean he's having a shot at winning it?"

"Of course I didn't. I meant just what I said."

"You mean he couldn't stop what he didn't start?"

"Mr. Saxton, you are bright! I don't see why he should mind telling you this. Jane Kanwhistle always hated him, and she stuck the codicil on to the will just to make him as mad as she knew how. Mr. Jellipot—he's her solicitor—said he knew nothing about it being there till she was dead. He said the codicil wouldn't have any legal value, even if anyone could fulfil such crazy conditions, as it was against public policy, and Fred's cousin, who's got the lot, couldn't be made to pay up.

"But you can be sure that it wasn't meant to be a way for Fred to earn ten thousand pounds. It was just to annoy him by dangling the money at the other side of a ditch that he couldn't jump. Unless she thought he might be mad enough to get into trouble trying—trying to jump the ditch, and fall in—and you can't tell that, unless you know how silly she thought he was, or how crazy she may have been."

"If you think she wasn't all there, you ought to contest the will. You might get young Kanwhistle to compromise, if nothing better than that."

"That was what Fred thought of at once. But Mr. Jellipot said there wasn't a chance. We should have had something to go on if it had been part of the will, but it was stuck on two years later.

"And besides, it would be said that it was evidently not intended to be taken literally. No one could expect to break the law once a day for a year and not be noticed by the police, and no one but a lunatic would be likely to try.

"Spiteful things are often put into wills, just to annoy, and that isn't considered any evidence that the people aren't sane. Anyway, Mr. Jellipot said that there wasn't a chance, and Fred could do nothing better than forget it. After all, she only exposed her own nasty character. I don't see why Fred should mind."

"No," Bill agreed, "that sounds the sensible way to look at it. I suppose you can't tell me what set the old cat's back up?"

"Only that she thought Fred hadn't enough vice in him, and she liked Percival better because he had. I don't see why Fred need be ashamed of that."

"No. He ought to feel just the other way. Good old Fred!"

Mr. Saxton shut his notebook. He felt that he had obtained the raw material for as long a column as the thing was worth. He added: "I think it's you who ought to have the ten guineas, Mrs. Corder. But I dare say you'll know how to look after that."

And then, just as he was rising to leave, he remembered something, and a cloud of doubt, "small as a man's hand," rose in his alert and curious mind.

"By the way," he said, "I heard that Mrs. Fortey's milk was stolen this morning."

Mrs. Fortey occupied the flat two floors below.

Fred had been silent since Adeline had taken the interview so firmly in hand, but now he felt that he played the right game when he looked up to say with a hint of righteous indignation in his voice: "I didn't steal Mrs. Fortey's milk, if you mean that."

Bill Saxton grinned. "No," he said dryly. "I know you didn't."

"Oh, Fred," Adeline said, as the door closed, "if only you could have kept still!"

"I don't see what there'd be wrong in that, even if it hadn't been true, as it was. It was Bill's milk I took. I didn't go down to hers."

"Neither do I. But there was something, all the same. It's made him suspect, if he doesn't know."

"Then what are we to do now?"

"What can we, except to go on? We don't want to be beaten, and we're just beating ourselves if we stop now without being sure we must."

Fred did not deny that. He said: "Then it's still to be Hampton Court?"

"Yes. Unless you can think of something better.

"Not if you can't. You've raked up fifty times more innocent crimes already than I thought there were in the whole penal code."

He did no more than justice to Adeline's systematic industry when he said that. She had analysed and tabulated an almost incredible number of offences separately defined and penalised by the complexities of English law. And though there were very many which Fred was, so to speak, ineligible to commit, there was a residue of many hundreds among which to select from week to week, and of a variety sufficient to avoid any danger of his finding monotony in his lawless deeds.

Now she consulted her chart anew, not to disturb the programme for the next morning, which, unless they should be closely mobbed (scarcely a reasonable anticipation) still seemed to her as good a selection as could be made, but to alter that which she had chosen for the following day. The deposit of waste matter on public land is not an operation which can be safely performed, even at night, by one who may be surrounded by prying, suspicious eyes. She must find something better than that.

She considered alternative iniquities with a frowning intentness, only interrupted by a brief door mat interview with a reporter from the *Evening Herald*. ("If you mean that my husband's a lunatic, why not say so straight out?"); and meanwhile Mr. William Saxton returned to Fleet Street to report to the feature editor of the *Morning News* the interview which he had obtained.

"Corder didn't say much," he concluded. "He let the missus do the talking, but it seemed sensible enough, and it seemed a crazy idea that he would be trying to win money in such a way. Besides, he'd have had to break the law about a hundred times already, or he'd have run himself off the course, and it isn't sensible that he wouldn't have been caught out before now.

"But, just as I was leaving, I remembered the morning's milk. There's always a pint bottle left at the door of our own flat—the Corders are on the floor above—and I pick it up and take it in when I get back in the morning, unless I'm home earlier.

"Well, this morning it wasn't there, and I supposed it had been taken in, but my wife said it hadn't, and I must be wrong, as she had distinctly heard the milkman lay it down when she had been going along the passage.

"So I went back to look for it, but it wasn't there. Then I went down to the floor below, and there were two bottles outside Mrs. Fortey's door, so I thought the man might have made a mistake, and left ours there.

"It was no use ringing to ask, because I know that Jill Fortey doesn't get up before three, unless she's got a rehearsal, so I took one, and told my wife to ask her about it later. Well, so she did. Jill said she always takes two pints. She needs milk for her complexion. I don't know whether it's for internal application. I thought she took something stronger than that. But there's no doubt that our bottle was delivered and disappeared. But who would have been likely to come up there and take it? There's only the Corders above us."

Mr. Cartwright listened to this tale. He rubbed his chin in a way he had when hesitation troubled his mind. It sounded to him a most improbable supposition founded on very slender evidence. But he had some confidence in Bill Saxton's scent for a story. Just possibly he might have made a good guess.

"We should want," he said, "a lot more than that before it would be any use."

"Yes, of course. But if you'd heard how Corder rose to the bait!"

"You haven't missed anything else, except this bottle of milk?"

"No. I don't think so. He borrowed an overcoat once, but Mrs. Corder brought it back."

"Because, if he's been pilfering from his friends every day for the last three months—"

"Oh, but he'd hardly have tried keeping that up all the time! He's been shoplifting more likely than not."

It was a conversation which, had she been able to hear it, would have confirmed Adeline in the wisdom of the programme of widely assorted, unrepeated crimes which she had been so diligent to arrange. Even Bill Saxton's imagination had not gone beyond a hand-to-mouth opportunism of casual, continual theft.

"Well," Mr. Cartwright concluded, "you'll know how to write the interview up. You must take what Mrs. Corder said at its face value now. No libel actions for us! But you can have any time off that you like to follow it up. There may come a time when we shall have something that we can use, and that no one else has."

Bill Saxton went off to write an article suitable to the occasion and the instructions he had received. It was innocent enough, and after the blue pencil of an expert sub-editor had been exercised upon it, it became of such a character that even Adeline's cautious alertness was led to doubt whether the allusion to the missing milk had been more than an idle jest.

CHAPTER VIII.

ADELINE CALLS ON MR. JELLIPOT

MR JELLIPOT was accustomed to tell himself, with some truth, and his usual diffidence, that he did not understand women. His acquaintance with them (if we except a timidly developing autumnal romance with a Quaker lady who can hardly be considered typical of her own sex) was certainly of a distant and professional rather than an intimate character. But, whatever the limits of his own understanding might be, it was common for them to approach him in more confident and confiding moods.

He had a good memory for names, and when he heard that a Mrs. Corder had called and requested an interview, he had no difficulty in associating her with Miss Kanwhistle's eccentric will. He said: "Show her in," rather reluctantly, anticipating that his time would be wasted, and his patience strained, by some vain appeal that he should persuade Mr. Percival Kanwhistle to a generosity which the will did not indicate, nor the law require. Perhaps he must listen sympathetically to some tale of misfortune or pressing debt, which only Percival's generosity could relieve. Perhaps—such things had been—it would end in his own cheque book appearing from the little drawer at his left hand, to make a loan of the character which is not entered in business books. But he hoped not, for the lending of money is always an embarrassment to a shy man. It may be considered the solitary exception to the fundamental law that it is more blessed to give than to receive.

Mr. Jellipot looked at a young lady dressed in a manner vaguely satisfactory to his masculine eyes, with a face that was intelligent rather than beautiful, but with the advantage of a clear, straight glance, a firm chin, and a ready smile. As he met her, his anticipation of the interview changed. Forgetting that he did not understand women, he judged her to be efficient, sensible, one on whom it would be safe to rely. Certainly not one who would pester him with absurd requests. Beyond that, he regarded her only as Frederick Corder's wife. He took little interest in contemporary fiction, and was unaware that Adeline Corder had a growing reputation for lightly-written mystery tales.

"I came to see you," she said, "about the codicil to the Kanwhistle will."

"Yes?" he replied tentatively. "I am sure that Mr. Corder understood that I had no responsibility for it, nor knowledge of its existence until after Miss Kanwhistle's death."

"Yes. I understood that. It's really about what's getting into the daily papers."

"It is a temporary annoyance, which is, I fear, unavoidable. A will, when probate is granted, becomes a public document, and any unusual reference or provision is commonly discovered by the news agencies. There is no remedy, apart from comment of a libellous character."

"Comment?" she echoed dubiously. "Do you mean that a libel can be inserted in a will, and then repeated with impunity in the daily press, so long as they avoid comment upon it?"

"No, that would be going too far. But does the question arise? Are you suggesting that the codicil libelled Mr. Corder in such a manner that any publication of it is actionable? That is arguable only on the condition that it is libellous to associate the name of any man with the possible commission of crime. It is one which I should regard with very great hesitation, but on which I would obtain counsel's opinion should you instruct me to do so."

"That was about what I supposed. But what do you think of this?"

Adeline drew from her bag a cutting of the paragraph in the *Talker* which had first come to her husband's notice, and Mr. Jellipot read it with his usual deliberation. Written in the jesting style characteristic of the periodical in which it appeared, it certainly visualised a possibility, if no more, that Frederick Corder might have embarked already upon a downward career of crime.

Mr. Jellipot pondered this for some silent moments. Then he said: "It is possible—it is barely possible—that a libel action might be brought successfully, and even result in the award of substantial damages. The costs of such an action would be considerable. If it were lost, they would be heavy. The award of damages does not necessarily mean that they will be paid, nor even that the plaintiff's costs will be recovered.

"It is—I am going to give you no more than my first reaction—a litigation which I should hesitate to advise, even if I were satisfied of the stability of the publishers and printers concerned.

"When I even consider its possibility"—Mr. Jellipot turned his eyes directly upon his visitor with a gentle and yet penetrating regard as he said this—"I am, of course, assuming, as you will expect me to do, that Mr. Corder was not tempted, for however short a time, to comply with the conditions specified in the codicil, for it is obvious that the defence of such an action might take the direction of strict enquiry into that possibility.

"You will, when I say this, allow that I do no more than recognise every condition, however remote or hypothetical, which must qualify the advice I give."

Adeline heard this without her glance falling before the solicitor's shrewd though friendly eyes, but a smile curved her lips as she answered: "From all you say, such an action would evidently be too hazardous for us to attempt, as we have very little money to risk."

"It is, I am sure, a discreet decision."

Mrs. Corder rose to leave. "I thought, somehow," she said, "that I should like you to know."

Mr. Jellipot, rising also, appeared to check himself on the threshold of speech.

Mrs. Corder hesitated. Her hand went to her bag. "What should I pay you?" she asked. She was unsure whether it were customary to pay for such a call at the time, or to wait for a bill to be sent to her.

But Mr. Jellipot gently shook his head. "There will be no charge," he said, "on this occasion."

She went out, wondering whether there were significance in those last words. Did he anticipate that she would come to him again, at a greater need?

Left alone, Mr. Jellipot was conscious of certain speculations which did not produce the full moral reprobation which was their due. He was mildly excited, mildly shocked, at his own thoughts. He had not judged Frederick Corder capable of such conduct. Probably that judgment had been correct. "The woman tempted me—" Mrs. Corder was an exceptional woman. She knew how to say enough—just enough—and no more.

Well, it was no business—certainly no responsibility—of his, and in the end he would surely know.

CHAPTER IX.

AN INVITATION TO TREES

MR. FREDERICK CORDER was partly, and not unpleasantly, aware of the change which had come to him as the result of his three months' course of criminality, so ably directed and abetted by his cool and resourceful partner. He had acquired a more upright carriage, a more confident glance from alerter eyes. In his private imagination he surveyed the world with a hawk-like glance, which may have been less evident to those upon whom it fell. At his side would hang, at times, an imagined sword: a short, straight, keen, lethal weapon, symbolising his private warfare upon the organised force of law. Had the inciting codicil not placed a period upon his course of iniquity, it is possible that a second year might have found him of willing capacity to continue even without Adeline's sympathetic support. Had they not been at one in avoiding anything really wrong, it is possible that he might have emerged from this year of intensive training as a veritable king of crime. Should he be discovered in anything which the law would regard as deserving serious penalty, it was possible, even so, that he would find himself in a position in which it would be difficult to continue to make a living by honest means, and he must decide between becoming dependent upon the precarious earnings of *More Jam for Jane* and his wife's subsequent novels, and changing his status from a mere amateur (if he could be described, even now, correctly by that inoffensive word) to that of a professional criminal.

Now, as he walked the streets, he looked round continually for new ideas which might be given to Adeline to be noted down for his future programme, and with a frequent envy for those around him, who were eligible for so many crimes which he could not hope to commit.

Could he water milk? The opportunity would be hard to find; and, even so, it was by no means clear that he would have done a

45

criminal deed, unless he were either the wholesale or retail vendor of the adulterated liquid. Rather than become a criminal himself, he might merely have created other criminals, who would be unaware of the legal status which had been thrust upon them. It was to save himself from such disastrous pitfalls, which might otherwise cause Mr. Jellipot's impartial acumen to decide at last that the conditions had not been fulfilled, that Adeline now spent two mornings a week regularly at the British Museum following the intricate mazes of English law.

Could he abandon an infant? It is a difficult enterprise for a partner in a childless marriage, and even had he been more favourably placed in that particular, it is improbable that Adeline would have approved the idea. Could he carry firearms without a licence? Well, perhaps he might. But would not the gunsmith object to sell?

It had become necessary to act with an increased caution—Adeline in the choice, and he in the execution of lawless deeds—since Mr. Saxton had so unceremoniously intruded upon them, for though the privacy of the lady's compartment had been violated without official protest, they had been disconcerted to observe the journalist alighting at Hampton Court from the farther end of the train, and to be subsequently trailing them at a timid distance, which they had abruptly shortened by turning a corner and then waiting until he had almost run into them as he came round it a minute later.

After that, they had kept together, showing a willingness for the journalist's company which, as he had been too distant to observe the "Ladies Only" upon the compartment window, had reluctantly convinced him, not of the innocence of the day, but that there had been no lawless object in the expedition which he had joined; and caused him to catch an annoying cold as he had watched during the later evening for Fred to issue from his upper floor for some evil deed which he might have in mind for the darker hours.

"That," Adeline said, "ought to teach the wretch that we've got nothing to hide." But would it? The more certain fact was that Bill Saxton's suspicions had been aroused, and that he had evidently been deputed by the editor of the *Morning News* to discover the truth. For they judged correctly that it would require more than a private curiosity to draw him to Hampton Court at an hour when he would normally have been taking the repose which his midnight labours had justly earned.

Until the following Tuesday, when she had called upon Mr. Jellipot, and for the two subsequent days, Adeline had felt it necessary to resort to the very cream of the schedule of possible delinquencies from which the daily selection was made; but in doing this she felt herself to be acting with a prodigality which might have disastrous ultimate consequences. Had she not been hoarding these with a view to some special difficulty, some urgent need? Suppose a time should come when Fred would be in bed with a cold, if no worse than that? Suppose—so many things.

It was Friday morning when she looked across the breakfast table to say: "I tell you what it is, Fred, we've got to clear out of London."

Fred looked doubtful. It was a method of escape which had already been in his own mind, but which he had not liked. For how long was it to be? It doesn't matter where you may wander if you have nothing more local to do than the next chapter of *More Jam for Jane*, but a brisk trade in book jackets is best conducted from an address which should not be far either from W.C.2 or E.C.4. Besides, with a shrewdness which for once may have passed that of his quick-witted wife, he saw snags. Away from their own home, their own resorts, and the crowded metropolitan streets, they might be more easily followed, more closely observed. Even occasion might be found to inspect their luggage, which would presumably include the fatal journal of evil deeds which it had become a constant evening practice to enter up.

"What," he asked, with the doubt evident in his voice, "should you say to going abroad? Say a week in Paris? They'd hardly follow us there, and we'd have a chance to think up some new ideas?"

"We couldn't do it. I don't suppose we could fulfil the conditions there. You can't break English laws while you're in France."

"No? I don't see why not. You could some, anyway. What about writing, begging, or perhaps blackmailing letters? You wouldn't say the police couldn't arrest me when I got back because they'd been sent from a Paris hotel? Not, I mean, if they were addressed here."

"I don't know how that would be. But you're not going to send such letters, so it's no use discussing that."

"No, of course not. I only used it as an illustration. There must be lots of things besides those."

"I don't know whether they are or not, but you won't risk it with my consent. I've got an idea, since I saw Mr. Jellipot, that we shan't have much difficulty in collecting, if we keep the rules of the game, and we should be crazy to risk anything over that."

It was a proposition which Fred did not seriously dispute, but they spent some time in academic discussion of the terms of the codicil, recalling the solicitor's criticism of its phraseology, which, perhaps even more than its purport, had been distressing to the exactitude of his legal mind.

In the end, they had neither finally dismissed nor adopted the idea that their career of crime could be continued in greater security if they should make a temporary migration to some distant part of the British Isles, when Fred changed the subject by asking: "What have you got cooked up for me today?"

"I've got something so simple," Adeline replied cheerfully, "that it's hard to think of it as a crime at all, and so safe that I thought you might offer to walk down to Fleet Street with Bill this evening, and do the deed while he's watching for any wickedness he may see you commit.

"And that reminds me that there's a letter for you on the window ledge. It was that coming which decided me to use the idea today, and if you open it before I explain, I want you to be very careful not to injure the stamp."

Fred got up with some alacrity to collect the letter. His correspondence was not heavy, most of his business being personally transacted. It consisted mainly of occasional dunning letters and less frequent cheques. Adeline's, as was natural to a semi-successful novelist, was more voluminous, and was already warning him of the possibility that he might come to be known, at no distant day, as Mrs. Corder's husband. It gave him a further incentive to attain the dignified independence which comes from the knowledge that the bank will honour your cheque for ten thousand pounds, a position hardly to be gained by the slow production of a thousand book jackets, however lurid. He saw a rather square business envelope of substantial quality on which his name and address were correctly typed.

He observed that he was described as Esq., which was not the invariable practice of the typists of the publishing offices for whom the most part of his work was done. He observed also that the postmark was E.C.2; but inspected the stamp in vain for any indication to justify the care with which he had been urged to preserve it.

Finally, he turned the envelope over, and saw that the name of the London & Northern Bank was embossed upon the flap. It meant nothing to him. His own small and reluctantly permitted overdraft was a source of quarterly profit to a rival establishment. He inserted a finger to tear it open, and withdrew it. "If there's a fortune in the stamp," he said, "I'd better slit it with a knife."

"There's no fortune," she said, "but there's the easiest crime that you've ever done."

Without waiting for further explanation, he cut open the envelope, gazed for one puzzled moment at the typewritten contents, and handed the letter to his wife.

"Perhaps," he said, "you know the meaning of this."

With no readier understanding than his own, she read:

Trees, Hither Dene

May 12, 1934

Dear Mr. Corder,

Your name has been very kindly given to me by my friend, Mr. Jellipot, as that of an artist particularly capable of undertaking a little commission which would involve your presence at Hither Dene for a few days, more or less.

If you should not be otherwise engaged, and could spare the time, perhaps you would accept my hospitality at the above address?

In that case, and if the 3:17 P.M. from Charing Cross on Saturday next would suit your convenience, there will be no occasion to reply to this letter. Our mutual friend, Mr. Jellipot, will be on the train, and my car will meet it at Hither Dene station.

Yours sincerely,

Reginald Crowe

P.S. Both Lady Crowe and myself will be additionally pleased should Mrs. Corder—whose last novel we much enjoyed—be able to come also. R. C.

"Well, anyway," Adeline said, "it's a very nice letter."

"I suppose you say that because they say they've read *When Maud Went Home*," Fred answered peevishly. "It seemed rather cool cheek to me."

Adeline understood very well the mixture of pride and jealousy which confused her husband's reaction to such evidences of her literary reputation. She answered with her usual tactfulness: "I suppose he just put that in to get us to go. The last man who said how much he'd enjoyed my last book hadn't read a page, and doesn't know how completely he gave himself away when I drew him on. But who is Mr. Crowe, anyhow? He seems to be a bank manager, more likely than not, unless he picked that envelope up in the street."

It was a point on which Fred was better informed. "The name of the Chairman of the London and Northern," he said, "is Sir Reginald Crowe. It isn't likely that there'd be two using those envelopes. The question is, are we to go?"

The question was not one to which Adeline felt it possible to give an instant reply. She saw that, if Fred were to go, she must do so also. It would be too great a risk for them to be separated during this year of crime. And that thought led to a passing wonder as to how far, and with what motive, Mr. Jellipot might have been responsible for the invitation.

She was sure that he had understood. She had a suspicion that, however little it might influence the cautious rectitude of his conduct, he was more interested than shocked by the information which, more by telepathy than explicit words, she had conveyed to an astute mind. Yet, from another angle, she saw reason to doubt this theory. Mr. Jellipot had disassociated himself with emphasis from that discreditable codicil, as the facts entitled, and his reputation rendered it imperative for him to do. This position had been confirmed by the press, which had given prominence to the fact that the codicil had been added subsequently to the drawing up of the will, and without the knowledge of the solicitor concerned. Yet, however vaguely, his name must be connected with the event, and, much more so if it should become known at some future date that he had been required to adjudicate upon the record of crime and should pronounce that the stake had been fairly won. Was it consistent with the legal caution which he had shown up to this point that he should risk the implications of having stayed in the same house with them during the period of the lawless deeds?

She saw another possibility. Might not Mr. Jellipot, on reflection, have decided that it was his duty to persuade them to abandon their nefarious enterprise? Might he not have enlisted the banker's powerful assistance to that purpose? Might they not find that they would have to face a vexatious weekend of persuasive argument, which would be difficult to endure, and might even fatally impede them in their daily practice? Suppose that this commission so unexpectedly offered were of the nature of a bribe to lure Fred from a life of crime? Sir Reginald Crowe striving as a good citizen should, somewhat after the fashion of the Discharged Prisoners' Aid Society, to enable her husband to make a sufficient living by honest means to induce him to abandon his fallen ways? Perhaps they thought that orders for book jackets rarely came, and that he was now stealing from actual poverty, as much as for the glittering prize ahead? With less than her usual logic, she flushed angrily at the thought.

So she hesitated, in a mind further confused by pleasure at the kind allusion to *When Maud Went Home*, desire to make the acquaintance of Lady Crowe, and cold fears that her wardrobe (even though it might be reinforced by that rose-coloured evening dress which she had coveted in Paul & Snelford's Regent Street window yesterday) would be inadequate for the occasion; and while she remained silent, Fred broke out with an exclamation which showed that his thoughts had started along the same road as her own, though they had turned in at a different gate.

"It's some trick of Percy's, more likely than not. I vote that we don't go."

"Percy's?" she echoed in a puzzled voice, and then: "Oh, you mean he's asked Mr. Jellipot to set a trap for you somehow? No, I don't think it's that."

"Well, I do. It's just what Percival would. I don't say he won't stump up if we stay the course. I feel sure he will. But he'd think it good sport to dish me in any way that he could. He'd do anything that isn't actually hitting under the belt, and it's the sort of case where it isn't over easy to see where the belt lies."

Adeline did not concern herself to question this metaphorical description of Mr. Kanwhistle's sporting code. But she felt sure that he would not have been able to obtain Mr. Jellipot's co-operation, nor was it probable that he would have gained that of the Chairman of the London & Northern Bank.

"I don't know what it means," she said. "I'm as puzzled as you are. But it isn't that."

"Well, it might be. They mightn't try to spy on us at all. They might just trap me in a locked room where there wouldn't be a possibility of breaking any law that was ever made, except committing suicide, and I'm not going to do that, even for you. I'm not even going to fail in the attempt."

No, they both saw that. Even failing in the attempt, at which people can become expert with sufficient practice, would be useless here, for there would be almost certain prosecution to follow.

"It wouldn't," he added gloomily, "even be a crime to smash up the room, when you were locked in like that."

But, however perversely, Fred's misjudgement of Mr. Jellipot, as she considered it to be, had resolved Adeline's wavering mind.

51

She might have been less confident of the solicitor's friendly integrity had she known that Percival Kanwhistle was to be their fellow guest at Hither Dene, he having actually accepted Sir Reginald's invitation before the dictation of the one they were now discussing. But, having no suspicion of this, she said: "You needn't worry about suicide. We've only got to keep together, and even if we get locked in, we shall have a good crime in reserve. But you needn't ask what it is. I hope it won't come to that. But we were saying that we ought to get away from Bill while this invitation was lying waiting for you to open it, and it would be silly not to go, now we've got just what we said we wanted. And it ought to be rather fun.

"Of course, we can come away any time we like, or, if it seems that there's any trick being played, I'd let you seduce Lady Crowe—I know how you've been hankering after that kind of crime—but the trouble is that it wouldn't be a crime at all! We've noticed times enough that the law doesn't bother much about things that are really wrong. That is, not unless you knock her on the head first, and if you do that she'll be almost certain to mention it when she feels better, and you'll get run in, and the whole thing spoiled, and I should say that she's worth a lot less than ten thousand pounds; besides that, you'd get all the pleasure, and I should lose my share of the cash."

Fred did not trouble to reply to this ribald suggestion. Hardened criminal though he must be, his mind did not respond blithely to the idea of such unceremonious treatment of Lady Evelyn Crowe. He rightly understood Adeline's words to mean no more than that she had resolved upon a weekend, or longer, at Hither Dene, and that she liked the idea. That was how she would talk when a pleasant excitement stimulated her mind. He said: "Well, if that's how it's to be, you'd better tell me about this crime of not tearing a stamp, and we'll get that out of the way now."

"It isn't a crime to tear it. It's only that it would make it useless for what we want. If you look at it again, you'll see that the postmark's missed it almost completely. When you've got it off, you'll have to look very closely to see that it's been cancelled at all."

"You mean I'm to use it again?"

"That's the idea. I've read that it's done so much in Australia that the Post Office there prosecutes people who try it on—that is, when it can prove a case. For some reason, English people aren't equally enterprising. But we've got to do it so that it couldn't possibly be proved that it's anything to do with you."

Adeline then proceeded to direct the operation with the careful efficiency which had brought them safely through so many previous ventures, and must multiply them so largely yet before they would be in reach of the golden bait.

She selected a sheet of notepaper from her own desk which could not be suspected of having Fred's fingerprints upon it. She folded it, inserted it in an envelope of equal virginity, and paused a moment with a poised pen. She had thought to send it to the Postmaster General. But suppose that letters so addressed did not require stamps? She was conscious, as so often now, of an ignorance which must not be risked. On an impish impulse, which reason told her could be safely indulged, she addressed the envelope to Percival Kanwhistle.

"There's nothing wrong in anything I've done yet," she remarked, "but you've got to do the rest with your own hands, and so that they can't possibly fix it on you, even though they put every detective in the Post Office—and I believe they've got scores—on to your track.

"You'd better put on some gloves, and soak the stamp off, and then gum it on carefully enough for it to look fresh and natural. If you make a good job of it, I should say that it will be about ten millions to one that it won't be noticed at all, and if it is, the odds would still be about that much more that they couldn't trace it back to me; and as to you, there'd be no chance at all, unless Bill's looking in at the kitchen window while you're at work, and he'll have to hold on to the wall with his nails to do that."

"He might hang down by a rope from the roof."

"The cat might have a litter of puppies. But I'll look out all the same, and make sure that he isn't there. You're quite right that we can't be too careful, being watched as we are."

Fred set to work with no further words. His fingers were sensitive, as those of a designer of book jackets should be. Even wearing gloves, he did a good job, and when it was completed it would have needed a closer inspection than any letter is likely to get in a busy sorting office to observe that the stamp was not being used for the first time.

It gave him the sense of satisfaction, of power, which was too often the consequence of unholy but successful ventures. But before he finished, he had found occasion to reflect that Australians must have more leisure than is to be found in an older country.

Adeline inspected, and approved his work. "You'd better not let Bill see you post it," she remarked, "it was a silly thing to suggest. And after the way I've addressed it, you'd better post it in the city. You'll be certain not to forget?"

Fred gave the required assurance, and departed eastward. Half an hour afterwards, Adeline set out in the opposite direction with more money in her handbag than she could afford to spend. She had that dress in Paul & Snelford's window in mind. And shoes. And—other things which bedroom servants must not regard with supercilious eyes.

CHAPTER X.

The Opinions of Sir Reginald Crowe

SIR REGINALD CROWE was a young man—singularly so for the position of Chairman of one of the great English banks. How he had come to that position has been told before, and is a matter with which we have no present concern. Having had cause for complaint against the manager of one of the bank's Lancashire branches, he had demanded his dismissal, and when the board had declined to listen to this request, he had used the fortune which the boom in the cotton industry had enabled him to acquire to gain a secretly plotted control of the majority of the bank's shares, sufficient, as they finally proved, to enable him not only to procure the discharge of the offending manager, but to take the office which he had now held for more than six years, during which his vigorous and sometimes unorthodox methods had raised the London & Northern to a position second to none in the English banking world, and caused the "big five" to regret that further banking amalgamations were impracticable in the present state of the English law.

It was after Sir Reginald gained this position that the transactions incidental to the exploitation of the Ralston invention, and the tragedy of the Bell Street murders connected therewith,[1] had brought him into contact with Mr. Jellipot and Inspector Combridge (Chief-Inspector, as he now was), as well as providing him, in Lord Britleigh's sister, with a charming wife, whom he had previously wooed in vain.

Since that time it had been his pleasant annual custom to invite the two gentlemen mentioned to share for a few days the hospitalities of his country house, at such times as the Chief-Inspector's leave and the solicitor's business obligations would combine to allow.

---

[1] See *The Bell Street Murders.*

Now they sat together in a first-class compartment of the 3:17 as it drew out of Charing Cross Station, their privacy secured by the key of an obsequious guard, and with a pleasant sense of having left, for a brief space, the cares of a tiresome world.

"I wonder, Jellipot," Sir Reginald said, "whether we've hooked the cartoonist. There ought to be some fun if we have, especially when he finds that Kanwhistle's on the spot."

Mr. Jellipot looked more serious. "I don't know," he answered, "that fun's quite the right word to use. I have been disposed to think, on the reflection which I should have given the matter at an earlier moment, that I acted with less discretion than the position required when I—"

You needn't blame yourself for that. The thing's public knowledge," Sir Reginald, who rarely had the patience to allow Mr. Jellipot to reach the end of one of his carefully qualified statements, interrupted cheerfully.

"The primary responsibility," the solicitor replied, with the tone of one who will not be diverted from the worship of abstract truth by any personal consideration, "was entirely mine. But I was about to say that your invitation has certainly been accepted (though I am not aware that I used the word cartoonist in describing a gentleman who is, unless I have bee materially misinformed, a designer of what are, I believe, commonly known as dustcovers or book jackets, for the protection, or perhaps for the advertisement of books as they leave the publishers' premises), as I observed Mr. and Mrs. Corder entering a carriage at the farther end of the train."

"Mrs. Corder? Evelyn will be pleased that we've got her." Mr. Jellipot looked faintly surprised. "I was not aware," he said, "that the ladies had met previously."

"No. That's what Lady Crowe wants. She's rather keen on her books."

"You mean," Mr. Jellipot asked, with quick intelligence, though with undiminished surprise, "that Adeline Corder is a writer of books which Lady Crowe admires?"

"Yes. That's it. I supposed you knew who she was, being, more or less, a client of yours."

"It is a fact of which I was ignorant, and which occasioned a surprise for which I can advance no logical justification. I must admit that I am not a frequent reader of contemporary literature, but the lady appeared to me, at the one brief interview which we have had, to be of a particularly alert and intelligent mind."

To this point Chief-Inspector Combridge had listened in silence to a conversation which he did not understand, and into which it might be unmannerly, to intrude; and his profession tamed him to a willing silence so long as other people would talk. It was only when the fluency of others failed that it would become his part to stimulate it with adroit remarks.

He was on holiday now, and among friends: as much off his guard as a man of such training can ever be. But the conjunction of the two names—Corder and Kanwhistle—had waked a memory which reflection confirmed, and which could hardly be a repeated chance.

"I suppose," he interposed confidently. "you mean you've invited the beneficiaries under the Kanwhistle will?"

"Yes," Sir Reginald answered. "You'll see the two jokers meet."

"They don't know yet that they're on the same train?"

"I don't," Mr. Jellipot answered, "suppose that they are. Mr. Percival Kanwhistle, when he calls upon me, is usually the sole occupant of a sports car, which I have understood to be his customary vehicle of locomotion. I doubt whether he ever uses any other. At least," he added, with his usual careful precision, "within the limits of our own land. I have no doubt that he may avail himself of the services of a ship for marine occasions."

"I suppose they don't love each other," the inspector asked curiously. He was puzzled, and instinctively aware of something more to be told. The Chairman of the London & Northern Bank was capable of surprising actions, sometimes of a mischievous, even boyish quality, but he was hardly of the sort to invite two incongruous or unfriendly guests that he might make sport of their antagonisms while beneath his roof.

"They are not," Mr. Jellipot replied, as the banker again left the conversation to him, "of congenial dispositions, nor was the nature of Miss Kanwhistle's will, either in its main provisions or that most regrettable codicil, of a character to improve them to cordiality."

Sir Reginald Crowe's nimble mind was working with its usual efficiency, though his words had been slower, to come. He was conscious that, although there might be plausible, and even veracious explanation, of those two invitations of which he had no reason to be ashamed, yet he had not been innocent of some thoughts of another kind. He had certainly looked forward with pleasure to observing the actions—or inactions—of the man who had been so temptingly lured to a career of diurnal crimes, with something shockingly approaching hope that actions might be the word. But it would never have entered his mind in his wildest dreams to betray anyone so sportingly occupied to the talons of an unimaginative and unrelent-

57

ing law. It had not occurred to him previously that, in inviting the cousins and Chief-Inspector Combridge to become fellow guests, he might be exposing Frederick Corder to a perhaps fatal peril, such as he would not otherwise have had to face.

He saw also that, apart from the realities of the position, the appearance of an important member of the Criminal Investigation Department upon the scene was liable to an interpretation little conducive to Mr. Corder's peace of mind, or consistent with the good faith of the invitation which that gentleman had accepted from him. Indeed, the coincidence of these two invitations, even without the complication of Percival Kanwhistle's added presence, was a carelessness which might not easily be believed, and placed upon him an obligation (as he looked at the matter) to see that no unpleasant consequence should follow from their common sojourn beneath his roof.

All this was, of course, on the assumption that Mr. Corder had accepted his aunt's mocking invitation to a year of crime. Otherwise, he might meet the inspector, ignore his cousin, and fulfil the commission he had been invited to undertake with a quiet mind. But that was not what Sir Reginald was inclined to expect, and perhaps hope, the position to be. He did not therefore anticipate trouble which he would be unequal to handle. He had some confidence in himself. He merely became alert to the position, as a general watches the deployment of foes whom he had gone too nearly to overlooking.

"You mustn't suppose," he said, "that I asked them because I thought they were bosom friends, and certainly not because Corder'd be likely to go for Kanwhistle on sight. The fact is, they're both business invitations, and quite separate, though they are concerned with the same matter in almost opposite ways. Tell him, Jellipot. It's your doing rather than mine."

"I am not aware," Mr. Jellipot replied, with a readiness to repudiate this construction which may have sprung from a conscience not entirely at ease, "that I have either deviated from or exceeded the very natural and proper instructions which I received.

"Sir Reginald"—he turned to the inspector as he went on— "three years ago, actuated by generosity rather than merely business considerations, and in excess of the limit to which he was professionally advised to go, lent a sum of four thousand pounds upon a property adjoining his residence at Hither Dene.

"Recently the owner died, and it became necessary to take possession of property which the executors concerned were unwilling to touch. Sir Reginald, who, as you may know, is rather obstinate in being unwilling to take a loss, and being advised that the amount was greater than would be likely to be reached at public auction, has been anxious to secure a private buyer.

"A few weeks ago, I had reason to think that I had found an American gentleman who would give the price we were asking, but he returned to his own country without reaching a decision, and he has now written asking that photographs or sketches of the property should be forwarded to him, for the approbation of the lady whom he is about to marry.

"It was Sir Reginald's own suggestion that some drawings in black and white, or perhaps a watercolour sketch, might be more attractive—mellower was the actual word he employed—than photographs, in presenting a house the antiquity of which is, to American eyes, its particular charm. I had his instructions to find a suitable artist, and it occurred to me that Mr. Corder might be able to undertake the work, which it is important to have properly executed.

"So long as our American correspondent remains an uncertain buyer, you will agree that it is my duty to Sir Reginald to remain alert to other opportunities. My client, Mr. Percival Kanwhistle, having inherited a substantial fortune, is looking round for a suitable residence. I have recommended Maidcote Manor to his consideration, and Sir Reginald has, very naturally, invited him to Hither Dene to enable him to inspect the property in a leisurely manner."

Chief-Inspector Combridge listened to this lucid but somewhat prolix explanation, and his mind, as Sir Reginald may have desired, was partially diverted from the consideration of Frederick Corder as a potential criminal. "You mean," he said, "that while Kanwhistle is looking over the house he'll see Corder there making a sketch for another customer, and that's to give him a leg up to the bid you want him to make?"

"It did occur to me," Mr. Jellipot modestly admitted, "that the position might be conducive to that result."

For the moment the conversation paused while discretion strove to restrain Sir Reginald from further speech. In the end it gave way to his habitual preference for the bolder course and the frontal attack.

"See here, Combridge," he said, "we're good friends now, and I expect we always shall be. But I don't invite guests to Trees to spy on each other, or make trouble after they leave. I suppose it's understood that you're off duty till you go back to the Yard?"

The inspector did not deny this, but answered cautiously and with some surprise: "You don't mean me to understand that Corder's breaking the law every day, and I'm to see it and just look on? I shouldn't have thought there was a mug on earth crazy enough to go in for a game like that."

"Of course I didn't mean anything of the kind. I don't know that he ever broke a law in his life. I'm told that that silly will was just to poke fun at him, because he wouldn't take tuppence if it fell into his hands because some other fool had forgotten to press button B. But what I mean is that it's his matter, not ours; and when you take a week off, I should say you've got less business than most men to be hunting after a bad smell."

Inspector Combridge could not fail to see that there was a reasonable basis for this argument. He was on vacation. His official duties were suspended. More than the average citizen, he might claim that such an interlude implied that he should not busy himself in pursuit of those who fail to honour their country's laws.

"Well," he said, "from what you say—and what's common sense—I don't suppose there's anything to be seen; and you're right that I needn't lose any sleep trying to turn it up. Of course, if one of them bashes the other's head, you'll call in the local police. You won't need any interference from me."

Mr. Jellipot felt that this was as much as any C.I.D. officer could be expected to say, and would have turned the conversation to other channels, but Sir Reginald's methods of verbal warfare were more aggressive.

"That," he replied, "is the right way to look at it, and no more than I should have expected you to say. But I'll say something myself which goes a bit farther than that. If Mr. Corder's been committing a daily crime for the last three months without anyone noticing what's been going on, you policemen can't do the law or your own bosses a better service than to leave him alone, and take care that no one ever makes a guess at a game he's busy playing so much better than you."

"I don't see that, Sir Reginald. I don't see that he ought to be treated any different from any other law-breaker just because he's hoping to make an extra rake-up at the end of his career."

"I didn't say that he should for that reason. I wasn't thinking of him. Suppose you do run him in on the last day of the year, and when he's been found guilty of impersonating a policeman, or not registering a bull calf, or selling a foreign egg as English new-laid, or shooting his neighbour's cat, or perhaps nothing worse than buying chocolates three minutes after hours, or wringing a crooner's neck—how will it look if he asks the bench to take his other crimes into account, and hands up the list of the three hundred and sixty four, and there's not one in the whole lot by which anyone's a penny the worse, and perhaps some that go down bang in the other scale?

"It might lead to Parliament being given six months to repeal nine-tenths of the laws we've got, and then a ten-year vacation on half-pay so that they shouldn't vex us with any more, and perhaps half of you johnnies going the same road."

Inspector Combridge met this proposition with no more than a silent smile. He had a great respect for Sir Reginald Crowe. If it pleased him to talk nonsense at times—

Having reduced the inspector to a satisfactory silence, the banker turned to Mr. Jellipot: "I'll tell you what, Jellipot. You're the only one of us who knows the Corders, and you'd do me a favour if you'd meet them and bring them along. There'll be the limousine at the station, and Combridge and I will go on in that. But Lady Crowe is bringing her car down as well, and there'll be room for you and the Corders there. I don't suppose they'll have over-much luggage, and if they do we can send down for it later. But it may spare Mr. Corder a bit of a shock if he isn't introduced to the inspector till you've had a chance to explain that he's not been brought here on a business visit."

CHAPTER XI.

MEETINGS AT HITHER DENE

IT was by deliberate design that Mr. and Mrs. Corder had reached the departure platform fifteen minutes before the train had been due to leave, and had then gone to the far end before entering a third-class compartment. The fact was that Adeline had expended so much upon some of the contents of the two rather large suitcases which the attendant porter, to her breathless relief, deposited safely upon the rack, that she had faced an urgent need for economy on counting her remaining notes, which had been no less apparent after she had enquired concerning her husband's willing but exiguous resources.

She had then decided that the tickets must be third-class, and though she had no expectation that Sir Reginald Crowe would be on the train, nor that the tickets for his travelling companions would be purchased from his own fat wallet, she had a well-founded doubt of the class which Mr. Jellipot would use, and a disposition to avoid meeting until the journey should be completed.

"Fred," she said, as the train slowed down upon the long green-bordered platform of Hither Dene, and her husband rose to get the two suitcases from the rack, "you'll be careful about the clasps, won't you? And don't trust the blue one to a porter, whatever you do with mine."

Her apprehension was based upon the fact that the suitcase, once her own, which she had allocated to her husband's use, was liable to burst open at most inopportune times, if handled by those who did not humour its failing clasps, and that case now contained—outcast from her own by the extent of those recent purchases—the detailed record of criminal conspiracy, its careful tabulations intended ultimately to satisfy Mr. Jellipot's conscientious if not unfriendly scrutiny, but most unsuitable for exposure to other, earlier eyes. "It would have been another reason," her mind wandered to observe, with a vague fear of the probing which personal luggage may receive from foreign customs' officials, "against going abroad. We ought to have thought of that."

She watched Fred secure one of the two porters on the length of a platform upon which about a dozen scattered passengers had descended, and his resolute refusal to let the man handle more than one of the cases. "Three months ago," she thought, "I wouldn't have trusted him. I should have had to deal with that myself, or the man would have had it out of his hand by now, and be scattering pyjamas along the line." It led her to wonder whether the most beneficial result of the majority of our countless laws may not be their effect upon the character of those who break them. Might not a correspondence course be—? No, the idea, for several reasons, was absurd. But that was surely Mr. Jellipot detaching himself from a little group at the other end of the platform, and waving his umbrella as he hurried toward them.

"Sir Reginald," Mr. Jellipot said, "was on the train, but he has another guest with him, and he has asked me to meet you. I understand that Lady Crowe is driving us up."

The last sentence, which was verbally correct, however misleading it might be, had the effect of removing any aspect of discourtesy from the one which had gone before it.

The limousine had already left by the time that Mr. Jellipot's little party reached the station entrance.

Lady Crowe, who knew the solicitor very well, having shared some exciting experiences with him before her marriage, had already received from her husband a quick word of enlightenment as to the present position, and now waved a beckoning hand from where she had drawn up to the curb behind two cars which were already in the act of moving away.

Her own, a light four-seater saloon, was sufficient, though no more, for the accommodation of her three guests. "James," she said to the porter, "you'd better fasten those on behind."

Mrs. Corder thought differently.

The porter evidently regarded Lady Crowe as the one to be obeyed, but the result was a compromise by which one was strapped on at the back, and one went inside. That was satisfactory to Mrs. Corder, and Lady Crowe saw no reason to object. "It's the gentlemen who'll get crowded, not we," she said equably, as she invited Adeline to the seat beside her.

She was no older than Adeline, and her figure only slightly more matronly. She alone knew the rigour of exercise, and the meagre dieting which maintained the youthful symmetry which she valued (Sir Reginald told her) at too high a price. Like most men who are leanly made, he considered generosity in a woman's figure a most venial fault. But Evelyn, though willing to please her husband, had some inclination also to please herself.

They had not traversed more than a tenth of the ten-minute drive to Trees before Adeline felt that she had found a friend. Lady Crowe talked while driving with careless ease on a road she knew. Adeline listened with a diligence which assimilated and responded suitably, while missing little of Mr. Jellipot's conversation with her husband in the rear seat.

By this means she learned something of the occasion for the surprising invitation they had received, and heard a casual and plausible explanation of the fact that a Chief-Inspector of Scotland Yard had been invited to meet them. She also caught the name of Percival Kanwhistle, in a half-heard sentence which prepared her for the sight of that gentleman, who, next moment, with his eyes only upon the road, caught and passed them in a low racing car at a rate which may have been less than eighty miles—or may not.

Meanwhile, Lady Crowe was telling her how the house to which they were going had been called Greenlands when Sir Reginald gave it to her as a wedding present ("Not a bad name if only you could say it without icy mountains coming into your mind "), and how she had renamed it Trees in honour of the winding avenue of chestnuts which, beyond a low dip in the undulating landscape, was already visible while she spoke.

Altogether, Adeline's ears and mind had a very busy time until the car came to rest before the central door of a low Tudor brick-and-tile residence—mansion would have been scarcely too pretentious a word—which enclosed three sides of a square courtyard, paved of old, but now broadly gravelled, greenly turfed, and gay with beds of tulips of unvaried gold.

"I'm running the car round into the garage myself," Lady Crowe said. "I never let anyone else drive it. But Janet will show you to your rooms, and there'll be tea in the rose garden as soon as you're ready for it. Mr. Jellipot, you might show Mr. and Mrs. Corder the way down the side stairs. You'll be in your usual room, and they're in the next one to that."

Adeline heard this with a divided attention, while she said to an astonished boy: "No, don't touch that one. Mr. Corder always likes to carry his own luggage. It's—it's a family habit."

But her interposition had been needless on this occasion. Fred had learnt of the coming of Percival Kanwhistle. He had learnt of the coming of a Chief-Inspector from Scotland Yard. He had received these items of information with a mind more suspicious and less buoyant than hers. Acutely conscious of the damning evidence within that ill-fastened case, only physical violence would have induced him to loose the handle, or raise the finger that pressed the catch.

The builders of the Tudor period and half the succeeding century had only two ideas for the layout of bedroom floors. Either they had avoided passages entirely by the simple expedient of making each room open into the next, or they had run a straight and narrow passage along the side of the series of rooms to which it was designed to give access.

The east wing of Trees had been constructed on the latter principle. Built over the kitchens, larders, dairy, and storeroom which occupied so considerable a proportion of a Tudor mansion, and probably designed for the accommodation of an inside and outside staff at a time when human hands were considered more valuable and machinery less so than now, it consisted of a long range of small rooms entered from a narrow passage which ran the whole length of the wing. The passage windows looked out over the stable roofs and to the gardens beyond. The bedroom windows looked down on the central court.

Electric lighting, central heating, and the provision of abundant bathrooms had transformed this wing into suitability for the reception of bachelor guests. The first room of all, larger than the others, perhaps meant originally for a steward's use, and which now had a private bathroom opening from it, had been allocated to Mr. and Mrs. Corder. Mr. Jellipot was next. After him came Inspector Combridge's room, and then that which was to be occupied by Jane Kanwhistle's sporting heir. The others were vacant on this occasion. It was not the idea of domestic bliss either of Sir Reginald Crowe or his wife to surround themselves with promiscuous guests, though there would be occasions when hospitality overflowed the accommodation even of that extensive mansion. For the most part, their own lives were too full to require the introduction of extraneous diversions.

Mr. Jellipot, looking through the passage windows, pointed over the stable roofs to the direction in which the rose garden lay. "You will find," he said, "that there is a flight of stairs at the farther end of the passage, and if you descend by that, rather than by the main flight up which we came, and will then take the path to the right after the stables are passed, you will come straight to the rose garden. There is a little lawn at the side shaded by a group of beeches, under which, if precedent be a sufficient guide, I have no doubt that the tea table will be set."

As he spoke, the existence of the further stairs was demonstrated by the appearance of a groom bearing Mr. Kanwhistle's trunk on his shoulder, followed by that gentleman himself.

His appearance caused a withdrawal of the Corders into their own room, too hurriedly to observe that he was followed by the Detective-Inspector whom they had greater reason to fear, and allowing only of the curtest recognition of Mr. Jellipot's leisurely explanation.

Adeline looked round the dark-toned beauty of the low-raftered room. It had the atmosphere of strength, of permanence, of unassertive dignity which is the antithesis of that of a modern home. The people who built thus would not have thought it enviable to whirl about at increasing speeds. They were content to be firmly there. They did not say: "Let us eat and drink, for the future is dark to see." They said: "Let us build strongly and well, that our homes endure in our children's days." Contrasting the atmosphere of that ancient house with that of the shoddy ugliness of the Bloomsbury flat which she had left less than three hours before, she felt that she would have been entirely happy in such an interlude but for the sordid programme of petty crime from which there could be no pause. But she did not therefore falter in resolution, or allow her mind to be drawn aside from the exigencies of the hour. As she closed the door, she said: "When I've hung up some of my things, there'll be room for that wretched book in my own case, and I'll transfer it at once. Thank Heaven that one's got a good lock."

"It isn't a good lock we need," Fred retorted, with gloomy wit, "if you ask me, it's a good bolt."

Adeline understood quickly enough, but she was less disposed to agree. "Oh, I wouldn't say that. 'The wicked fleeth when no man pursueth,' you know. It's a good verse. It all seems to have happened naturally enough."

"You really think that? Percy here and Jellipot, and a cop from the Yard at the same time? I wonder they had the cheek to suppose that we shouldn't see through so bare a trap!"

"No. That's just it. If they'd been laying a trap it wouldn't have been done in such an obvious way."

"But if they only mean to make it impossible for us to go on doing things without being caught, it doesn't matter to them how obvious it is. It's just as good for Percy if they frighten us into stopping as if they get me caught and convicted. The money'd be done for just the same, and he might prefer it that way."

Adeline had no difficulty in following this rather ill-stated argument, but she still held to her own opinion: "I haven't seen Sir Reginald yet, so I can't say, but I don't think Mr. Jellipot would be a party to anything of the kind, and I'm absolutely certain that Lady Crowe wouldn't. She'd be on our side if it came to that, more likely than not."

"But suppose they all think—I mean except Percy—that it's being done for our own good? They may have asked the cop to give me a talk about jails not being properly warmed."

"Yes, there is that. But it's no use guessing. We've just got to wait and see. And, at the worst, we've got return tickets, and there ought to be plenty of trains. We've got today's good deed done already, and tomorrow's all properly fixed up. If it wasn't for this book—which they're hardly likely to guess we've got, and it may have been foolish to bring—I don't see why we should have a care in the world."

"It might have been just as bad if we'd left it. I dare say they've got detectives searching the flat now."

"Well, that's one cheerful thought, anyway! And I hope they are, for they certainly won't find anything there."

CHAPTER XII.

The Extremes Meet at Tea

MR. KANWHISTLE'S car, having outdistanced that of Lady Crowe with the contemptuous indifference of continual habit—for the cars were few indeed that he sighted and did not leave in a dusty rear—rapidly overhauled Sir Reginald's limousine, which he might also have passed without ruffling the feelings of a chauffeur too conscious of the dignity of his own position and the latent power of the smooth engine which he controlled to give emulous attention to any antic of the inferior denizens of the road, but that they had entered the narrow byway which is the only approach to Trees from the main road that runs through the village of Hither Dene. The lane twisted, and Sir Reginald's chauffeur knew that Mr. Kanwhistle could neither pass him nor proceed at a faster pace than his own with reasonable safety, and therefore, when he heard the impatient honk of the horn of the sporting car, he took no notice at all, unless it were to move out a foot or two farther across the centre of the lane, changing into the impossible that which would have been merely hazardous before.

It followed that the sports car remained closely in the rear of its more imposing cousin. Sir Reginald, not holding Inspector Combridge on a footing of ceremony, told the chauffeur to drive straight into the garage yard, and Mr. Kanwhistle, not being one who lost any sleep over the finer points of etiquette, took the same way.

Sir Reginald, alighting, looked at Mr. Kanwhistle and at Mr. Kanwhistle's car, and had no difficulty in guessing his visitor's name. Introductions followed. Sir Reginald, handling a delicate situation too lately visualised, added with habitual boldness: "We've got some other friends of yours coming this afternoon, Mr. and Mrs. Corder. Mr. Corder has kindly undertaken to do some sketches of Maidcote Manor for a possible American buyer."

"Oh," Mr. Kanwhistle answered easily, taking this information without showing any great surprise, or appearing to regard it as of importance to him, "you've got Fred coming here? And of course you know he's the man my aunt teased in her will. Jellipot would have told you that. And you thought it would be prudent to have someone here from Scotland Yard who'd be able to count the spoons! Well, I don't blame you for that. But I don't suppose he'll find anything wrong. Fred may have had a shot at winning the stakes. I half thought he would. But he'll have chucked it long before now. He's not the sort who'd stay such a pace as that. Miss Kanwhistle knew well enough what she was doing when she put that joker on to the will."

Sir Reginald spoke with as much sharpness as he cared to use to a guest: "I hope you will put any such idea out of your mind. It has no foundation at all. Inspector Combridge is here solely because he is an old friend, and his visit was arranged before I even heard Mr. Corder's name."

"That," the inspector confirmed, "is the fact, Mr. Kanwhistle. I've come here to forget business for a few days, and I hope nothing's going to happen to make me wish I'd taken my vacation elsewhere."

"Oh, yes, of course. Sorry. Of course, that's what you've got to say! Clumsy of me. But you won't find me blowing the gaff. I only wonder you didn't bring him down dressed up like a groom, or a maiden aunt. I thought that was the usual way."

"You will oblige me," Sir Reginald replied coldly, "if you will accept my assurance in a more literal manner. I would neither spy on a guest nor invite anyone for Lady Crowe to receive against whom such an occasion could be expected to arise."

"Sorry, again," Mr. Kanwhistle repeated, but in a tone which gave no confidence that his previous conclusion had been disturbed. "I know Fred's one of the best. And as to looting anything that's not his, why if he took a shilling out of his right-hand pocket, he'd be too conscientious to put the change back in his left. That's just why my aunt used to get mad."

The banker saw that, for the time at least, there was no more to be said. To protest too much might only confirm Mr. Kanwhistle in his mistaken opinion. He turned his attention to giving the necessary order for the disposition and comfort of the two guests who were immediately on his hands, and then went to his wife's room, where he explained the position to her in more detail than had been possible previously.

"It might," she said, "be rather fun."

"It might be a damned mess."

"So it might. We've got to hope that it will be nothing at all. But I've no doubt you'll be equal to handling it. Anyway, we've got to give the menagerie tea, and it's time to go."

With these loyal and hospitable words Evelyn threw away the cigarette in which she was too prone to indulge when in the privacy of her own room, and led the way downstairs.

On the half-landing she paused and looked at a scarred finger-tip where a bullet had left a mark which would never entirely go: "When I ever have any doubt of whether you'll be able to pull things through, I just look at this. Or if it's too dark for that, I think of the walls of a particularly nasty jail."

"Well," he said, "if it comes to that, you didn't do so badly yourself. And we may be up against something now that you'll handle better than I."

"It's more likely that it will be just nothing at all."

With these confident exchanges the two went out into the sunshine of a May which was to prove the best month of a subsequently inclement year, to await the appearance of their incongruous guests. Under the low-spreading shade of beeches, beautiful with the fresh green of their half-grown leaves, Evelyn adroitly arranged the little party so that its more inflammable elements should not be brought too closely together. She wished in vain that she had had the forethought to import two or three additional girls whose attractions and wits (stimulated by the right word from her) might have been sufficient to pass the time safely away. But it was too late for regret. And she had not known that Mrs. Corder—nor even certainly that her husband—would be there.

Rather, she had anticipated a party of men only, certainly innocuous, probably a little dull. Talk—dinner—billiards—perhaps bridge. Pleasant reminiscences. The business prospect of getting rid of Maidcote Manor. But this was a horse of another colour.

She seated Adeline at her right side, with Inspector Combridge beside her, careless that she embarrassed, and went far to alienate them by suggesting that the inspector would be a mine of information that no novelist could afford to miss. Sir Reginald, at Inspector Combridge's farther side, was a safety barrier between him and Mr. Corder. Beyond him was the solicitor, and Mr. Kanwhistle at her left hand completed the circle, spread widely enough to support a reasonable hope that they would converse with their immediate neighbours rather than engage in a general conversation, while Janet, a particularly neat and efficient parlour maid, waited deftly

upon their material comforts. Beyond petitioning a too-probably re-
gardless heaven, what more could a hostess do?

For a time everything went well. Inspector Combridge was not
a man who scintillated in social circles, but he had a wide knowledge of human nature, and a long experience in mixing with all
manners and degrees, both women and men. When he learnt that
Adeline Corder did not write detective fiction, and that he was not
expected to talk shop to a gushing or probing woman, he became
genial enough; and if the force of habit caused him to study with
some attention one who might be wife of a peculiarly active criminal, it may be doubted that he was more adroit or alert than was the
lady novelist, either in maintaining her own guard, or in probing
him.

Meanwhile Sir Reginald explained to his right-hand neighbour
the reason for his invitation, in more detail than he had heard it before.

"I don't want to rush you," he said, "and I've no idea how long
two or three sketches ought to take you to do, but if you *can* have
anything ready for Tuesday's mail, I shall be glad to get it off; or, if
not, you've got till Friday, when the next goes. You must use your
own judgment of the best aspects to choose, but I'd like you to show
the general elevation, and get in some of the mullioned windows,
and the sundial, and the yew garden—it's got trimmed walls of yew
all round, ten feet high—and the back porch, which is said to go
back to the fourteenth century, and the swan pond, and at least one
interior, either the great galleried hall, or the dining room (it's got an
exceptionally interesting open fireplace and irons, and the escutch-
eons are rather good), or perhaps both."

"Well," Fred replied, rather breathlessly, "I'll do what I can, but
you know this isn't really in my line at all. I've done scarcely anything except book jackets far the last three years."

"I've no doubt you'll make a good job," the banker answered
confidently. "I've got Jellipot's word for that, and I've never known
him make a mistake yet when he picks his man. What I want most of
all is something that will show the age and character of the house in
a way that photographs never will. They're too cold. I want something mellower, if you know what I mean."

Fred said, with more confidence than he felt, that of course he
did. He was beginning to feel, under the influence of the banker's
eloquence, more belief in the good faith of the invitation that
brought him there. He reminded himself that Adeline had expressed
that opinion, which he knew to be at least as valuable as his own.
But he looked round and saw his cousin—his cousin's solicitor—a

Chief-Inspector of the C.I.D. Sir Reginald might not be in the plot, but it was hard to think that no plot was there! And then Sir Reginald went on to open another aspect of the matter by saying: "There's another thing you ought to know, and that is that it's the same business that's brought Mr Kanwhistle here—"

"Yes, Mr. Jellipot told me that."

"I dare say he did. But what I want to point out to you is this. I don't mind how much Kanwhistle hears about what you're doing, or what it's for. It might easily bring him up to scratch, trying to get his bid in before it's too late, and perhaps adding a thousand, more or less, to the price he'll pay. The fact that he's your cousin won't make you unwilling to do that, will it?"

"No, not in the least."

There was a heartiness in this reply which led the banker to add: "And if that's what happens, you needn't mind putting an extra tenner or so on to your bill when you send it in. You'll find I shan't cavil at that."

Fred, receiving that gratifying assurance, raised his eyes to where his cousin sat nearly opposite to him, talking to Lady Crowe and being talked to by Mr. Jellipot in about equal proportions. The eyes of the two men met, and it may have occurred to both that no previous sign of greeting had passed between them. Fred had no love for his cousin, but it would have been poor policy to make open quarrel with one whose given word or sporting code was his sole assurance that he would be able to collect the rich prize for which he perpetrated so many unlawful deeds.

He said: "Hullo, Percy," cordially enough, and Mr. Kanwhistle, almost at the same instant, said: "Hullo, Fred," to him. Unfortunately, he said more. It may have been merely a genuine recognition of what was actual fact, joined to the levity of disposition the deceased Miss Kanwhistle had approved, which caused him to add: "You're looking a different man from what you did three months ago. The old lady knew what she was doing. If I get a bit off colour, I'll ask you to give me a few lessons in the profession."

"Janet," Lady Crowe's voice broke in, rather more emphatically than would have been appropriate under normal circumstances, "I think Inspector Combridge is needing another cup."

CHAPTER XIII.

ADELINE PLAYS BRIDGE

MR. JELLIPOT said that he had never played contract. The conventions were too elaborate for one limited as he was both in leisure and mental power. Mrs. Corder said the same, though without offering similar explanations. She added that she liked auction, but understood that it was considered by contract players to be no more than a childish game. Lady Crowe said, with truth, that she and Sir Reginald preferred it; and Mr. Kanwhistle, with no truth whatever, but unexpected politeness, said the same.

They sat down accordingly, Adeline as Sir Reginald's partner, and Mr. Kanwhistle opposite Lady Crowe. Adeline, being asked if a shilling a hundred would suit her, and observing, with a slight feeling of concealed annoyance, that she was regarded as the only one necessary to consider, said that of course it would. She spoke with an inward dread, for her purse was lean, and a penny was her usual limit.

Mr. Jellipot said, by their leave, he would watch the game. He was always willing to learn.

Inspector Combridge and Mr. Corder went to the billiard room. They both played a moderately bad game, running each other closely, and winning about equally. Good temper prevailed.

Inspector Combridge could not avoid giving some consideration to his opponent in the light of a particularly persistent and successful criminal, but all his experience did not assist him to a correct conclusion. He had no intention of breaking his tacit pledge to their common host, but he felt that, if he could obtain a direct assurance from Mr. Corder that he was living a blameless life, he could take his word and put an absurd idea finally out of his mind.

"It was a rotten trick," he remarked, as he chalked his cue at the commencement of the third hundred up, "making the will the way that woman did. I don't wonder you felt sore. She couldn't even have meant it to be taken seriously."

Fred, always inclined to nervousness when under the eyes of his vigilant and sometimes critical wife, met the danger in a way that she would have approved, and perhaps somewhat more coolly than her presence would have allowed him to do.

"I've never been quite sure of that," he said easily, "it read to me rather as though she wanted to encourage me to try, and at the same time to make sure I should fail."

"It was a sum that would make a good many of us think once or twice," the inspector admitted, "before they decided to let it go."

"Yes," Fred agreed, with the delusive frankness of the half-truth, "we talked it over a bit ourselves—Mrs. Corder and I. It would have been doing the old girl one in the eye, so to speak, for if anything's sure, it's that she didn't intend me to pick up the money.

"We talked about sleeping out, which I'm told is a dreadful crime, though I don't know why. But there wasn't only the difficulty of keeping anything up for twelve months without getting caught, there was the risk that I might have lain awake, sooner or later, and come unstuck."

Inspector Combridge considered this from the standpoint of his professional knowledge, and saw how a layman's ignorance must obstruct him in the pursuit of a life of crime. "It isn't the going to sleep that matters," he explained. "It's enough if you're wandering about at night with no money in your pocket—no visible means of support."

Fred thought he saw the way here to an easy method of law-breaking which Adeline's and his own half-knowledge had put too lightly aside. He answered boldly: "You mean, I should have been breaking the law sufficiently if I'd walked out every night for a few minutes without taking any money with me?"

"Yes, that's the law."

"Well, I didn't know that three months ago, or I might have done it. It would be too late to start anything now.

Inspector Combridge accepted this assurance as saying more than it exactly did, and it was a merely abstract respect for accuracy which caused him to qualify his previous statement. "I don't quite mean that," he said. "I don't say it would be a crime to be in the street during the night without money. Not if you gave your name and address and a proper account of yourself you were asked."

"You mean," his now thoroughly puzzled opponent asked, as he missed an easy shot at potting the red, "that if I walked about at night, with some money in my pocket, and refused to give my name and address, it would be no more than I'd a right to do? But if I'd got no money, and didn't give them, it would be a crime for which I could be put in jail? It seems to me that you've got to arrest the men first, according to that, and find out whether they're criminals only after they've been searched."

"Oh, we don't make many mistakes."

"All the same, there doesn't seem to be any crime until you're questioned. You can't be passively refusing a name that no one's asked you to give. So I shouldn't have been earning the money until I was getting caught, and the chance of winning it gone. It shows what a mug I should have been trying it on."

"Yes," the inspector agreed seriously, as he missed a fairly simple shot, "it's always best to go straight." His own mind had become somewhat confused as to the moment and circumstances under which wandering during the night with empty pockets becomes an outrage of English law. Mr. Jellipot would have expounded it to him with prolix exactitude, but Inspector Combridge, to whom it had been quite simple before, now felt that it was too much for him. Or, at least, as a theoretical proposition. As a practical one he had no doubt that, in any probable circumstance, he would know what to do.

The two men settled down to a rather less talkative and slightly higher standard of play. The inspector had come very near to certainty of opinion that Mr. Corder was a law-abiding and therefore respectable citizen. Mr. Corder had had a fright. Suppose he *had* tried the iniquity of sleeping-out, and, even though Adeline had been able to testify to authentic snores, it had been pronounced by Mr. Jellipot, when the hour of enquiry should arrive, that he had been a blameless, and must therefore be a disqualified man? Having come so nearly to this mistake, into what other fatal innocencies might not Adeline's too-confident guidance have led his blundering feet? He determined that he would not sleep before he had reviewed the written records of guilt, and relieved his mind of this dreadful doubt.

The sooner, therefore, that Adeline and he should retire, the better it would be for his peace of mind, and their fitness for the next day. At the second time of his proposing it, the inspector put his cue back into the rack, and the two men crossed the hall together to rejoin the bridge party in the lounge, where the game still went on.

Mr. Jellipot had seated himself on a low hassock between the two gentlemen's chairs. He was an ideal spectator, seldom speaking unless directly addressed, and then offering no more than diffident though acute opinions, discriminate praise, or sound excuse for the blunders of bidding or play that became apparent as the last trick was lost.

In his position he could see Mr. Kanwhistle's hand entirely, and had sufficient glimpses of Sir Reginald's. He must guess or wait to learn the cards that the ladies held.

The play had gone steadily in favour of Mr. Kanwhistle and Lady Crowe. Percival Kanwhistle was a swift and practised player. He set a pace which the others inclined to follow with results less satisfactory to themselves than him. Also, he and his partner had held the cards.

Sir Reginald played a sound game. There had been times when Adeline had been praised for hers. But it had not been their night.

Mr. Jellipot, watching silently, had formed the opinion that Adeline was worried by what she lost. That was a guess which had no supporting evidence beyond the fact that her eyes went frequently to the score which her neighbour kept. Sir Reginald had twice asked her if she were tired, and she had replied no. It was quite early yet, wasn't it? They were down 2,700 points when the billiard players entered the room.

Sir Reginald had just dealt. Not having raised his cards, he asked: "Shall we stop now?" The others had looked at theirs. Evelyn was silent, waiting for her guest to speak. Adeline said: "It's as you like, of course. I don't mind going on." Her voice implied more willingness than her words. Mr. Kanwhistle said: "That's all right with me." There was no doubt of his meaning.

Evelyn said: "Perhaps another half hour." Sir Reginald picked up his cards. He said: "One spade." Evelyn passed. Adeline bid: "Two hearts."

Mr. Jellipot saw Percival Kanwhistle's cards. The king and queen of spades. The ace of hearts bare. The king and ten of diamonds. Eight clubs, including the five honours. Not surprisingly he said: "Three clubs."

Sir Reginald hesitated. Being auction, he knew that his partner had told him plainly that she could not support spades. Mr. Jellipot caught a glimpse of a poor hand. But after a pause he confirmed his previous choice, "Three spades."

Lady Crowe passed again. Adeline bid: "Four hearts," no hesitation at all.

For ten seconds—long for him—Percival Kanwhistle gazed at his cards. His partner had offered no support. It would be game and rubber to their opponents to win the hand. At the worst, he could not be much down, and he had the five honours to score. He said: "Well, six clubs."

Sir Reginald passed at that. So, of course, did his wife. Adeline, with a shorter pause than Mr. Kanwhistle's had been, said: "Six hearts."

Percival Kanwhistle doubled. There were two more passes. Adeline said: "Just a moment, please." ("What will it mean?" she thought. "I'm one pound seven down without this rubber. I've got about thirty shillings, and Fred's got about ten or twelve. And it's only the first night! I ought not to have bought half I did.") She said aloud: "Redouble."

That finished the bidding. Mr. Kanwhistle led the king of spades. Sir Reginald laid down his cards. Adeline saw seven spades, headed by ace and knave. The rest was rubbish. There were no trumps. Mr. Kanwhistle smiled.

Adeline smiled also. She addressed her partner: "I banked on that—on your having the ace of spades."

After three tricks had fallen, she laid down her cards. There was no more to be said. She had held ten trumps, the ace and eight of diamonds, the four of spades. Only the ace of hearts could have been made against her by any but the most blundering play on her part. She heard the two men agreeing the score: "That will be one hundred and ninety-two below the line, and—" Yes, it was the rubber as well. Several shillings recovered, and renewed confidence to go on.

After that the luck changed. When they broke up Adeline learnt that she was three shillings to the good. She valued them much more than if she had not been in peril of a widely different result. She retired in a confident, happy mood, little disposed to listen to Fred's doubts and fears, and emphatic in her refusal to produce the key which would give access to the written evidences of their lawless conspiracy. "There's only one thing," she said, "that you've got to remember now, and that's that these old houses are said to carry sound from room to room in the most curious ways. I believe it's the wooden beams. Probably everything you're saying now is being shouted into the red-headed detective's ear. It's lucky for us that we've got no one worse than Mr. Jellipot in the next room, but we should be silly to trust to that."

Fred saw the wisdom of silence, for more reasons than one.

CHAPTER XIV.

BREAKFAST AT TREES

ADELINE waked to the sound of birds that quarrelled upon the eaves, and with a slant of sunshine across her bed. She remembered that the obligation of getting breakfast would not be hers, and that she had won three shillings the night before. The memory gave her some pleasant confidence that she would not fail to win a much larger sum at a later date.

She knew as little about sunrise as most Londoners do, but she judged correctly, by the ray of light which shone through the low, diamond-paned casement, that it would be some time before Janet would appear with the tea which was to come at seven-thirty; and until then she could lie at ease, making such plans as the occasion required, while Fred remained, at the other end of the room, in the quiet sleep which criminals and condemned murderers know, while it is sought vainly by better men.

Reviewing the position in this leisurely atmosphere, she could not fail to see that the assembly of Mr. Kanwhistle, Mr. Jellipot, and a detective officer from Scotland Yard around them, whether with deliberate hostile purpose, or that delusive aspect of coincidence which is the result of converging circumstance, could scarcely fail to increase the dangers of what they did; while, on the other hand, to resort to sudden, ignominious flight might confirm suspicion against them, or even rouse it while it might not seriously exist. It was a choice of evils, but inclination supported judgment in the decision that, for the day at least, they should hold their ground. At the worst, could not Fred declare that he felt unequal to producing the very numerous or comprehensive sketches that Sir Reginald required, and retire from the scene tomorrow in a natural manner? Or, better still—for, after what he had said already, that might have an unconvincing sound—might he not injure his right hand (a single finger would do!) sufficiently to incapacitate it for the required work?

The position might have been less ominous had she been willing to resort to a mere repetition of such minor delinquencies as can be committed with a privacy almost impossible to oversee. Profane oaths, for instance, may be uttered in public places with almost absolute safety, if their moment be chosen well. But there had been three occasions already when it had been necessary to resort to this form of iniquity, and though the objection which she had first raised against the frequent repetition of any one legal offence had been based, perhaps soundly, upon the increased probability of detection which might result, she had been influenced subsequently, and more than she was herself aware, by an artist's pride. As one of her own ancestors may have taken pleasure and pride in the arrangement of the many-coloured remnants which went to the making of a patchwork quilt, so did she desire that the variegated record of iniquity, when it should finally be presented to Mr. Jellipot's critical examination, should be worthy of her imagination and organising capacity: a gay defiance of the ubiquitous tyrannies of English legal enactments, wide-visioned and well-displayed! And as to profane oaths, there was another, though perhaps minor objection, in her own fastidiousness. They had been selected with care, but it had been necessary to make them objectionable enough to ensure that the conditions of the codicil would be fulfilled, and for her to witness and record their utterance, and it was a part which she did not like.

Her mind wandered for a moment to a list of legal offences which she had held in reserve, but been too cautious to risk—offences for which penalties were no longer exacted, but which were forbidden under old statutes, forgotten but unrepealed. There are so many of these that few men can go through a week without some act of unconscious crime. Particularly on Sunday, the sins of omission and commission lay snares round us on every side. She knew, for instance, that the cooking of meat on the first day of the week throws the shadow of the jail continually over a million homes, and she had once seriously considered allowing Fred to graduate on Sunday morning in this manner, but had put the idea aside through fear that Mr. Jellipot might rule that the will had not contemplated the mere breaking of obsolete laws—and, besides, Fred would have been almost certain to spoil the joint.

Well, perhaps she might be able to get a ruling from the solicitor on this point, if it were asked in a discreet way, and when Percy was not about. At this moment of her reflections, Janet came in with the tea, and after that Fred waked and became annoyingly talkative, in spite of all she could say respecting the sound-carrying qualities of a wooden beam. He was particularly inopportune in his suggestion that they should review the list of accomplished crimes for any possible innocence into which she might have led him through failure to take legal opinion more reliable than her own. He hadn't made a successful redouble the night before.

Fortunately, bathroom separations interrupted a conversation which approached more nearly to quarrelling than they had come since they had had a common interest to engage their minds, and after that they agreed to postpone the subject until they should have reached the secure solitude of a walk in the open air; and so, in a recovered amity, they descended to breakfast.

This, on other mornings of the week, when there would seldom be guests to consider, was a brief and punctual meal. Sir Reginald would arrive in the breakfast room at 8:15, and Evelyn was usually there about ten minutes before. At 8:43 precisely his car would come round to the front entrance, giving him time (with one spare minute) to catch the 8:55 to Cannon Street; while Evelyn, after the interview with the cook which, to most country house mistresses, is the most portentous and inevitable, and often the most dreaded event of the day, would usually order a horse if the skies were clear, or otherwise resort to the gymnasium, to indulge in such exercises as are said to be most beneficial in reducing weight.

But on Sundays the procedure was different, and breakfast was a meal to which all could help themselves at their own times, from the heated dishes the sideboard bore.

Adeline, entering the room in advance of her sinful spouse, was greeted with shy geniality by Mr. Jellipot, whose breakfast was nearly done. Inspector Combridge was represented only by a used coffee cup and a greasy plate. As Adeline paused to weigh the rival attractions of fried eggs and bacon, devilled kidneys, and Dover soles, Percival entered the room.

He uttered a sufficiently respectful good morning to Mr. Jellipot, a slightly too-familiar one to Adeline, and a good-humouredly contemptuous one to his impecunious and unadventurous cousin, at whom, however, he looked again at a later moment with a direct and questioning stare, which only Mr. Jellipot fully observed.

The suspicions of Inspector Combridge might have been turned aside, and those of the solicitor and Sir Reginald and Lady Crowe might be of a curious rather than an aggressive character, but those of Percival Kanwhistle—who was more directly interested—had become widely awake. Somehow, Fred looked *different*. What—but one thing—could be the meaning of that?

Mr. Percival Kanwhistle contemplated the possibility that his cousin might have plunged into a year of crime in pursuit of that £10,000 which he might so easily have handed over from a full purse, without resentment or thought of blame either to his cousin or to himself.

It was primarily a sporting event, and if he fairly lost he would fairly pay. But he did not intend to lose, if he could intervene to enforce innocence or secure the conviction of guilt. If Fred were really so occupied, he had had three months' start, which is more (proportionately) than a fox will get. But now the hunt was up, and he must look to himself.

"I understand, Mr. Kanwhistle," Mr. Jellipot said, "that Sir Reginald has arranged to drive you over to Maidcote Manor this afternoon."

"Yes, that's the ticket."

"We," Fred said, "have been asked to go at the same time."

"The intention is, I believe," Mr. Jellipot explained, "to leave the morning clear, on the assumption that all or any of us may wish to attend the service at the village church, or other forms of devotional exercises for which there are facilities in this vicinity. But I will confess that I am not so greatly drawn to attendance at a strange church that I am willing to forgo the pleasure of a country walk on a spring morning of such exceptional charm. Perhaps, Mr. Kanwhistle, you would care to join me, unless you would prefer the alternative?"

Mr. Kanwhistle said with emphasis that the alternative was not for him. With greater moderation, and rather to the solicitor's surprise, he accepted the invitation. He had two objects in doing this. He wished to discuss his cousin's possible delinquencies, and it had occurred to him also that he would like a quiet look at the surroundings of Maidcote Manor before he was in the hands and under the guidance of the vendor. For, as may have been already apparent, Percival Kanwhistle was very far from being a fool. He added the query: "Policeman coming as well?"

"Chief-Inspector Combridge," Mr. Jellipot replied, with more formality, "is, I believe, proposing to attend the congregational Church at Sleigh."

"Sounds queer for a cop."

"It is a proposition which might be argued from several angles," Mr. Jellipot replied, with the vagueness of one who had no inclination to argue at all, or at least not with Mr. Percival Kanwhistle on such a subject as that, and as he spoke their host and hostess entered the room together, and the conversation terminated.

CHAPTER XV.

Mr. Kanwhistle Seeks Advice

"WHAT I want to know," Mr. Kanwhistle said, when he had enquired concerning the position of Maidcote Manor, and assured himself that they were proceeding in that direction, "is whether Fred's really trying to make the haul."

"It is," Mr. Jellipot admitted, "a very natural curiosity, but it is a matter on which I feel differently. It is one about which I cannot know less than I wish to do."

"Well, if you don't care to ask him, there's no reason I shouldn't?"

The remark was clearly interrogative, and Mr. Jellipot answered it with characteristic precision: "If you intend to ask me whether you would transgress in any way the conditions of the will of your aunt, as they apply to yourself, by addressing such a query to Mr. Corder, I must give you a negative reply. You are apparently free to do or say anything that you will. I cannot tell you that any form of interference is barred. But I do not say that its propriety might not be questioned on other grounds. And you will, of course, observe that there is no obligation upon Mr. Corder to give you a truthful, or indeed, any reply whatever. Considering the conditions which have been laid upon him, a measure of reticence—I might say a severe measure—would appear to be an essential element in any plans such as you contemplate the possibility that he may pursue."

"I might get it out of her, if not out of him."

"Yes," Mr. Jellipot agreed dubiously, "you might—or you might not."

"You think Adeline's deep?"

"I think Mrs. Corder to be an exceptionally intelligent and attractive woman."

"Oh, she's all that. What she saw in Fred—!"

Percival was fluent enough for most purposes in the use of his own peculiar vocabulary, but words appeared to fail him as he contemplated his cousin's deficiencies as they should have appeared to a woman's eyes.

Mr. Jellipot, still maintaining his own intellectual integrity while declining argument on a serious plane, replied vaguely that they appeared to be mutually contented with the union into which they had entered, and his companion's mind reverted easily to its previous subject.

"I suppose," he said, "that there's no end of laws that Fred might break, if he's got into the habit; as I suppose he has, more likely than not."

Mr. Jellipot admitted that they were numerous, but he added modestly that he was not a criminal lawyer, and even such a one might hesitate to assert familiarity with every form of wrongdoing which has been particularised by English legislative enactments, even without their retinue of departmental regulations and local by-laws.

"But, perhaps," he added judicially, "the fault is less in the number and detailed nature of these sometimes arbitrary prohibitions than in the customary infliction of financial penalties which must obviously press unequally upon rich and poor. And this is most particularly so in connection with traffic offences, in relation to which a wealthy man may put a hundred or two aside at the commencement of the year as a fund to cover any illegalities he may commit, and then contemptuously disregard the law, knowing that nothing short of murder or habitual drunkenness will exceed the licence purchased, so to speak, in advance, by what may be no more to him than a trivial sum."

"I never heard of Fred running a car."

Mr. Jellipot perceived without taking offence that Percival kept to his point, and that abstractions were not for him. "I don't think," he replied, "that, if Mr. Corder were aiming to put himself into a position to claim the legacy, he would endeavour to reach his goal by breaking the traffic laws, numerous and sometimes irritating though they may be. The risk of being caught and convicted would be too great."

Percival saw reason in that. He asked another question which showed that he had been giving the matter some thought during the night. "Suppose," he said, "the beggar's running what you might call a continuous crime. Something that when you've started it, just goes on and takes care of itself without him doing anything more—should you say he'd be earning the dough by that?"

"Suppose," Mr. Jellipot countered cautiously, "you would give me an illustration of what you mean?"

"Well, say he tapped the electric main, and left the light on in the cellar for the twelve months?"

Mr. Jellipot hesitated. He was on the point of saying that it was a problem on which he would advise the taking of counsel's opinion, when he recalled the basic lawlessness of the whole matter. "The codicil," he replied, "was drawn up without legal advice, and I can have no responsibility for it. I hope that the question may not arise. Indeed, if you will excuse me, I should prefer not to discuss the problems which that unfortunate codicil raised, or to contemplate the regrettable possibility that I might ever be asked by either of you to adjudicate thereon."

"Then I'll only say that if he isn't trying on some trick like that, he'll find he's got his work cut out to carry this thing through, if that's really his game, as I've got an idea it is. You wouldn't say there are many ways he can break the law, try how he may, without being seen while he's staying among us here."

"No, I certainly wouldn't. I wouldn't say anything about it, if you don't mind," Mr. Jellipot replied, with that note of mild obstinacy in his voice which those who knew him best had learnt to respect, and sometimes to dread. He turned the conversation resolutely to the antiquity of Maidcote Manor, now showing its dark-brick chimneys among the trees.

He explained to an inattentive listener that the first syllable of the name of the residence did not allude to an unmarried woman, but was a contraction of "Mayday," as was proved by the evidence of most ancient maps.

CHAPTER XVI.

THE DAILY CRIME, AND SOME DETAILS

FRED and Adeline also went for a Sunday morning walk, which not only gave them the benefit of private consultation upon the difficulties of their position, but opportunity for a sudden crime, which relieved them from any further anxiety for the day.

There is a single railway line running through this sparsely populated part of West Sussex, which carries so little traffic that the owners have not yet been able to persuade the Southern Railway Co. to acquire it at the price which they are determined to get. In the neighbourhood of Hither Dene, it runs through a deep cutting, the Southern Line crossing it at a higher level.

Fred and Adeline, walking more rapidly than Mr. Jellipot was accustomed to do, and making a larger circuit, took a field path which led them to a level crossing obviously intended for the private use of the farmer whose fields stretched upon either side of this line.

Adeline frowned at the notice regarding the closing of the wider gate in a moment's doubt, which resulted in a reluctant decision that it would not do. It had become a point of honour with both of them, so far almost absolutely observed, that the long record of criminality should not contain anything that had done real harm either to man or beast. There were sheep in the farther field. They looked too somnolent to stray anywhere. They were probably too sensible to leave a luscious pasture to nibble at the sparse coarse grass which thrust upward through the black clinkers of the line. At any time someone of more normal morality might come along and close the gate. Even should they stray, it was improbable that any serious harm would result. There was no night traffic upon the line. Today being Sunday, there was none during the day. But their eyes met in silent recognition of the fact that it would not do.

Adeline looked up the line. As it curved into the cutting, there was a signal, and it was down. It was sufficiently high to be seen for some distance by an approaching engine driver, but lower than the sides of the cutting, so that, if it were raised, its movement could not be observed by anyone out of their own sight.

It is a grave offence for any unauthorised person to interfere with railway signals. Adeline felt that she could be certain of that without reference to the bylaws of this obscure line, which she had not seen. "But to raise a signal cannot result in any serious catastrophe. It will mean, at the most, some delay to a train which should have been allowed to proceed, and half an hour, more or less, to anyone content to use that line—!

"Quick, Fred! It's too good to miss. I'll 'coo-ee' if anyone's coming, and they'll never guess what you were meaning to do."

Three months ago—even two—there might have been hesitation and argument, but not now. Fred saw the idea as quickly as she, and before she had settled herself into an attitude of seeming indolence upon the stile which enabled pedestrians to cross without opening the heavy gate, he was hurrying along the line.

It was twenty minutes later when he came back. His hands were filthy, and his handkerchief was busily employed in wiping the blood from a skinned hand.

"I shouldn't think," he said, "that they'd moved that signal for twenty years."

Possibly not. The traffic would not pay for a large staff, and the signal had been found redundant on a line which seldom had more than one train on its whole length. Local residents could have told them that that signal was always down.

So the day's crime was done; and though they were both disposed to doubt the wisdom of the impulse on which they had acted, as they considered the possibility of having been followed by those who might have surrounded them for the express purpose of spying upon their movements, they had good cause to think that the risk had been safely taken; and when they came upon Percy and Mr. Jellipot at the turning which leads to Maidcote Manor, they were in the confident good spirits which they commonly found to be the result of accomplished crime.

Mr. Kanwhistle, observing that Mr. Jellipot was indisposed for further conversation on the subject of his aunt's codicil, had given his outward attention, and his audible remarks, to the ancient mansion of which they had obtained views from the road at several angles, but his thoughts had continued to dwell upon the problem of his cousin's conduct. He saw that, if Fred were really endeavouring to qualify for the nefarious prize, there must still be nine months of remaining criminality, and it was hard to think that, if he were put under sufficiently close observation, he could continue so long and regular a course of undetected lawlessness. Still, there was no time like the present. There might be no opportunity so good. He decided that he would take advantage of Chief-Inspector Combridge's presence to discuss the matter with him. Even if Sir Reginald had spoken no less than the truth when he had protested that there was no connection between the inspector's visit and his cousin's dubious deeds—even though the banker might really think it beneath his dignity to suspect his guests—Mr. Kanwhistle was under no such self-imposed restraint. They were not his guests. If one of the chief officers of the C.I.D. would not interest himself in a suspected criminal—and one whose violations of his country's laws were of such continuity, past, present, and future—what on earth were they for?

He looked at the happy pair converging upon him, and speculation approximated to certainty. They had been out together and done their crime! Mr. Jellipot, though trained to reach his conclusions with greater circumspection, was inclined to the same view. He noticed that Mr. Corder had a handkerchief twisted round an obviously cut hand. He would have said nothing, but Adeline had noticed the direction his eyes had taken.

"Fred," she said, "grazed his hand helping me over a stile, and I've told him to keep it covered till we can give it a proper wash. I'm always afraid of tetanus in these country fields with all the cattle about."

Mr. Jellipot, privately wondering whether the germs of tetanus were supposed to float about in the air of a cattle-infested land, contented himself with replying that it was always well to take precautions against infection, and that it was difficult to be too prompt or too diligent in washing a wound.

CHAPTER XVII.

INSPECTOR COMBRIDGE GIVES SOME ADVICE

MR. KANWHISTLE did not find it possible to speak to Inspector Combridge until after lunch, for the Congregational Chapel at Sleigh is three miles from Hither Dene, and it indulges in morning services which, whatever their relative quality may be, are certainly longer than those of the parish church which was favoured by the support of Sir Reginald and Lady Crowe, so that lunch was already served when the inspector returned.

Even afterwards, the opportunity was not easily made, and the time was short, for Sir Reginald had ordered his car to be at the door at 2:45, to take those of his guests who were sufficiently interested to Maidcote Manor. But Mr. Kanwhistle was a persistent man. He learnt that the party would consist of Sir Reginald, Mr. Jellipot, Mr. and Mrs. Corder, and himself, and that Lady Crowe and the inspector were remaining at home. There was a short interval during which the guests separated to prepare for the expedition, and Mr. Kanwhistle, deciding that his own preliminaries need be no more than the picking up of a hat in the hall, used this opportunity to hunt the inspector down. Lady Crowe being occupied with some detail of domestic control, Inspector Combridge was alone in the lounge.

Mr. Kanwhistle opened the subject at once. "I suppose, Inspector, that you'd be rather interested if you were to learn that Corder's trying to win that ten thousand pounds?"

Inspector Combridge did not like Mr. Kanwhistle, who had an offhand manner which the C.I.D. is not accustomed to meet. Neither did he like the question. He had been listening to a sermon that morning on the text: *Judge not, that ye be not judged, for with what measure ye mete, it shall be measured to you again*; and the preacher had not dealt with it as a matter of pious conduct with a promise of reward in some future existence, but as enunciating a fundamental natural law. This may have had some influence on his mind, and, apart from that, he remembered that he was Sir Reginald's guest, and that that gentleman had made it clear that he did not expect that any superfluous detective work would be carried on in his house. He remembered that he was on holiday. Not the least, he remembered his own dignity, which he might put aside at the call of duty, but not necessarily therefore at that of Mr. Percy Kanwhistle. Was he going to suggest that he should occupy these brief holiday hours in spying upon Frederick Corder, in the hope that he might detect him in the commission of some petty crime?—and that, most probably, to no purpose whatever, for, as we know, he had already formed a fairly confident opinion that Mr. Corder had put that fantastic temptation aside, as the vast majority of the law-respecting population of London would be likely to do.

He answered coldly: "No, I don't know that it would be any business of mine."

Mr. Kanwhistle was surprised by this reply, but he was not one to be lightly rebuffed. He said: "I thought it was the job of the police to stop people breaking the law."

"If you know of anyone breaking the law, it will become your duty to inform the local police, who will know how to deal with it, and you should do this even though it be your own cousin, which would, I suppose, make it unpleasant for you, especially if it were likely to mean a personal profit. Still, it would be very risky not to make your report. If you should omit to do so, you might be charged as an accessory after the fact."

Mr. Kanwhistle was not the man to give way because he disliked the implications of this reply. He said, with some logical shrewdness: "Well, I suppose we're all in the same boat. If it's my duty, I suppose it's yours just as much, if you have any reason to be suspicious, and you can't say there aren't a cartload of reasons here."

"Perhaps it would if I agreed with you on the fact. But I see no reason at all. We assume that people will keep the law unless we have evidence in the contrary direction, I don't see how that codicil can be considered evidence against anybody, unless it's the old lady herself, and she must have been rather weak in the head."

"She wasn't that. She was a very lively old bird."

"Well, you knew her. I'm judging by the silly trick that she played. But, as far as I can see, Mr. Corder's behaving just as a quiet respectable man, and one of Sir Reginald's guests would be likely to do. And perhaps you'll pardon me saying, Mr. Kanwhistle, that you may not look at the matter with absolutely impartial eyes."

"You can say that, if you like, but it isn't true. If Fred can win that ten thousand, I'll say good luck to him, and give him the cheque. But he's got to win before he picks it up, and I mean to see that he has a hard run. It isn't breaking the laws, it's not getting caught at it, that's the snag, and that's where I come in, as I suppose my aunt meant me to, more likely than not."

"Well, you knew the old lady, as I said before. But as it stands at present, the matter's between Mr. Corder and yourself. You can see the local superintendent of police if you think it's worthwhile, but what he'll probably tell you is that if you want to spy on your cousin, you'd better hire a private detective. He'll tell you he hasn't got a man to spare for a job of that kind."

As he received this advice, Mr. Kanwhistle was interrupted by the entrance of Janet, who informed him that the other members of the party were now awaiting him in the car, and he retired from an interview in which he did not think he had wasted his time, though he felt that he might have been met in a more sympathetic manner. He said: "Thanks. That's an idea. I might do worse," and went hurriedly out.

He left Inspector Combridge to be expertly handled by Lady Crowe, in a manner which confirmed his disinclination to constitute himself an official spy upon the movements of Mr. Frederick Corder.

It was the inspector who introduced the subject. He said: "That fellow Kanwhistle will make trouble if he knows how. He was trying to persuade me before he left that Corder has been breaking the law for the last three months, and is going on doing it every day. He seemed to think that it was my duty to interfere."

Evelyn looked interested. "Did he tell you what Mr. Corder's supposed to be doing wrong?"

"No. He expects me to find out."

"You mean he's really got nothing to go on at all?"

"That's how it sounded to me. I suppose he thinks he'd have a shot at it if he were in Corder's position, and judges him by himself. But I should say he's a different sort."

"Yes. I should think he is. I shouldn't think most artists would be much good at breaking the law like that."

Inspector Combridge looked puzzled. His opinion of artists as law-abiding citizens was not high. His mind rapidly reviewed the crowded memories of his official life: night clubs, drink, ugly muddles with women, one or two emotional homicides, a disposition to write cheques without enquiry into the prosaic detail of the bank-balance available to meet them. No doubt, he admitted fairly, there were some respectable artists who did not come to the notice of Scotland Yard. But the fact remained that Lady Crowe's remark was Irish to him.

"I didn't mean that," Evelyn went on, in ready interpretation of the blankness of his expression. "I've no doubt that lots of artists can break the law quite easily. What I meant is that they wouldn't have the—well, the continuity which such an occasion requires."

Inspector Combridge considered this. He was not brilliant, but his reply illustrated the patient thoroughness with which he would study every angle of the problems with which he dealt, and which had brought him to the responsible position he held. He said: "I don't know that that applies to Corder particularly. He seemed rather level-headed to me. And besides that he's got a very capable wife."

"You think being level-headed makes it more likely that he'd try to carry out the terms of the will?"

No, he certainly hadn't meant that. He only meant that the element of instability commonly attributed to artists was not conspicuous. The adroitness of the flank attack reminded him that he had already formed an opinion that Mr. Corder was an innocent disciple of his country's laws.

"No," he said, "I think any man'd be a fool trying a thing like that."

"I'm sure Mr. Corder isn't a fool. He couldn't go on day by day doing wicked things without his wife knowing, could he?"

"He might with some women. Not with Mrs. Corder. I should say no."

"I've had one or two little talks with Mrs. Corder, besides reading her books. I'm sure she wouldn't be a party to anything really wrong."

Inspector Combridge was impressed by this opinion, much more so than would have been the case had he heard it from Sir Reginald's lips.

He had the respect for Sir Reginald which was due to such a successful man, and one who had shown exceptional judgment and resource in more than one emergency in which they had been associated. But he was not what he would have called *sound*. He had, at times, a confusing levity in his handling of serious matters. It would be inexact to say that the inspector sometimes thought that the banker made silly remarks. Rather, he made remarks which had no meaning at all.

But Lady Crowe was, by all standards, an exceptionally sensible and truthful woman. If she said that Mrs. Corder wouldn't have anything to do with law-breaking, it must go far to support the opinion he had already formed. It was true that she hadn't said exactly that. She had said "anything really wrong." But the distinction was not one which would readily occur to the inspector's mind. Anything which the law prohibited must, in his unconscious judgment, have been wrong in itself, or the law would not have frowned upon it. Having been declared illegal, it had acquired a double measure of turpitude, such as all decent people would recognise, and most surely shun.

"That," he said, "is just how it looks to me. I told him that if he knew of anything that Corder was doing wrong he ought to inform the local police, or he might find himself charged as an accessory after the fact. But if he didn't know anything, he'd only be wasting time, and they'd show him the door."

"It seems to me," Evelyn replied, with some ingenuity, "it might be more serious than that. Isn't it a more serious offence if anyone's an accessory before a crime, than only after it's done?"

The inspector admitted, with some qualifications needless to follow, the soundness of that legal proposition.

"Then if he lets Mr. Corder know that he'll pay him ten thousand pounds if he breaks the law, which he's not legally bound to do, isn't that very much what it would be?

The inspector would have been pleased to charge Mr. Kanwhistle with being an accessory at any stage of his cousin's hypothetical wrongdoing, but his sense of equity rebelled against this construction. "I don't quite see," he replied, "how you can put it like that when he's anxious to catch him out."

"But he could tell him he wouldn't pay anything under such a claim, even if it could be proved, and that would end it at once. And he could do much better than that by handing over the money at once, as any decent man would. When he won't give it unless Mr. Corder's committed three hundred and sixty-five crimes, but says he will if he does, I should call it being an accessory from one end to the other, unless, of course, Mr. Corder isn't doing anything wrong. I suppose nobody could be an accessory to something that isn't happening at all!"

The inspector did not dispute this. He felt rather confused. It was too much like the sort of argument in which Sir Reginald would indulge, to the silencing of simpler and more sensible men. There was a sound of reason in Lady Crowe's contentions, but it seemed an apparent absurdity that Mr. Kanwhistle should be a criminal if his cousin were breaking the law without his knowledge, and while he was anxious to catch and bring him to justice, but an innocent man if

Mr. Corder were living a blameless life. He contented himself with saying that, having all the money he had, Mr. Kanwhistle, in withholding the ten thousand pounds from his cousin, was doing rather a lousy thing.

"Well," Evelyn concluded, "it's no business of ours, so long as nothing nasty happens while they're here, which I hope it won't. I don't think Sir Reginald would easily forgive himself, or anyone else concerned, if that happened. He'd feel it came from asking you all down together, and that it was a careless thing to have done."

Hearing this, Inspector Combridge felt an added satisfaction in the recollection that he had sent Mr. Kanwhistle away empty-handed. And yet—had he? He had made a random suggestion that a private detective was his requirement, and Mr. Kanwhistle had responded as though that suggestion had compensated him for any previous discouragement he had received. But even so, private detectives are not easily obtainable on Sunday afternoons at Hither Dene. Lady Crowe had said that so long as peace reigned while the cousins were her guests, she would be content. That seemed likely enough, and the inspector would be very slow to do anything to disturb it, unless at a call of duty too direct to be ignored. So much Evelyn had done, without the clumsiness of asking a pledge which he would have been unlikely to give. She had used the influence of a woman's attractions with the wits which can arm them (fortunately not often) unfairly against mankind.

CHAPTER XVIII.

CONCERNING AN ANCIENT SEWER

WHILE Lady Crowe was adroitly influencing Inspector Combridge in the right direction, Sir Reginald and his guests were inspecting the ancient edifice of Maidcote Manor, Mr. Jellipot having attached himself to Mr. Kanwhistle, to whom he was discoursing upon its historic interest and other attractive features with a quiet prolixity which neither failed to maintain a standard of careful accuracy, nor to bring the best features of the property into prominent consideration; while Sir Reginald, who was not talking to a possible purchaser of the property, pointed out its most picturesque and venerable features to Mr. and Mrs. Corder in a lighter and less responsible manner.

Shepherded thus, the little party proceeded without any outward display of hostility to survey the remains of the ancient moat, the sundial, the yew tree hedges, the mullioned windows, the wide fireplace and great beams of the raftered hall, and many other evidences of an age which made modernity of Sir Reginald's seventeenth-century residence.

The visitors responded according to their various dispositions and artistic sensitiveness. It occurred to none of them to contrast the flimsy instability of modern buildings with this evidence of an age which had better reason for confidence both in itself and in the materials with which it wrought. Fred saw most, looking with frequent admiration, but with an artist's critical and comparing eyes. Adeline, with an admiration no less keen though sometimes less discriminating than his, perhaps got the most enjoyment from what she saw, though having room for a thought that such a home might have many disadvantages in a period which eats and works less heartily than its ancestors were content to do, which seeks comfort first, condemns abundance of youthful life, and conserves age. Mr. Kanwhistle, less impressed than Mr. Jellipot would have liked him to be, remarked upon the quantity of fuel which would be needed to heat the hall.

It was a fact that the bare emptiness of the house gave it an aspect of melancholy which even the fitful May sunshine, baffled too often in its approach to the mullioned windows by the sombre yew trees without, could not dispel. The house needed suitable furnishing. It needed blazing logs in its ample hearths. Not the least, it needed the bright mural paintings which, in that remote day when it had been fresh from the builders' hands, had been more warmly decorative than are paper or pictures on modern walls.

Mr. Kanwhistle, looking for trouble, saw or imagined a dark stain on a shadowed wall. He suggested damp. Sir Reginald overheard the remark, and interposed before Mr. Jellipot, gravely studying the alleged blot, had commenced his reply: "It's no use saying that, Kanwhistle. You can say lots of things about this place that wouldn't be pleasant to hear, and I should say you'd as good a right to your opinion as I to mine; but damp's one thing that it hasn't got. Why, even the cellars were bone-dry last autumn in about the worst floods that I've ever known. We'll look at them next, if you don't mind. The smugglers' cellar alone ought to put a thousand pounds on the price—I'm not asking you to pay that. Mr. Jellipot's told you what I'm willing to take, if you care to close before I hear from Pittsburgh again. But you mustn't miss seeing it all the same."

No one objecting to the proposal, Sir Reginald led the way to the cellars, which are often so extensive a feature in houses of that antiquity.

The electric light, being supplied from a private plant, was still available, and by its aid they descended a flight of much-worn stone steps to a series of vaulted chambers which certainly sustained the character of dryness which the banker had given them.

As they proceeded he explained that by a well-established tradition, old enough, but yet far more recent than the house itself, these cellars had once been used as a smugglers' depot, the house being about midway between the Sussex coast, where the contraband was landed, and London, which would be its ultimate destination.

"The tale is," he added, "that the place was searched more than once without anything of an illicit character being found, which may be explained by a discovery made some years ago by children who visited here when the house was tenanted."

He led the way to the farthest cellar, at the side of which was a narrow, stone-paved channel about eighteen inches deep, with an opening under the wall at the end, into which a boy might crawl, or a small man.

"They went through there," he said, "and found a large chamber beyond, which doubtless had a separate entrance, well concealed, of which no trace now remains. At least, that is what I am told. I can't say that I have wriggled under to see."

"They must have been mugs who searched," Mr. Kanwhistle remarked with contempt, "if they didn't have a look through a hole like that."

"So it may appear," Sir Reginald answered, with the courtesy which a host should observe, even to those of inferior manners, "and if we conclude that they were bribed not to look too hard, we may be making a good guess; but there is a presumption that the moat had then been drained, if at all, only on the lower side of the house, and that this gutter, which carried away the sewerage of the house, according to the primitive sanitary methods of that period, could be completely flooded, or shut off, as occasion required."

This explanation was received without further comment. It had been demonstrated to Mr. Kanwhistle that the cellars, whatever they might have been in medieval days, were now dry. Adeline, finding no food here for the one subject which had come to preoccupy her thoughts, even to the exclusion of *More Jam for Jane*—for how could Fred smuggle anything without going abroad, which they had agreed that it would be foolish to do?—felt that, however dry the cellars might be, they were uncomfortably chilly. Only Mr. Jellipot, leaning forward on his invariable umbrella, made an abortive effort to gaze through that one-time sewer.

"I believe," he said, "that it bends sufficiently to prevent anyone seeing anything without penetrating to the chamber to which it leads."

No one challenging this opinion, they returned to daylight and more genial air, and were soon being driven back to Trees in time for an afternoon tea which was served somewhat later than usual, but was no less pleasant for that.

CHAPTER XIX.

MR. KANWHISTLE EMPLOYS A DETECTIVE

IT was while returning from Maidcote Manor that Sir Reginald, who was driving himself, being one of those car owners who believe that chauffeurs, like other men, should not be required to work more than a six-day week, swerved to the right-hand side of the lane to avoid a man who was coming from the opposite direction, and who made no motion toward the hedge.

Mr. Kanwhistle, who in the cause of peace had been invited to the seat beside the driver, said: "Filthy swine! I'd have made him jump if I'd been you," to which Sir Reginald replied: "I suppose a good many would. But if there's no footpath, I always reckon the pedestrian has the first right to the road. And suppose he hadn't jumped fast enough? It might have been awkward for me, though there are some people round here who would have been rather glad."

"Not a very popular character?"

"Not with everyone, particularly not with Lord Barton's game-keepers. The man is the most notorious poacher in the district—boasts of it in fact—and they haven't caught him once in the three years he's been living here."

Mr. Kanwhistle said no more, but he thought that one who could poach with such bold immunity must have at least some of the qualities necessary for successful detective work.

He recalled the man's appearance as well as the brief encounter enabled him to do: a small, neatly-dressed, alertly confident figure, with an almost insolent jauntiness of manner. Not, he thought, a typical poacher. But then he was not said to be that. Mr. Kanwhistle believed, with some reason, that typical poachers are caught and convicted at frequent though irregular intervals, which this man was not. He determined to seek him out during the evening, and offer sufficiently liberal terms to induce him to keep a close watch upon his cousin's movements, so long as he should be remaining at Hither Dene.

But to do this, it became necessary to learn his name and other relevant details, and with this object he brought up the subject when seated beside Lady Crowe at tea, which the kindness of the weather allowed to be served in the rose garden again.

"Do you get many poachers round here?"

Evelyn said vaguely in answer to the abrupt question: "Oh, I don't know. Not more than most country districts, I suppose. We're not much concerned ourselves. We've only got a few acres of wood, and no one interferes with that."

"But Lord Barton preserves, doesn't he?"

"Oh, yes, he takes it very seriously indeed." The next moment her attention was drawn in another direction, and Mr. Kanwhistle saw that he must be more explicit if he were to obtain the information he sought. When he was able to capture his hostess's attention again, he said: "We almost ran a man down in the lane, and Sir Reginald said he was a poacher who never gets caught."

"Yes? Oh, you mean Cutmore! He's said to boast that Lord Barton's keepers will never catch him if they sit up every night for a month."

"He didn't look quite the type to me. I thought poachers were more down at heels."

"Not always, I believe. They are said to poach now in a wholesale way with cars to take the game into London the night it's snared, and making more money in a single night than the gamekeepers get for a month's wages. But I don't think Cutmore works in that way. He's said to have some private means and to poach more as a hobby than for any profit he makes."

Evelyn became aware, as she said this, that the conversation of the little group had paused, and that they were all listening to her. The tale of the oddness of the Cutmore household was one which was commonly told to visitors. It had become one of those stock topics of which most dwellers in country houses have a routine supply to provide conversation for successive guests with the minimum of intellectual effort on the part of their hosts. It was a tale in which she only half believed, knowing how rumour grows from a small seed. But what of that, if her guests were entertained? She would not omit to say that it was only gossip of an unreliable kind.

"The Cutmores—there are two brothers, or at least that's what they say they are, and a sister, but three people more entirely different from one another it would be difficult to find—came here three years ago and bought an old cottage about a quarter of a mile from

Maidcote Manor. It was one which had been in the occupation of a retired cowman—an old-age pensioner and his daughter—too large for them, but in such a ruinous state that it was expected that it would be condemned at his death as unfit for human occupation. But the Cutmores repaired and modernised it, not with much taste, but in a way which showed they had money to spend. Report said that they had won a huge sum with a lucky coupon in a football pool, and if Bob Cutmore—he's the one you saw this afternoon—hasn't actually confirmed this, he has certainly heard it talked of before him without saying it isn't true.

"The elder brother, if that's what he really is, is an elderly, benevolent-looking man who walks with a limp. If you were told that he was a Doctor of Divinity, you'd think it natural enough. Whatever poaching goes on certainly isn't being done by him. His principal occupation seems to be sitting in the sun, so far as this climate makes it possible to pass the time in that way. It's said that he composes chess problems when it rains. But I don't see how anyone can know that. No stranger ever enters the house, and they keep no staff.

"By the way, his name's Caldwell. The sister's Sara. She looks about thirty years younger than he, though her birth certificate might make it a bit less. The aborigines of Hither Dene don't approve of her. They say she goes about with too much paint on, and too little of anything else.

"She is also said to have been seen kissing Bob in a way which sisters seldom affect. The rector's wife was very shocked about that, and Sir Reginald asked her if she would have thought it a more Christian act if she had been seen battering his head with a poker, and the lady said of course that might have meant a lot less. It's because Reginald will say things like that that he isn't approved at the rectory, even though I do get him to church about three times a month."

"I told Mrs. Primer," Sir Reginald interposed, "that I should have thought it would have meant about the same thing, but she hadn't the least idea what I meant. A woman oughtn't to be allowed to marry a clergyman until she's passed a course in psychology."

As no one questioned this novel method of qualifying for becoming a curate's bride, Lady Crowe went on: "There's nothing really against them. Nothing more than I've said, and nine-tenths of that probably isn't true. It's just that they're not congenial to the people round here, and of course this poaching business makes a lot of talk. Not merely that Bob Cutmore poaches, though, as Mr. Kanwhistle says, he's not quite the ordinary type, but the open way he seems to like people to talk about it, and makes a joke of the idea that he might ever get caught."

"Perhaps," Mr. Kanwhistle suggested, "he doesn't do as much as he makes out." He had no wish to engage an idle blusterer for the detecting of his cousin's crimes.

"Perhaps not," Lady Crowe conceded readily, "but I believe it is a fact that if the Cutmores make a present to anyone it's usually pheasants, and always game of some kind; and there was a tale once that Bob nearly got caught by the keepers, and the next day the postman was called into the cottage on some pretext, and there was a brace of roast pheasants being served up."

Mr. Kanwhistle thought that he had heard all that was likely to be useful to him, and as the other members of the party showed no interest in the subject, it was allowed to drop.

Reviewing what he had learnt, he was inclined to doubt whether Bob Cutmore would be likely to accept the commission, or, at least, not without a more substantial fee than he had previously contemplated offering. But he reflected that the stake for which he played was not small. A hundred pounds, more or less, should not be too closely regarded when its employment may ultimately save just one hundred times that amount. Percival Kanwhistle was accustomed to take risks which his judgment approved with a gambler's freedom. He decided now that he would see Bob Cutmore, and if he thought him the right man for the job, he would engage him, even at a high figure.

This matter did not admit of delay, for his cousin's visit was not likely to last for more than a few days, and even that might be curtailed if he himself should make an acceptable offer for Maidcote Manor, and thereby remove the occasion for the sketches which were being made. It was an additional reason for not doing that against which he might have decided on other grounds. He had already resolved not to buy the house unless it could be obtained at a bargain figure, such as would leave a margin for altering it to his own ideals, which were not those of Sir Reginald or Mr. Jellipot. He would make a very low offer now, and if the American buyer bid up—well, there were many other empty country houses among which to choose. But if this buyer withdrew—which would be likely enough—then Sir Reginald might think of his rejected offer again, and Mr. Jellipot would be a ready intermediary for reopening the negotiations. But even that first low offer should not be immediately made, lest its reception should leave him with no reason for prolonging his stay. Meanwhile, he would seek the elusive poacher at once, and arrange terms. He may not have heard the proverb that every man has his price, but had he done so, he would have accepted its truth as almost too obvious for words. He might have added that those who are resolute not to overpay find that the price of most men is quite low.

To the surprise of more than one of his fellow guests, but the annoyance of none, he announced that he was disposed for a second walk that day, and set out in a direction which made oblique approach to the Cutmore cottage.

CHAPTER XX.

MR. CUTMORE CONSENTS

MR. KANWHISTLE, having started out in the direction of the Cutmore cottage, had a mental pause of hesitation. The employment of a private detective is of itself a matter which should be privately arranged, particularly in a rural district. He saw that to call at this cottage, which was not commonly visited by its neighbours, and to request a private interview with Mr. Robert Cutmore—even if it should be granted, which was by no means certain—would be likely to cause comment in a community which had both leisure and inclination to give at least as much attention to the doings of others as its own concerns.

It was by no means improbable that the fact of the call might be carried to Trees, in which case it would be likely to be mentioned before the Corders, either casually, or in a deliberate warning, for he had gained a correct impression that both his host and hostess and fellow guests were more friendly to them than to himself, or, at least, that they would not welcome any exposure of evil-doing while they were assembled at Hither Dene.

He remembered the demeanour of Bob Cutmore also, as it had impressed him in the lane, and this, with the character subsequently attributed to him, did not suggest an easy approach. He had confidence in the power of his money when he should come to discussing remuneration, but he saw that it might be difficult to arrive at that point, if he should not secure a leisurely and confidential hearing.

He considered the feasibility of strolling round the cottage on the chance of meeting the man he sought. But this was a slow, uncertain method, besides being open to the construction that he was spying upon the Cutmores, rather than requiring one of themselves to act in that capacity, which they might not approve.

Still less would it be likely to lead to the conversation he sought, if he should attempt to follow or intercept the poacher in the course of his moonlight activities. He had an absurd imagination of himself plunging through bush and bramble in pursuit of a dim flying figure, to whom he shouted vainly to stop, protesting that it was the desire to hire a detective, not to act one, that had led him to follow the poacher's tracks.

But while these hesitations disturbed his mind, he had a stroke of good fortune such as is surely due to those who seek to uphold the laws of their native land. He saw Bob Cutmore, a hundred yards ahead, entering the saloon door of the "Flower-in-Hand."

Mr. Kanwhistle prided himself on being at home with every grade of social life, arriving at this satisfactory result through being densely indifferent to whether others were equally at home with him. Now he had no hesitation in following through that swinging door.

He looked round a low, oak-beamed room which had three or four small, marble-topped tables scattered about its sawdusted floor, and some partitioned recesses with leather-covered seats against the left-hand wall. It was only a few minutes before that the inn had opened for its Sunday evening session, and the sole occupants of the room were three or four farm workers who had been waiting for the key to turn, and were now engaged in carrying mugs of beer from the bar to the corner where they had chosen to sit.

Bob Cutmore sat in a recess at the opposite side of the room, and Mr. Kanwhistle, observing his solitude with satisfaction, and avoiding an immediate approach, settled himself at a neighbouring table, within the view of the man he sought. A moment later, the barman crossed the room, bringing a whisky-and-soda to Mr. Cutmore's table, and receiving an order from Mr. Kanwhistle for a glass of beer.

It was not until this had been laid before him that he made a direct approach, looking at Mr. Cutmore and saying, while the pot man was still within hearing: "I am a stranger here. Do you mind if I sit with you?"

He asked with some fear or even expectation of a rebuff, for his second observation of Mr. Cutmore had confirmed the first. He saw a small man, neatly and quietly dressed, with black, close-cropped hair, small, black, sharp-glancing eyes, and a latent assertiveness of manner, as though aware of suspicions against himself which he had no wish, or knew it would be vain, to deny. Mr. Kanwhistle thought again that he had little of the appearance or manner of one who wriggles through dark undergrowth setting illicit snares in the moonless nights, unless it were in a heavily knobbed ash stick which he had thrown down on the opposite seat, as though claiming it for the time that he would be there.

Indeed, but for this stick, Mr. Kanwhistle might have felt it the better chance to take the seat without giving him the opportunity of refusing a nearer acquaintance, but to have removed it without permission—? No, he thought he had chosen the better way.

Mr. Cutmore looked at him indifferently. He looked at his own stick. He said: "You can put it there," pointing to the further corner. There was certainly no courtesy here. But there was nothing of which Mr. Kanwhistle could complain. If he asked for the seat, he could not stipulate that the man should remove his stick with his own hands. Nor was he in a position to take offence. He had a favour—or what he feared might be so regarded—to ask. He removed the stick and sat down.

He felt the less reluctance to do as he was told, because he had formed an opinion with which Mr. Cutmore would certainly have agreed. He regarded him as one of his own class, which he may have been. He would have said that that was synonymous with calling him a gentleman, which is a more disputable proposition.

He sat down to a conversation which even he did not find it easy to begin, and to which he could not reasonably expect that Mr. Cutmore would give an opening lead. Yet it was he who opened the conversation, with a remark which Mr. Kanwhistle was unable to understand.

"I have arranged," he said, "for the eighteenth of next month. I shall be at the usual place between two and three."

The words were not whispered or said furtively, but the tone, though casual, was low. There was no expression beyond a vague indifference on the speaker's face. No one, even at the nearer tables, could have caught the words, or supposed that anything of importance was said.

Mr. Kanwhistle, in his own shallow way, was a keen-witted man. He saw that he had been mistaken for someone else whom Bob Cutmore had expected to meet. He thought that, if he should allow the error to develop further, he might be in a better position for the bargain at which he aimed. Perhaps curiosity also influenced him to reply in a manner as indifferent as that of Mr. Cutmore: "Do you mean in the afternoon, or during the night?"

The question brought a puzzled look into Mr. Cutmore's black eyes. He had to restrain himself to maintain his previous air of indifference as he answered: "Night, of course. I never risk anything during the day."

"Can't you manage anything before the eighteenth?"

"No, I can't. And, besides, you know the bargain was that I shouldn't be asked more than four times a year, and it'll be the fifth in the last twelve months, even at the date I've fixed."

While these exchanges went on, Mr. Kanwhistle had formed the opinion that he was being let into a secret respecting sales of poached game for the London market. To carry the deception further might annoy Mr. Cutmore without adding materially to this confident guess. And besides, there was the risk that they might be interrupted at any moment by the illicit game dealer whom he was supposed to be.

"I ought to tell you," he said, "that I'm not really concerned with getting anything on to the London market. I wanted to ask you whether you could do something for me for which I am prepared to pay liberally."

The statement was potent enough in disconcerting Mr. Cutmore. He controlled himself with difficulty to answer: "London market? Who said anything about London market? Perhaps you'll tell me what you mean by that? And who you are? And why do you come seeking me here?"

Mr. Kanwhistle, looking into the blank mask of the man's face, felt that he detected hostility and perhaps fear. Had he blundered upon something more serious than the taking of game in the night? He did not greatly care if he had. He was in search of his cousin's crimes, not those of the community in general. Besides, to set a thief to catch a thief was proverbial wisdom. It made Bob Cutmore appear more eligible than before for the office of detective which was to be thrust upon him.

Only, it was necessary to establish a shaken confidence on a fresh basis. Surely, if Cutmore understood that he was not interested in exposing whatever nefarious activities he might pursue, the fact that the veil had been so nearly lifted should incline him to accept the commission which was to be offered, and endeavour to satisfy the man who had come so nearly to penetrating his guarded secret.

"That," he said, "is what I want to tell you, if you will give me a chance. I don't care if you poach all the game between here and Croydon. It's no business of mine. I want to ask you to watch a man who's up to no good, and find out how he's breaking the law."

"Well, I'll listen."

With this laconic encouragement Mr. Kanwhistle went on to explain himself, his cousin, his aunt's will, and the service which he asked Mr. Cutmore to perform, and that gentleman kept his promise almost too well. He listened with no word of interruption. When Mr.

Kanwhistle paused, he still said nothing. He remained attentively silent, as though asking for more.

After talking for fifteen minutes, Mr. Kanwhistle was still unsure whether his proposal was destined to be accepted, or (which seemed more probable) rejected with curt contempt. He would have preferred to have had some indication of his hearer's attitude before entering upon the scale of remuneration which he would consider, but being faced with this blank, though attentive silence, he went on to say: "I'm willing to pay well, if the job's properly done. I don't mind twenty-five pounds, or even thirty, if—" and stopped abruptly as he became aware that Mr. Cutmore's attention had left him to observe a stout man, with the aspect of a prosperous commercial traveller, who had just entered the room.

But the deviation was only momentary. He turned back to ask, as laconically as before: "How much did you say?"

"I said twenty-five, or even thirty for a good job. "

"*Shillings?*"

Mr. Kanwhistle was disconcerted by the sarcasm of this query. He said: "No, I meant pounds, of course."

"To save you ten thousand?"

"You mightn't find anything out."

"Oh, but I should say that I should."

Mr. Kanwhistle was again rather disconcerted. There was an implication, in tone and manner rather than words, that if Mr. Cutmore undertook to look for a crime, and had a sufficient fee, he would not fail to deliver the goods.

"I don't want," Mr. Kanwhistle protested weakly, "anything planted on him."

"Who said that?" Mr. Cutmore's voice had become impatient as well as curt. Mr. Kanwhistle made a correct guess that, since the newcomer had entered, he was in a hurry for him to be gone. Mr. Cutmore added: "Two hundred certain: half now, five percent if we get him run in."

Observing the hesitation with which these terms were received, he added: "You can take it or let it go. I don't haggle. It's you came to me."

Mr. Kanwhistle was accustomed to carry a substantial sum in banknotes, as habitual gamblers often do. Feeling somewhat as one who is mesmerised by will, he pulled out his wallet. Mr. Cutmore took the ten ten-pound notes openly, as though seeing no occasion for any reticence in what he did. He counted them quickly, but carefully. He said: "All right. When you leave here, let me know your address, if you haven't heard from me before then."

He got up as he spoke. Offering no more formal leave-taking, he moved to another recess. As he did so, he threw his stick on the opposite seat to the one he took. Mr. Kanwhistle had the sense to withdraw without further ceremony, and as he passed out, the corpulent gentleman crossed over to Mr. Cutmore's recess, and made the same request that Mr. Kanwhistle had made half an hour before, was told to remove the stick in the same way, and sank wheezily down on a leather seat that creaked under his weight. It was a formula of approach which was unlikely to be duplicated by a stranger once in a thousand years, and would yet rouse no suspicion of previous appointment, though it should be observed by a thousand eyes.

But on this occasion it *had* happened twice, and this event became the first topic of conversation between the two.

CHAPTER XXI.

INSPECTOR COMBRIDGE
MUST SHOP IN KETTLEWELL

MR. KANWHISTLE returned to Trees in time for dinner, his evening expedition, if not entirely disregarded, having occasioned neither curiosity nor regret. The little party had indeed benefited by his absence, Mr. and Mrs. Corder blending better with the other four when the embarrassment of their cousin's presence was lifted, and a greater conversational intimacy had resulted.

It occurred to no one to ask him where he had been walking abroad, and he had a reasonable presumption that his engagement of Bob Cutmore would remain unguessed by any of the party, unless he himself should select a confidant, as, in fact, it did.

The next morning Sir Reginald departed for the city at his usual hour, and Mr. Jellipot, though nominally taking the short holiday as Sir Reginald's guest which had become the annual custom, said that he had matters on hand which he was reluctant to leave to the discretion of his office staff, and that, if he also went, he might have an easier mind for the rest of the week.

Fred said that he would need all the daylight hours if he were to have anything adequate to Sir Reginald's expectations ready for the mail of the next day, and Adeline suggested on his behalf that he should be provided with sandwiches, so that he need not return to the house for lunch. With Lady Crowe's permission, she said that she would go also. Sitting quietly beside her husband, she hoped to make substantial progress with *More Jam for Jane*, which had dragged during the criminal preoccupations of the last three months, and which the conditions of her publishing contract now rendered it urgent that she should finish.

Evelyn said that she would drive them over to Maidcote Manor as soon as Sir Reginald had left, and would fetch them back at their own time.

Mr. Kanwhistle, finding that it was politely assumed that his visit was not over, accepted this position, being disposed to wait the result of the watch on his cousin for which he was paying such a substantial price. Left with Inspector Combridge for company, he readily accepted a proposal that they should pass the time at the billiard table, where the inspector found him to be a far more formidable opponent than Fred had proved on a previous occasion. But Inspector Combridge was always a good loser, and there are few circumstances that make a man more satisfied with himself and creation in general than successful competition with an opponent who neither abuses the gods of luck nor excuses himself. Percival Kanwhistle made winning shots, and Chief-Inspector Combridge admired his skill.

Under this genial influence, Mr. Kanwhistle became expansive. He remembered that it was on the advice of this expert in detecting crime that he had set out to engage a detective for his own use. What more natural than that he should repay that excellent advice with a confidence as to how promptly it had been taken, how surely he had selected, and how successfully he had sought and engaged perhaps the only man in the place who would be equal to such a task?

So, at least, he did, and it was a garrulity of vital consequence to others, if not to himself.

Inspector Combridge, a much-practiced expert in abstracting truth by the process of speaking the fewest words which would suffice to sustain the flow of confidence he desired, heard the whole tale of how curiously the conversation had begun, which he considered to be even more interesting than the presumption that Frederick Corder was steeped in crime. But, having a habit of silence on such matters, unless there were clear occasion to speak, he said nothing of this also, not even to Mr. Jellipot, who had more of his confidence than anyone except his official colleagues, and not even under the dramatic events of the later day; and this reticence also had its momentous consequences.

It was at lunchtime that Mr. Kanwhistle mentioned his intention of strolling over during the afternoon for another inspection of Maidcote Manor. He raised a question about the keys.

Evelyn, frowning inwardly behind a hostess's smiling face, admitted that there would be no difficulty about entrance. She had given a set of keys to Mrs. Corder, and she and her husband would presumably be upon the premises. But she remembered that

Reginald had said, during their usual goodbye ritual on the front steps: "Keep that bounder off the Corders as much as you can, till Jellipot and I get back to take them in hand again." Now she said: "If you care to put it off till tomorrow, when Sir Reginald or Mr. Jellipot could go with you, I dare say Inspector Combridge would like a game of clock golf, at which he is rather good."

Mr. Kanwhistle did not respond readily to this suggestion. His first thought was that there must be something about Maidcote Manor that they were afraid he should find out if he went alone, which it therefore became all the more his business to do. But he was not averse from showing the police officer that he was as expert at outdoor as indoor contests of skill, and this inclination was fortified by a doubt as to whether it might not be best to keep away from his cousin while he was under the supervision of Mr. Cutmore.

He would have replied, after that ungracious pause, agreeing to the suggested game, but Inspector Combridge unexpectedly demurred. It was true that he was on holiday. It was true also that he had implied assent to Sir Reginald's emphatic desire that the Corders should not be subjected to police interference while they were guests at his home. True also that it was no part of his duty at any time to interfere with the local police work of the district in which he might happen to be. But in spite of all these admitted facts, he had decided that a few words with headquarters would ease his mind, and that it would be best to use a line for this purpose which would secure his conversation from the possibility of being overheard at the local post office, or on one of those lines which so often make irregular contacts at rural exchanges.

He said: "I'm sorry I can't play this afternoon, but the fact is that I've got a bit of shopping to do in Kettlewell, if you won't mind me running in."

Evelyn frowned doubtfully. "Of course," she said, "if you wish to go! But do you know how bad the local service is? You'll have to catch the two-eighteen—I'll get you to the station for that—but even then you won't get a train to bring you back much before dinnertime."

She thought the shopping must be important indeed which would reconcile him to spending four or five hours in so dull a way—and the shopping facilities of Kettlewell were scarcely better than those of Hither Dene!—but he replied that he had already bargained with the under-gardener for the loan of his motorbike, and expected to be back within a couple of hours. Evelyn saw that she had gone perilously near to spending the afternoon on the lower lawn in a solitary duel with Mr. Kanwhistle, and even in the cause of peace, and the protection of law-breaking guests, it was more than she was disposed to do. She said: "Oh, well! If you've both got something better to do. But I thought it was such a fine afternoon—"

They murmured the thanks and apologies that the occasion required, and the wheels of destiny, which she had made so ineffectual an effort to turn aside, continued on their appointed course.

CHAPTER XXII.

THE AMOROUSNESS OF MR. KANWHISTLE

THERE may be as much art in painting a picture which will do justice to mullioned windows and include a sundial at the best angle of obtrusion as there is in the writing of such novels as *More Jam for Jane*, but there is a difference in their manner of production.

Mr. Corder, having spent some time in artistic hesitation as to the position in which his portable easel should be erected for the first sketch, settled down to work, and Adeline would have been surprised had he suddenly risen and declared that the fountain of inspiration had dried within him, and that, whatever urgency there might be to catch the mail of the next day, he could do no more until that inspiration returned; but she did not consider that it merited a corresponding criticism upon herself when, after she had sat beside him on her mackintosh for some hours, and the pleasant interlude of lunch time had come and gone, she declared that she could do no more, and put her writing case definitely aside.

After that, she began to wander about. She explored a little wood of birch and oak which came close to the east side of the house, brushing the stable walls. It might be no more than five or six acres in extent, but it was no less enchanting for that, clad now in the freshest green of the opening year. The pale gold of its primroses had not faded; its breaking hyacinths were a blue mist between the white boles of the slender birches, and beneath the spreading arms of the darker oaks.

Little paths ran through the woods. There was no wonder in that, the ancient house being so close, nor, perhaps, that they were so well-defined. In that dry weather they showed no traces of recent feet. Yet she looked at them in puzzled thoughtfulness, having the observant habit that a novelist who uses the material of her environment must possess or acquire. They lacked, in a way she could not define, the abandoned aspect of the solitary neglected house; and when she heard the undergrowth stir at no great distance away, she was not startled or alarmed—she was not, indeed, the sort to shy from a doubtful sound—but rather expected to see someone, woman or man, advance upon a path they were accustomed to tread. But the noise died away. Grey squirrels ran from before her feet. Disturbed wood pigeons broke noisily through the boughs above. A hen pheasant scuttled from bush to bush. She thought: "They are not used to being disturbed. This is how it should be expected to be." She went back to Fred, who had moved his position, and was well advanced with a second sketch. He worked rapidly, emphasising the essential features, and putting detail aside, as a designer of book jackets would be likely to do.

"I shall have a try at the inside next," he said, "though I doubt whether I shall get there this afternoon."

"I'll have a look round," she answered, rather from lack of something to do than supposing he needed the help from her, "and choose you a good place to begin on."

"Thanks," he said, "if you will. But I think somebody's in the house now. I'm nearly sure I've heard them moving about."

"Rats, more likely," she answered lightly. "Anyway I've got as good right as whoever's there, possibly more. I've got the keys."

The remark reminded her that, in strict accuracy, she had not got them. She had opened the house on their arrival, and left the keys in the lock of the front door. There was excuse for that in the fact that they were a heavy bunch, and, anyway, she thought, with the assurance of a student of much criminal law, there isn't much that anyone can do wrong in an empty house, unless they set fire to it, or there's some lead piping to steal. But perhaps she shouldn't have left them, all the same. She went round to the front with the resolved step of one whom the law supports, which, during the last few months, had become a part which she did not always play.

She found the front door standing open, which she felt sure had been closed, but an umbrella she had put down in the hall was undisturbed. Unalarmed but faintly curious, she went through the empty rooms, her mind divided between the idea that a stranger might be there, and the selection of a position from which Fred might make an attractive sketch.

She found the latter, in a corner of the long hall from which a view of the dining room might be obtained through an open door, before she was conscious of any sound to indicate that she was not alone; and it was only as she was ascending the broad shallow steps of the main staircase that she heard the unmistakable noise of someone who came up from the cellars, with a tread on the stone steps that was quick and loud. It was evident that he had no care that he might be overheard. She looked down from the top of the stairs, and saw Percival Kanwhistle come up through the cellar door, which was at the rear of the great hall. He did not observe her, as she stood still, making no sound. He glanced down at the lock of the door, in which there was a heavy key, which he turned with some difficulty and a grating noise.

"Who," she asked, "are you locking up in the dungeons there?"

The words were idly said, with no more purpose than to make her presence known, but they caused him to start violently, and to answer her in what seemed at the time to be an excessively embarrassed manner. "I heard something moving down there. I don't know what it was. I always had a loathing of rats. Some men do."

"Oh, well," she said, "so have I. But they won't come through a locked door."

Nor, she thought, would they have come through one which had been firmly closed. His manner and reply caused her to give more attention to the incident than she would otherwise have been likely to do. If he had found the door locked, it would be natural and proper for him to lock it again when he came up. But had he? Had it been locked yesterday? She could not be sure. But the noise and difficulty with which he had turned the key made it improbable. She could not remember any similar ritual, which she did not think she would have failed to observe.

But the incident passed from her mind next moment, and though she recalled it afterwards, the course of events was such that no explanation ever came from Mr. Kanwhistle's lips, and what he may have heard, or seen, or imagined, in those deserted cellars became a matter on which all could guess, but no one would ever know.

But whatever may have startled or disturbed his mind was evidently dismissed from it easily enough as he turned the ponderous key, and saw Adeline descending the stairs.

He was not one to neglect such an opportunity in an idle hour such as was now his, nor could he easily have supposed that Adeline, deplorably wedded to his unexciting cousin, would fail to welcome the chance of spending it in the society of a better man.

Beyond that, he had no intention of going further than her own attitude might encourage.

It was mere habit with him to make amatory advances to the ladies he met wherever circumstances should be favourable, for which he had a crudely bold and abrupt technique, beginning by praising them for alleged beauties of form rather than face, and judging by their reactions to this line of approach whether it would be profitable to pursue them further.

It is not a method to be recommended either for itself or its probable consequences, but it is a deplorable fact that Mr. Kanwhistle could recall instances where it had been successful among the women with whom he mixed.

It was that year that skirts were at their shortest, and as Adeline came down the stairs she gave anyone who might look up with sufficient particularity an unobstructed view of a pair of legs of which she had no reason to be ashamed, and concerning which Percival made a remark which, as she heard it imperfectly, there is no need to record.

Had she asked him to repeat it, the subsequent course of events might have been substantially different, but, unfortunately, a too-fearful imagination caused her to guess the words which she did not hear, and her guess was wrong.

Thinking that he had alluded to the raising of the signal on the previous day, she became warily alert. Her heart gave a sudden beat, with the fear that discovery had ruined all the thought and enterprise of the last three months. Her colour rose. Controlling her lips to smile, and her voice to a casual levity, she asked: "What exactly might you mean by that?"

Mr. Kanwhistle felt that his first advance had been favourably received. He knew the game he played to be one at which those who parley usually haul down their flag. Few things would suit him better than a little fun with Fred's wife, while his cousin laboured unsuspecting without. He asked: "Where's Fred?" which seemed to him a natural query with which to reply to hers.

So it seemed to her also. She supposed that he wished to make his accusation to Fred direct, or for them both to hear it together. But she did not wish to appear to understand, where understanding must be very near to a confession of guilt.

"Fred's busy," she said. "He's doing a sketch that won't be finished for another hour yet, and he won't want to be disturbed."

"Well, then we all feel the same." She had completed her descent of the stairs by now, and was standing beside him with a somewhat heightened colour, and a look which he misread. It may have been as complete a misunderstanding as ever occurred in the age-old duel of love, or that which may deserve a worse name.

"I never could understand," he went on boldly, "what you could see in that little worm. With all the men there are in the world!"

She was bewildered by this, but supposed that he was in the mood to boast over Fred, having caught him out in his career of crime. She would have liked to say: "At least, he isn't a cad like you," and still more to have boasted how much the element in her husband's character which had excited the contempt of Jane Kanwhistle had been modified in the last three months; but discretion urged her to reticence until she had ascertained what Percival really knew. She was not one to throw in her hand before the last card had been played.

"Men like you, I suppose you mean?" she answered, with a smile curving her lips, and aiming only to lead him to further speech, but he caught a note of contempt which she had not intended him to hear. It puzzled him slightly, but he was not one to retreat through lack of confidence, having gone (as he thought) so far.

If she hesitated, or showed caprice, he must be equal to bear it down. At that moment, he had a vision of robbing Fred of his wife for a sportive episode, if no more, which he rightly thought would be more troublesome to his cousin even than the failure to win the prize that their aunt had so mockingly offered.

"Yes," he answered, as boldly as before, "men like me! I'd give you a better time than he ever will. And I might let you have that ten thousand that there's all this fuss about, if you gave me as good a time as I'd give to you."

That was a plain proposal enough, though it still left her confused as to whether he had Fred at his mercy, and were offering this abominable—this absurd—bargain as the price of being silent on what he knew. But it must be her business to find out that, even at the cost of seeming to entertain the insulting offer which he had made.

"Let's get this straight," she said seriously. "We're to give each other a good time, whatever you mean by that, and I'm to have ten thousand pounds, if you think that the time has been good enough. And is that all? Where does Fred come in? And what's to happen to him?"

"He doesn't come in at all. He stays out."

"And suppose—just suppose—that, without either of us guessing it, he'd really done what your aunt said, would there be another ten thousand for him, or should I have robbed him of that too?"

It was a question which she regretted even before it was completely spoken, but it had already gone too far to be broken short. She regretted it more when she understood by his reply that she must have misheard what he said before, and that, whatever he might guess, he knew nothing of the career of iniquity in which Fred and she were daily engaged.

On his side, her question was one on which most men would pause for a moment to weigh reply. When he had spoken that vaguely conditional promise he had no more definite thought than that, if Adeline should consent to leave her husband for his obviously superior attractions, she should not forfeit any nebulous prospects she might have of benefiting from a sum which he had always regarded as earmarked for a particular risk, and which, though he had not seriously expected to lose it, he was prepared to part with lightly, in a gambler's accustomed way.

But even a gambler does not scatter such sums promiscuously about without consideration of what he gets. *Two* sums of ten thousand pounds? No, he certainly hadn't meant that.

All the same, he could not fail to see that the obligation of the codicil—and that it had no legal validity did not enter his mind as a factor of any importance; every man has his code, and it would have seemed to him an impossible baseness to plead such an excuse for non-payment—would not be satisfied by relieving his cousin of a wife from whom he had no desire to part.

The question also appeared to reveal Adeline in an aspect of hard bargaining which was—well, disconcerting. Not that he was unfamiliar with such demands. The class of women of whom he knew most, and with whom he was most at ease, were not disposed to forget what a man's cheque book is for. He did not object to that. He had a theory that, in all dealings with women, it is best to pay as you go, and make it very clear that there is nothing to be claimed on a further day.

But he had not expected Adeline to show such an instant appreciation of the business side of the escapade to which she had been invited. Indeed, five minutes before he had not anticipated that such a position would develop at all. It only showed how fundamentally alike all women are, especially when you praise their legs. Not that it wasn't natural that, when she found that she could change Fred for him, she should jump at the chance. Any sensible woman would.

But ten thousand pounds? He wasn't a quitter. If he'd said it, he wasn't one to draw back. But had he? Not unconditionally; he was clear on that. But if he were now asked to repeat the promise in a more binding form? (Was she going to ask for cash in advance? He thanked his discretion that he never carried his cheque book with him. He had learnt the folly of that. A good sum in cash, which, at the worst, you could afford to lose, yes. But a too-ready cheque book is a snare that a wise man shuns.) Well, if she must have that, he might, at least, ask for some indication of what the consideration would be likely to be.

He felt resentfully that he was being rushed, and yet admitted, fairly enough, that the proposal, even the mention of this confounded ten thousand pounds, had been his, not hers.

His sporting instinct, his admiration of Adeline, whose attractions were not lessened by the way in which the excitement of the moment (so utterly misunderstood by him!) had brightened her eyes and flushed her cheeks, and perhaps not least the contemptuous dislike of his cousin, which rendered it a particularly amusing thing to deprive him of his one desirable possession, combined to influence Mr. Kanwhistle to conclude the bargain, even on more onerous terms than he felt he should be asked to pay.

So, for a long moment, they faced one another in a pause of silence, during which Adeline felt some most annoying difficulty in controlling her breath to its normal quietude. ("This is absurd," she thought, "when I'm only playing with him, to draw him out.") And then he answered her with a note of irritation in his voice: "You needn't worry about anything Fred's going to claim. If he's really being fool enough to try to win that money the way the will said, you'll find that he'll come unstuck. I've put someone on his track who will settle him. But you'll find, if you chuck him up, that I'm not mean. Not to a pal like you. You'd better come and talk things over upstairs. There's a seat there, and we should hear Fred coming up."

The suggestion appeared natural, and even innocent, to Mr. Kanwhistle. It was a fact that a seat of polished oak was a fixture beneath the window of one of the principal bedrooms, and if there be occasion to talk to a lady it is surely more polite, and even more conventional, to ask her to sit down than to keep her standing at the foot of the stairs.

The bargain which she had shown such willingness to discuss was not one to be decided at arm's length. If Adeline stood uncertainly without responding to this suggestion, it was fair to remember that she was probably without previous experience of such adventures. Such shyness may not be unattractive. Mr. Kanwhistle had known women who would have been the better for a little more. But it is to be resolutely overcome, and this it was his business to do. He put his arm round her, to lead her on the upward way.

And then, in a sudden panic at the folly of what she had done already, and revulsion at the touch of a man she loathed, she struck him hard on the face.

"You utter fool!" she said bitterly, as she wrenched herself free. Free, at least, so far that his arm was no longer round her; but, as she would have pushed past him, with her eyes on the front door, and her thoughts on rejoining Fred, who had never seemed more desirable to her than he did now in contrast to Mr. Kanwhistle's more predatory characteristics, he took a firm grip on her arm.

"Look here," he said, with an anger for which justice must observe some excuse, "you're not going to treat me like that and get away with it. Two can play at that game, you know." (He rubbed a reddened cheekbone in sufficient indication of what he meant.) "If you felt like that, what did you mean, leading me on?"

She had stood motionless while he said this, conscious that the grasp on her arm would not easily be broken by any force that she could exert, and with a sound instinct urging her to avoid an undignified scuffle, and lead the encounter back to the war of words in which they were more equally matched.

"I didn't lead you on," she answered indignantly. "You tried leading me."

It is a question on which two opinions are possible, and neither of them was in the mood to apply the logical analysis with which Mr. Jellipot might have elucidated it for them. Neither, in fact, was very clear as to how they had arrived at the position in which they stood. But Mr. Kanwhistle had no doubt that he had been badly treated. According to his view of the proprieties of female behaviour, she should have shown indignation, if at all, at a much earlier stage of the conversation.

But she had stopped to talk, after he had praised her legs with the familiarity which only a most favoured cousin-in-law could expect to be well received, and after that she had actually considered with smiling lips a proposition that she should leave her husband in consideration of a payment of ten thousand pounds. And when he had proposed talking it over further, as the importance of the subject surely deserved, and had merely put his arm round her to lead her to a seat he knew, she had struck him—a hard venomous blow.

"I don't know," he answered, "what you call leading me on, but I know I'm going to put you over my knee and give you the best thrashing you ever had, and after that perhaps you'll know who you are, and talk sense."

There may have been some lack of precision in the wording of this announcement, but Adeline had no difficulty in understanding it, nor can it be criticised for any lack of clarity in its central threat. Nor, to be just, was it a decision for which Mr. Kanwhistle should be gravely blamed. It was his habit to sit through about three hundred screenplays annually, and in an actual majority of these the young American heroine would be chastised in that undignified manner, with the invariable consequence that she would become docile and sweet-tempered and surrender herself, with or without the formality of a marriage ceremony, to the man who wooed her by this unceremonious method. How was Percival Kanwhistle to know that this was no more than a peculiarity of American womanhood, and that English girls could not be guaranteed to react in the same way?

It is true that he had not tried it previously, but the occasion had not arisen with equal acuteness, no woman whose legs he had admired having hit him across the face.

Actually, the point remains unproved, and everyone may form what opinion they will. Had he thrashed her as he proposed, it is possible that Adeline might have vindicated the psychology of Hollywood's directors by rising to kiss his hand, and following him afterwards like a docile dog; but the event took a different course.

"Percy," she said angrily, "don't be crazy. You wouldn't dare. You'd be put in jail, more likely than not. And besides, if you don't loose my arm, I shall call Fred."

"He won't hear, if you do."

That was, unfortunately, too probable. Adeline remembered that he was in the courtyard on the other side of the house, at its extreme end. No, he probably wouldn't hear. She must rely on herself now. Her reaction to this thought was prompt and direct, though lacking in originality. His grasp was on her left arm. As he spoke he made a motion to get her more completely under control, doubtless with no worse or better purpose than he had warned her to expect. But she was half a second quicker than he. Her right arm came round as before, but with the added vigour of desperation. As a cause, it may be what the lawyers call too remote, yet it is probable that she owed her escape from what must have been an ignominious experience to the fact that she had run the Bloomsbury Street flat without keeping a maid. No great development of the muscles of the right arm is necessary for the writing of *More Jam for Jane*. But the daily care of a flat, even with the aid that electricity will give, is a different matter.

Adeline struck almost on the same spot as before, but with the difference that her thumb went into Mr. Kanwhistle's left eye. For half a second his grasp relaxed. She wrenched herself free, as she heard him say: "Damn you, you beastly bitch," for which again we must observe some excuse. He snatched at her, and caught no more than the neck of a blouse which ripped as she tore away.

As she ran for the front door, which she had left open when she entered, he followed a few paces along the hall, and then stopped, either because he was a sensible man, or because of the pain in his left eye—or, perhaps, both.

CHAPTER XXIII.

Mr. Corder Is Not a Worm

ADELINE may not have been quite as indignant as she supposed. A cynic might say that, under such circumstances, few women are. They must consider that the iniquity of the aggressor is in inverse proportion to the irresistibility of their own attraction, and it is therefore evident that only an excess of self-depreciation can lead to the conclusion that the men who so molest them have committed excuseless sin.

But Adeline knew the attitude proper to the event, as a lady novelist surely should. And a blouse which had cost nineteen and eleven pence three farthings three days before was ruined beyond repair!

Fred looked up from his nearly finished sketch with a natural astonishment, as his wife appeared before him, bright-eyed, highly-coloured, rather rapid of breath, and with her blouse hanging in silken tatters to her left side.

"Just look," she said, "what Percy has done to me!"

"Percy?" he echoed in a puzzled voice that changed next moment to comprehending indignation. "Oh, you mean it was he who was in the house. How did it happen? He surely couldn't have meant—"

"*Meant?*" she echoed in turn. "He only got hold of me, trying to drag me upstairs, and did this when I struggled to get away."

There was no doubt that Fred was roused now to an anger which she was not unwilling to see.

"If he thinks he can do what he likes with us," he said furiously, "I'll give him a lesson he won't forget."

"He'll certainly be surprised if you do. He said you weren't a man, only a worm. He seemed to think I ought to be glad to leave you and go to him."

Fred made no further answer. He was looking round for a weapon. He was not silly enough, even in his present anger, to suppose himself equal to tackling Percival with his bare hands. His cousin was three inches taller than he, and there was a rumour that he had once stood up to an amateur lightweight champion of somewhere or other for half a dozen rounds without losing his feet. By what seemed a happy chance to Fred in his present mood, but was to prove of a contrary kind, his eyes fell on a stout stake which had been thrust into the ground to support a rosebush which, in the neglect of the last two years, had fallen from it, leaving it conspicuous, solitary, and easily to be pulled up.

Was it too rotten for his purpose? At least it felt firm to his hand.

"Fred," Adeline said, "don't do anything silly. There wasn't any real harm done, and I've no doubt he'll be glad to apologise when he thinks it over."

She might enjoy seeing Fred roused to indignation on her behalf, but she had an uneasy consciousness that, however reprehensible Percival's conduct might have been, the impression she had given was rather wide of the truth. Yet a feeling which the Hollywood studios might find it difficult to understand made her curiously reluctant to add: "He wasn't really attempting what the law calls a criminal assault: he was only trying to put me over his knee." And even so, most husbands would object to that method of correction being applied to their wives by other men, however satisfying its results might be when inflicted themselves with a better right. And an offer of ten thousand pounds for the privileges of his wife's society, however flattering to herself, is also something at which the average husband may take offence. All the same, she didn't want any physical violence. She had nothing worse than a ruined blouse, and a very probable bruise on her upper arm; and there was sufficient satisfaction in the thought that she had marked her assailant in a more conspicuous manner.

Seeing that her words had no effect, she added: "If you do anything silly, you'll lose that ten thousand pounds, more likely than not. I'll never forgive you if you do that."

But Fred had become deaf to argument since he had heard Mr. Kanwhistle's contemptuous reference to himself. He was a worm, was he, and no man? He would make Percy swallow that. He would have resented it three months before, but now, with that period of successful criminality bracing his mind, it was an insult to be retracted or else avenged.

Adeline, seeing the anger she had aroused, might have made a further effort to avert the consequences of her own words had she not seen Mr. Kanwhistle disappear into the little wood on the east side of the house, which was, in fact, the most direct way to the main road to Hither Dene. She did not think that Fred had seen him, and by when he had gone through the house for a man who was not there, the distance between them should have become sufficient to prevent any mischief before there would be opportunity for a further and quieter talk. But, unfortunately, on this point she was wrong. Fred had seen him go, and started directly upon his track, and at a pace which was likely to catch him up long before he could reach the protection of the house of their common host.

When she saw this, she started to follow, but stopped herself with the thought that her presence might do more harm than good. Probably Fred would only try to show off the more! And if Percy did get a few good bruises about the head, she didn't see why she should mind. He might even be glad for people to think he had got that black eye from Fred rather than her!

Contenting herself with this charitable and cheerful thought, she had leisure to remember that the hour must be very near at which Lady Crowe had promised to come for her and Fred, to drive them back to Trees. She looked down at the torn blouse. She sought pins. She had to discover how far the damage could be concealed. (But certainly not from a woman's eyes! There would be no getting away from that.) She had to decide how much or little it would be prudent to tell. And she must not forget that Lady Crowe might meet Fred before there would be any further opportunity for consultation between them—which made anything less than, or different from, the facts as they were already known to him of a probable futility, even if concealment were otherwise worth the attempt.

And then, as she thought this, she heard—she was almost sure she heard—the voices of angry men. Yet how could Fred possibly have caught Percy up so soon, or so near that their voices would come to her? But there was no mistake about the cry of fury and pain that followed. She thought—but that might be fancy—that she recognised Percy's voice. Well, if he had got hurt, it was no more than he deserved, and he would not be likely to call Fred a worm again. Certainly not to her!

The satisfaction she felt in the thought that Fred had vindicated his manhood in her defence caused her to forget for a moment the question of how this violence of quarrel might affect the prospects of ultimately collecting the fortune for which so much had been adventured already of cunning plan and hazardous deed. But she was so far concerned to know what had happened within the wood that she stood motionless, listening with the torn blouse (which she had taken off to investigate the full damage it had sustained) in her hand, and did not notice Lady Crowe until she was close upon her.

Evelyn had left the car at the front gate. She had looked in at the open door, called without response, I and then walked round the house, seeking her guests.

She saw Fred's campstool and deserted easel, and Adeline standing motionless beside it, bare-armed, with the tattered blouse in her hand.

She thought first that she saw no more than a tragedy of brambles or briars. Adeline had scrambled too carelessly through the thickets of the neglected garden, and the thin silk had been caught and torn.

"Can I be any help?" she asked.

She had come so silently over the short soft grass that she was close enough to see, as she spoke, the black bruises on Adeline's left arm. Finger marks she rightly thought them to be. Her idea of what had occurred altered sharply. She had not supposed Fred to be a man who would mishandle his wife! And Adeline must be as strong as he. Still, you never know.... And besides, Fred was not here. Perhaps Adeline had chased him away, and now stood on the field of victory, counting its cost.

Adeline turned at the voice. It was evident that there could be no concealment now! "There's been," she said, "a bit of fuss with Mr. Kanwhistle. He's been rather troublesome. But it's all over. I was just thinking how I could fix this up so that it won't show till I get home."

"We ought to be able to manage that," Evelyn answered cheerfully. "It will only look as though you've got caught on a thorn."

She saw that her first idea should be explanation sufficient to turn curiosity away from anything her guests might prefer to conceal. Adeline wondered why she hadn't thought of the same thing. It would have explained everything in a word. But it wouldn't now. She had said too much. And here was Fred coming back at a run. He slackened his pace as he saw that Adeline was no longer alone. But he saw, as she had done, and with another reason than hers, that it was a tale which must be told.

"I think," he said, "we ought to help Percy. He's bleeding rather badly. I broke the stick over his head. It had a nail in it which I didn't see. I—I didn't know what to do."

"Oh, Fred, you don't mean—you haven't killed him?" Adeline exclaimed anxiously.

"No, of course not," he answered, with the irritation of a man who is sufficiently troubled by what has occurred, and doesn't thank anyone for suggesting it's even worse.

"But you mean he was too bad to move?"

"He wasn't even unconscious. I left him sitting against a tree. But it was bleeding, and wouldn't stop."

"That doesn't sound very serious," Evelyn interposed. "But, if you'll wait a moment, I've got a first-aid outfit in the car. It seems to be a lucky thing for Mr. Kanwhistle that I came when I did."

They had reached the edge of the wood as the conversation came to this point, and Fred and Adeline waited there while Lady Crowe hurried to the car. They both avoided the subject of the extent of Mr. Kanwhistle's injury, on which their minds had been somewhat relieved by Evelyn's matter-of-fact attitude, and the offer of assistance which would have been beyond their own capacities.

"I can't think," Adeline said, "how you caught him up so quickly. He must have gone scarcely any distance at all."

"He hadn't gone far. He wasn't walking. When I came on him, he'd got out a pocket mirror, and was looking at his black eye."

Adeline was amused at this. "Had it really gone black? I felt sure it would," she said, with unholy triumph.

Evelyn was back now, and they hurried together along the evening peace of the woodland path.

CHAPTER XXIV.

Evelyn Takes Control

BUT Percival was not sitting under a tree. He lay face down-wards upon the path, still as a dead man. There was blood—a good deal of blood—upon the grass and the rotting leaves of last autumn. His hair was matted with blood.

Evelyn broke a moment of silent consternation with the sharp words: "It's no use standing gaping here. We've got to see what we can do."

Careless of her skirt, she knelt in the sodden leaves.

"He isn't dead?" Adeline asked fearfully.

"No. He isn't dead, and the bleeding's stopped."

Her fingers searched in the clotted hair. She looked up at Fred to ask: "Where did you say you hit him, Mr. Corder? How many times?"

"I only hit him once. On the forehead. Where you can see how it bled."

Evelyn said nothing to that. She had a different opinion. But it was no time to discuss that. She said: "Help me to turn him over, as gently as you can. We don't want the bleeding to start again."

They gave the help for which she asked, the head hanging limply if it were not held. He might be alive, but he had the weight, the slackness, of a dead man. The eyes were staringly open. He did not revive for anything Evelyn could do, nor did she lose much time in the attempt. She took the torn blouse from Adeline's hand to ban-dage the wounded head, in which particular it might be said that Mr. Kanwhistle got more than he fairly deserved.

She looked frowningly at the narrow path. "We've got to get help quickly," she said, "even if we carry him to the car. But I may get it through the wood. If I can't, I shall drive for help. The cottage hospital isn't far. You'd better wait here, though there isn't much

126

you can do till I get back. Not if he doesn't come round, and I don't think he will. Keep him quiet, if he does."

She went off at a quick pace, leaving the two facing one another over the unconscious man.

"It's all my fault," Adeline said. "I shouldn't have told you what I did. There wasn't as much to make a fuss about as I made you think."

"I don't see that you could have helped telling me, with your clothes torn as they were. And I don't say now that I gave him more than he deserved. Lady Crowe thought that I hit him more than once, but I'm certain it isn't true. You wouldn't think that stick could have knocked him out like this, even with the nail. It broke so easily on his head."

"You must have hit him harder than you meant."

"I hit as hard as I could. Anyone would. He came at me like a mad bull. He was wild because I caught him with that pocket mirror examining his eye. But you can see how rotten the stick was."

He picked up the pieces. The end which had come down on Mr. Kanwhistle's head was fairly solid. It was stained with blood, and the nail which had done the damage was still firmly embedded in it. But the other end had been rotten, as Fred said. Looking at how it had snapped, it was hard to think that it could have struck with a great force.

"That," Fred went on, pointing to a half-grown oak at the other side of the path, "was where I left him. He didn't seem so bad then, only that his head was bleeding and wouldn't stop."

There were evidences to support Fred's account here. The weeds and brambles showed the depression of where Percy had sat. They were spattered with blood. A blood-soaked handkerchief lay beside the place. Under what impulse had he risen, taken some paces on the path, and then fallen forward like a dead man?

Adeline had formed a theory of which she was frightened to think. The nail had penetrated to the brain, causing an injury to which, rather than loss of blood, he had succumbed—from which he might be dying while they stood helplessly by. They had played for three months at the comedy of crime, and it had led them to—this. But when she looked at the nail, she saw that it had not projected far enough to make that explanation probable. It had dragged along scalp and forehead, tearing such a wound as would be likely to bleed freely, but it could not have gone in deeply. And surely such a blow on the forehead would not fracture the skull?

But it was no use guessing. Here—thank Heaven!—was the sound of the approaching car. It came slowly, lurching, tearing

127

through the undergrowth, backing at times. Brambles scratched it. Snapping boughs scraped the varnish from its sides. But it came on.

With difficulty enough, they got the wounded man into the back of the car, where they laid him across the floor, his head propped on Fred's coat against one door, and the other half-open to give place to his projecting feet.

At a walking pace, its passage made no easier by the swinging door, the car lurched its way back to the road.

But on the road they made so different a speed that it seemed no more than a moment before they had rung the bell of the cottage hospital at Hither Dene, and the matron had come out, not so much at the report of an injured man, as because Lady Crowe was at the door.

A quiet, efficient woman, unused to be flurried by any emergency, she looked at the occupants of the car without any sign of curiosity in her eyes. A road accident was her first and most natural supposition.

She saw Fred without his coat, Adeline blouseless, and with blue-black marks on her arm which the quiet eyes did not miss. Lady Crowe herself had her dress sodden in front from where she had knelt on the rotten leaves, but she appeared unconscious of that. When you know that two-thirds of the cost of running a cottage hospital comes from your own cheque book, you can afford to appear before it in any condition you think well.

"Matron," she said, "we've got a man who's badly hurt. There's been an accident in the wood. His head's injured. I think he ought to be looked at quickly. Is Dr. Danks here?"

"He's over at the surgery now. I can get him here in five minutes."

"Then tell him it's urgent from me. I don't know that we ought to have brought him like this. It might have been better to send an ambulance, but I thought it would be the quickest way."

"It's always best not to lose time," the matron answered quietly. A man who combined the duties of ambulance driver, gardener, and several others, and the two nurses who completed the staff, had appeared by now, and the car was soon relieved of its unconscious burden.

"Mr. Kanwhistle," Lady Crowe said, as she got back into the driving seat, "was staying at Trees. Will you ask Dr. Danks to telephone Sir Reginald as soon as he conveniently can and let us know how he is getting on?"

She drove away with no further explanation of what had occurred. If things were as she feared, there would be much more to be

said. But that could keep till a later hour. Sir Reginald and Mr. Jellipot, she was glad to think—yes, and Inspector Combridge—would
be back by now. There would be no lack of responsible advice as to
what should be done next. But the first thing was to hear what Dr.
Danks had to say. She felt that, if anyone were to be blamed, there
should be a full share for herself. Had not Reginald told her to keep
them apart till his return? And a nice mess she had made of that! But
she saw, all the same, that whatever had happened was different—
queerly different—from what they had been watchful to avert.

CHAPTER XXV.

MR. CORDER DENIES

SIR REGINALD and Mr. Jellipot had returned, as Evelyn had anticipated, but Inspector Combridge had not. He had sent a wire from Kettlewell, which must have been dispatched almost as soon as he could have arrived there, saying that he might not be back till rather late. Apparently, his shopping was not only an urgent, but a lengthy, process.

Evelyn read the wire in the hall with frowning satisfaction. It was puzzling, but no business of hers, and perhaps it was just as well that the inspector should be absent till the whole tale had been told, and the extent of Mr. Kanwhistle's injuries ascertained.

"When you're ready," she said to her two dishevelled guests, "you'll find tea waiting in the lounge. It's near enough to dinnertime now, but I expect we shall all be glad of a cup first." Having disposed of them for the moment, she sought her husband.

"Reggie, something's happened. But I'm a filthy mess. I've got to change. Yes, of course you can see that. But I want you to come with me. I want to talk to you while I get straight."

Being followed to her dressing room by an obedient husband, she went on: "Reggie, I didn't manage to keep them apart. You can say what you like about that. Mr. Kanwhistle followed them to Maidcote. He interfered with Mrs. Corder—so she says—and Mr. Corder went after him with a stick, and they had a fight in the wood by the house. The point is that Mr. Kanwhistle is badly hurt. He's got a fractured skull, if I'm not wrong. I shouldn't wonder if he were to die."

"Where is he now?"

"At the Cottage Hospital. I didn't tell them anything there. Dr. Danks may be ringing up any minute. "

"Then the police don't know?"

130

"No. I thought we ought to know what injuries Mr. Kanwhistle has first, and hear what the Corders have to say."

"Yes, of course, but if it's as bad as you think, we can't be too quick straightening it out. Tell me what you can now, and we'll go down and hear what they have to say." Evelyn gave a concise but sufficiently clear account of the event as she had seen it, and of the accusation which Adeline had made against the injured man. She added: "I've no doubt that's substantially true. Mrs. Corder isn't one you'd expect to lie, and she's not the hysterical sort. Not the sort who make up that kind of tale out of next to nothing. But when Mr. Corder said that he only hit the man once—well, it isn't true. But I didn't contradict him. I left the doctors to do that."

"If he hit him several times, he'll be very silly not to admit it straight out. It's the sort of thing that it's no use to deny, and he may prejudice himself in the attempt. But aren't we taking it rather too seriously? Unless Kanwhistle prosecutes—and he's hardly likely to do that if he'd been interfering with Corder's wife—it's most likely that there'll be no question of any investigation at all."

"Yes—if he lives. "

"You really think it's as bad as that? I shouldn't be too quick to expect the worst. I've known men get over some nasty cracks on the skull."

Evelyn said nothing more in reply to this cheerful optimism. She knew Sir Reginald well enough to be assured that it would make no difference to the discretion with which he would handle the event. It was an attitude of courage with which he would face all the crises of life, his own or others, having an aspect of recklessness which was not there.

They went down together to find that the Corders had joined Mr. Jellipot in the lounge, and were already giving him a narrative to which he was listening with a very serious face.

"I think," he said, as he rose punctiliously at Lady Crowe's appearance, "our young friends had better begin this tale again from the beginning." He turned to Adeline to add courteously: "You have a faculty of lucid narrative, as is natural to one of your profession, but there are one or two points which may emerge more clearly if you will kindly tell it a second time."

Adeline understood that well enough. Mr. Jellipot, however friendly to herself, however willing to suspend judgment he might be, had not found her first narrative to be entirely convincing. She was not surprised at that. She had felt that it was rather lame herself. When she began again, she attempted a more absolute frankness, seeking the muddled truth, and letting plausibility go.

"I'm afraid," she said, "I wasn't lucid at all. It's difficult to talk clearly about anything that isn't clear in your own mind, and the more I think it over, the less I seem able to make it out how it began. But I'm sure we misunderstood each other at first. I thought he was talking about that silly codicil, and he thought from my replies that I was what he called leading him on, and so he came to make a downright offer to me that I could have the ten thousand pounds for myself, if I'd leave Fred for him; and then I asked if there was only one such amount, or if there'd be another for Fred, if he made good his claim, or something like that. It was a silly thing to ask, for more reasons than one, but I just wanted to see what he'd say.

"And then he put his arm round me, and wanted me to go upstairs to talk it over, and I hit him on the face, and he said he'd thrash me for that, and Fred wouldn't hear if I called; and I hit him again out of absolute funk—he was holding on to my arm, so that I couldn't get free—and I think my thumb went into his eye, and I broke away, and he tried to catch me and my blouse tore. And like a fool I ran out to Fred and complained to him."

"It was," Mr. Jellipot conceded, "a most natural thing to do."

"I don't see," Evelyn supported him, "what else you could have done with your blouse torn as it was."

"But I needn't have told Fred that Percy'd called him a worm. It was that which made him so mad."

"Of course it wasn't," Fred protested unconvincingly. "It was the way that he'd treated you."

"I don't suppose," Mr. Jellipot said judicially, "that anyone can separate motives with absolute accuracy under such circumstances. But I should advise you to keep the blouse."

Adeline echoed: "Keep the blouse? It would be rather a mess now!"

Mr. Jellipot listened to the history of its demolition, and recognised, with less surprise than regret, the lack of foresight which is liable to affect the lay, and particularly the feminine, mind.

Well, it could not matter very seriously, unless—no, it was to be earnestly hoped not. Lady Crowe was an important, presumably impartial witness to its condition immediately after the alleged incident. The provocation, such as it was, should be capable of sufficient proof. The still more important question remained—what had happened between the two men, and what degree of injury had Kanwhistle sustained? He was about to ask Fred for his version of the encounter when he was interrupted by the entrance of the butler, who said to Sir Reginald: "There's a phone call for you, if you please, sir. Will you have it put through here, or to your own room?"

The man knew that Sir Reginald did not take calls of business importance in the reception rooms, where conversations were liable to be overheard by any casual guest. Only social calls, usually to Lady Crowe, were put through to the lounge. What he thought of this one as best known to his own mind. News travels quickly in such quiet backwaters as Hither Dene.

Sir Reginald asked: "Is it from Dr. Danks?"

"It may be, sir. It's from the Cottage Hospital."

"Then put it through here. Mr. Kanwhistle has had an accident, Hickson."

"Yes, sir."

As the man left the room, Sir Reginald moved to the desk on which the instrument stood, and in a few minutes was taking the call.

"That you, Danks?" the little group of intent listeners heard. "Yes, so I supposed. I'm sorry to hear that. Yes, of course. Bligh? You think he's the right man? You needn't spare expense if. Yes, I've no doubt you're right. You'll ring up again as soon as there's anything to report. Yes, any time. I should like to know."

As he said this, Sir Reginald made a motion to put the receiver down, but his hand paused, and it went back to his ear as it became evident that the doctor had more to say. He listened for what seemed a long minute, and then replied, with some impatience, and authority in his voice: "Look here, Danks, I understand all that. But the fact is that it's a case in which as little ought to be said as possible, in the man's own interest as much as anyone else's.

"The fact is that he got no more than he deserved. Someone broke a stick over his head, and if I'd been there I'd probably have done more. Know who did it? Yes, of course. He's here now. I've told you what I think of the whole affair."

There was another long pause, and then Sir Reginald answered, in a graver tone than before: "Well, of course, if you say that, that's how it must have been. But there's more than one side to most tales, and I've no doubt it can be explained. Well, Chief-Inspector Combridge of the C.I.D. will be here any minute now. That ought to be good enough."

Apparently, so it was, for the conversation terminated with a repetition of the arrangement that Dr. Danks should ring up at a later hour.

Sir Reginald put the receiver down, and remained gravely silent for some moments, as though weighing what he should tell to those who were most concerned.

At length he said: "Danks was just a bit awkward till I choked him off by using Combridge's name. The fact is that they are going to operate, and till they've done that they can't be sure how bad the damage is. Mr. Corder, before I say more, I wish you'd tell me just what happened, particularly where you hit him and how."

"I hit him on the front of the head. I'd meant to all along. I won't say I hadn't. But when I did, it was really in self-defence. We had a few angry words, and then he came at me like a wild beast.

"I hit him over the head, and when the stick snapped I thought he'd got me for sure. But he yelled out, and then staggered a few steps forward putting his hands to his head. I could see blood was coming from his forehead, quite a lot. I got him to sit down with his back against a tree, and tried to stop the blood with my handkerchief. He said: 'It's no use doing that. Get some help for me, you swine. Do you want me to bleed to death?' That's as near as I can remember. And I got frightened, and thought what he'd said might be the best thing to do, and ran for Adeline, and—you've heard what happened after that."

"You say you hit him once, and no more?"

"Yes, and that was only with a stick that had rotted through. I couldn't think how it had hurt him as it had, having felt it snap, till I saw the one half of it lying on the ground with the head of a nail sticking half an inch out, and all covered with blood."

"You say you're sure you hit him once, and no more?"

"Yes. I could swear to that. It's a fact."

"Dr. Danks says he was struck twice at least. The worst blow was on the back of the head. He is unconscious from a depressed fracture. They are going to operate at once, because it's the only chance, but he can't guarantee what the result will be."

"I never hit him on the back of the head. I can swear to that."

"Well, Danks says you did."

"Couldn't he have got up, and felt faint, and fallen and hurt himself?"

"A depressed fracture? That's for the doctors to say. But I should say you'll have to think of something better than that."

"Perhaps," Mr. Jellipot suggested gently, "it would be best, Mr. Corder, if you think it over carefully, and, for the immediate present, say nothing further on that point. But can you tell me what has become of the broken stick?"

"I suppose it's still there. We didn't bring it away."

"No, I suppose not. I expect it will still be there."

Mr. Jellipot became silent. No one else was quick to speak, and next moment dinner was announced.

CHAPTER XXVI.

SILENCE AT DINNER

DINNER was a silent and awkward meal. Mr. Jellipot found sufficient mental occupation in considering the narratives which he had heard, and endeavouring to build upon them a structure of truth, which, as previous experiences had taught him, might have a different appearance.

Adeline, miserable for the danger to which Fred had exposed himself by championing herself—"And," she reminded herself, "because Percy called him a worm; what a fool I was to repeat that!"—had now an additional cause of worry, in the revelation of the extent of Mr. Kanwhistle's injuries. Had Fred really lost his head so far that he had battered his cousin with repeated and murderous blows? And, if so, was that frenzied outburst to be attributed to his criminal activities of the last three months, for which she knew that the major responsibility had been hers?

Looked at thus, she felt herself to be doubly responsible for what had occurred—immediately so for the way she had complained to Fred and repeated that exasperating "worm," and more remotely for having incited him to a life of crime—and if Percy should die, what would the penalty be?

Not hanging. That horror, at least, she could put from her mind. Her reading of criminal law had been sufficient to make that clear. But a term of imprisonment—even a long term—was a very probable consequence. That was to be the fruit of the three months' folly which she had believed that she could bring to such a different result.

But much as she blamed herself, she had also an anger against her husband which reduced sympathy, and put upon him the blame of folly which had no passionate emotion for its excuse.

Whatever he had done to Percy, however violent, even brutal, it might have been, was beyond denial, and such an attitude was absurd. Explanation—yes. Excuse—yes. Perhaps some suggestion of a blow which fell as he had not meant it to do. And of course he could make the most of his fear of Percy, who was the larger and stronger man. But denial—no. It was pure folly. And she knew that it was that attitude of Fred's which was responsible for the uneasy silence around them.

These people, who, except Mr. Jellipot, had been utter strangers three days before, had acted the part of generous and most loyal friends. Even in the face of whatever Dr. Danks had said, Sir Reginald had not withdrawn the emphatic advocacy with which that half-heard telephone conversation had commenced. She saw clearly enough that, apart from the actions and attitude of Sir Reginald and Lady Crowe, Fred might be in a very much more unpleasant position. He might have been arrested by now! As it was, his precarious immunity might not extend beyond the hour of the operation which might be already in progress.

But if Fred had told the truth in a franker way, she felt that the friendship of these people would still have been freely given, and might have been powerful enough even to mitigate the severities of legal process. They had not liked Mr. Kanwhistle. They had recognised the provocation which she and Fred had received. But if Fred would not tell the truth, even among friends—what could he expect?

Her fears did not outrun the fact. Sir Reginald's first inclination had been to give them wholehearted support, which would have meant that his purse, his influence, and—perhaps most valuable of all—his buoyant and dominating personality would have been unreservedly theirs. But he had not liked what Danks had said, which had gone beyond what he had felt it necessary to repeat.

Percival Kanwhistle lay in critical danger, not from a forehead wound but a savage blow struck from behind. There was no doubt about that. Danks would not speak so confidently if it were not true.

Dr. Danks was a young man whose appointment came from his own patronage. He would be very slow to act in a way which Sir Reginald would not approve. But that was not a position of which the banker would wish to take an unfair advantage. He liked him no less for the way in which he had held to his own opinion on the telephone. It was a matter of which the police ought to be informed.

Sir Reginald was conscious also that he had bluffed him by mentioning Chief-Inspector Combridge's name in the way he had. He had not said that he was coming in connection with this affair. But Danks had naturally taken it that way. He had inferred that Sir Reginald was already in communication with the police on the matter, and that responsibility was removed from his own shoulders thereby.

Well, he could set that right by putting the matter into Combridge's hands when he appeared, and that might be what he ought to do.

Had Corder chosen to be franker with him, he could not tell what his course would have been; but in view of his attitude—well, he could tell Combridge the same tale, and see how it would go down with him!

Only to Evelyn did it occur that Mr. Corder might possibly be telling the truth, or what he honestly thought the truth to be. She might have said this, but for the advice she had heard Mr. Jellipot give that Fred should say nothing more on that subject. She had a great respect for Mr. Jellipot's judgment. She presided silently at a silent meal.

Fred was conscious of the atmosphere of disapproval, if not of hostility, by which he was now surrounded, but what could he do? Evelyn's instinct, against all logical probability, was right in thinking that he had told the truth as he believed it to be. He wanted to speak to Adeline alone. He wanted to hear the result of the operation, on which he saw that his liberty might depend. He went on miserably with the silent meal.

CHAPTER XXVII.

Mr. Jellipot Does Not Believe

EVELYN considered that guests must be entertained, even while they wait the news of an operation upon a cousin they have knocked on the head.

No one making a better suggestion, they sat down to the card table, Evelyn partnering the sanguinary Fred, and Adeline opposite Sir Reginald as before. Mr. Jellipot watched, as he said he preferred to do. It was an arrangement which relieved the Corders of any anxiety as to the financial issues of the game, for one must gain what the other lost, and this may have been fortunate in a contest which was neither cheerful nor serious, and in which Mr. Jellipot observed Adeline to lead up to her opponents' strength, and then Fred to revoke, without protest, though not necessarily therefore unobserved.

They had been playing less than an hour when Dr. Danks telephoned again. The operation, he said, had been "successful," which meant little, if anything, more than that Mr. Kanwhistle had not immediately died. His operating colleague had left, after expressing the opinion that there was a chance for the patient, who had been favoured by nature with a robust constitution and a thick skull. Dr. Danks was of the same opinion. A bare chance. He would not put it higher than that. There had been laceration of the brain. No, Mr. Kanwhistle showed no sign of returning consciousness. That condition might continue for many hours, perhaps days. It might never return at all.

Sir Reginald repeated this. It was little comfort, and yet might have been worse. While he was doing so, Inspector Combridge entered the room.

He had expected some difficulty in explaining his prolonged absence, and had prepared one or two specious lies, which courtesy, if not conviction, would be obliged to accept. But he found himself to be engaged in an unheeded mendacity. No one appeared to care where he had been, or why it had been necessary to shop in Kettlewell more or less from midday until 10:00 P.M.

He saw that something serious had occurred, with which he was quick to connect the absence of Mr. Kanwhistle, though he was naturally unable to guess what it could be; and as he became silent, Sir Reginald said: "You'd better tell him what's happened, Jellipot. You'd do it better than I."

Adeline rose, and interposed with: "If you'll excuse us, I think we'll go to bed now. I think we're both tired. We've had," she laughed foolishly, "rather a bad day."

Sir Reginald looked surprised. He thought the Corders should have stayed to discuss a matter in which they were most concerned. Yet perhaps some aspects of it could be dealt with more freely if they were not there. Mrs. Corder might be doing the right thing.

So it appeared that his wife thought. She said: "I'm sure it's the wisest thing you can do. You'll both be all the better for a good night." He observed that the two women kissed, a habit to which his wife, from whom the initiative had come, was not always disposed, even with intimate friends. He took it for a signal that she was still on the Corders' side, which had some effect on the conversation which followed, for he knew that Evelyn had a level, though not always a very logical, head.

Fred observed that he was being taken or sent to bed without his own opinion being asked, but he did not object. He disliked the presence of Inspector Combridge even more than he had done yesterday, and with far more reason than he had had then. He had a vague feeling that he would be less liable to immediate arrest if he should retire—that he would be safer in bed. And he wanted to talk to Adeline.

When they had gone, Mr. Jellipot gave a very accurate account of what had, or what was said to have happened, in a colourless manner, with little indication of his own opinion, and Inspector Combridge listened in a characteristic silence. When the tale ended, he gave no more than a noncommittal "Humph." He seemed more disposed for thought than speech. When he spoke at last, he turned to Lady Crowe and said surprisingly: "They must have made a mess of your car."

Evelyn agreed about that. The varnish was deplorably scratched. There were deep grooves in the panelling. The back seat and floor had been soaked with blood. "It's a queer thing about blood," she said, "that it gets everywhere. You wouldn't think anyone could have so much inside as comes out when it gets a chance."

Inspector Combridge agreed in turn. It was, he explained, the distributive action of the heart. Then he came to the point with the remark: "I'm rather sorry for Corder. It sounds like five years for him—or perhaps three."

"There was," Mr. Jellipot pointed out, "considerable provocation. And he says that Kanwhistle was coming for him."

Inspector Combridge appeared to have little sympathy for this view. "It wasn't done," he pointed out, "in the heat of the moment. He followed Kanwhistle into the wood."

"You don't," Mr. Jellipot asked, "believe Mr. Corder's statement that he only struck him once with a rotten stick?"

Inspector Combridge countered this with another. "You're not going to tell me you believe that, are you?"

Mr. Jellipot answered deliberately: "No, I'm not. I regard it as an improbability." He paused, weighing his words. "Perhaps an extreme improbability would not be too much to say."

Inspector Combridge agreed: "Yes, it's a lame tale."

Evelyn said: "If Mr. Corder sticks to that, I should say it's true."

Mr. Jellipot looked mildly surprised. "The legal experiences," he said, "both of Inspector Combridge and myself have unfortunately taught us that men placed as Mr. Corder now is do not always tell the exact truth."

"No," she said, "it isn't likely they would. But I think he believed what he said."

"Well," Inspector Combridge was definite, "he'll have to stand his trial on that. It's wonderful what counsel can make a jury believe. But I don't think that will go down. It's to be hoped, for his sake, that Kanwhistle doesn't die."

Mr. Jellipot spoke again. He seemed anxious to give any support he could to that which he did not himself believe. "A good deal," he said, "will depend on the stick—I mean whether it was really as fragile as Mr. Corder asks us to believe. I suppose it will still be lying there. Perhaps an early morning walk to the scene of this unfortunate encounter would not be wasted."

"If you think of doing that," Inspector Combridge said, "perhaps I'd better come too."

"So," Mr. Jellipot responded, "I had no doubt that you intended to do."

"It's got to be inspected, of course. But it's the kind of case that we may prefer to leave to the local police. If you'll allow me, Sir Reginald, I should be glad of an opportunity of telephoning to headquarters—privately, if I may. I expect, as they were your guests, you'll prefer to keep out of it, as far as possible?"

"On the contrary," Sir Reginald replied, seeing that Evelyn's eyes were upon him, "as they are my guests, I mean to see that they have a square deal, which means that the law will do just as much of its muddle-headed interference as I can't prevent, but no more. But you can telephone to anyone you please, and you'll find the instrument in the library put through direct to the exchange at this hour."

With this permission Inspector Combridge retired to the library, upon which an obstinate though friendly argument arose between Evelyn and Mr. Jellipot regarding the nature of Fred's defence, and whether it were reasonable that he should be believed.

"The legal proof of an act of homicide," Mr. Jellipot remarked, "is very often a matter of considerable difficulty, even though there may be no reasonable doubt concerning the nature or perpetration of the deed, or the motive which urged the blow. It would approach impossibility if it should be held sufficient for an accused man to make an unsupported assertion that the final blow had been mysteriously dealt by an unknown hand, as he had withdrawn from the vicinity of the man whom he had struck down. In the absence of any supporting evidence, it is not reasonable to expect such a statement to be believed."

"But suppose it's true?"

"Then I can only say that Mr. Corder is a most unfortunate young man."

The controversy, into which Sir Reginald declined to be drawn, had not concluded when Inspector Combridge returned.

"It's as I thought it would be. I'm wanted back in London as soon as my leave is over on more important business than this. I'm afraid Corder must expect to be arrested, even if Kanwhistle pulls through, but it's a matter for the local police.

"It isn't as though there were anything about the case that they won't be able to handle. It seems to be quite simple, and there really isn't any defence to the fact, unless you accept Corder's assertion that he only gave him some gentle taps, although, of course, there'll be plenty of argument about extenuating circumstances. But that's nothing to make a stir with the C.I.D. We're not anxious for him to get a heavier sentence than he deserves."

"Well," Sir Reginald replied, in some doubt of whether this decision implied any favour to himself, but with a clear perception that his influence with the local police was stronger than any he was likely to be able to exert upon Scotland Yard, "I'm glad you look at it in a sensible way. I'll have a word with the superintendent here in the morning, and see what can be done."

He thought that, especially if Mr. Kanwhistle's condition should improve, he could arrange for proceedings to be by way of summons rather than warrant, on his assurance that Mr. Corder would not fail to obey the call; and, after that, if the case were properly put to the local magistrates, a fine, or even a binding-over might meet the case—provided always that Corder would have the sense to say that he lost his temper and laid on as an angry man would be likely to do.

"The fact is," he went on, "that I feel an uncomfortable responsibility for the whole affair. I'd no business to ask the two men down here together."

The remark brought back to the inspector's mind the allegation of continuous criminality which Mr. Kanwhistle had made against his cousin, and his statement of the earlier day that he was setting a detective upon his tracks. It suggested motive of a very different and less defensible kind than that which was now put forward, and which husband and wife might well have concocted together, to make excuse for the crime.

Suppose that Kanwhistle had been led to admit that he was determined to frustrate the attempt to win that conditional legacy? Was that not a twenty times more probable cause of quarrel than this sudden infatuation with Mrs. Corder, of which there had been no previous sign?

There was a possibility of mercenary motive of another kind. Even the fantastic possibility of committing three hundred and sixty-five separate, unsuspected crimes could result in a no greater prize than ten thousand pounds. But Percival Kanwhistle was a rich man. If he had made no will—and he was young enough to make that a very probable omission—by how much larger a sum might not a cousin benefit, in the absence of nearer relatives, of whom the inspector had not heard?

This might be a matter for legitimate enquiry also, but he had said no more than the truth when he had expressed himself as not being anxious to make Corder's penalty heavy. He preferred that whatever happened now should be without interference from him. He only said: "I've done one thing. I've arranged for them to send Sergeant Solomon down to question Kanwhistle if he comes back to his senses. He'll do it a lot more intelligently than one of the local men would be likely to."

Mr. Jellipot said nothing to that, though he observed that Inspector Combridge was telling them nothing which they would not be otherwise certain to learn, and the thought crossed his mind that it was a singular proceeding in a case with which the C.I.D. did not think it necessary to interfere. But Sir Reginald broke out into one of those indignant protests which the ethics of police procedure were always liable to arouse in his lively mind.

"You mean," he said, "that you're going to station a policeman beside his bed to badger him the moment he opens his eyes, in the hope that he'll say something that'll make it worse for another man?

"I know you'll tell me it's the regular procedure in such cases as this, but I don't care if it is. It doesn't make any difference if it's done every day. It's a monstrous thing."

"I don't say," Inspector Combridge answered with unexpected mildness, "that it's a very nice thing to do. But we try to be fair to everyone. And the best way to be able to do that is to get at the truth, and that's all we're after."

"When people express sympathy for some poor criminal whom you're hounding to death," Sir Reginald went on, the mildness of the answer having had no power to deflect his wrath, "you say they ought to think more of his innocent victims and less of the guilty man. Well, perhaps you may be right there. But do you practise the thing you preach? Not a bit.

"When a man's had his skull cracked, he doesn't want to make statements the first moment he sees the light. He wants to lie quiet, if I'm any good at a guess, and that's what he ought to be let to do.

"I dare say you've killed men before now who might have pulled through if you'd let them have any peace, and then hanged some poor wretch for what's really been your own work."

"I hope," Inspector Combridge answered, with the same resolute determination not to take offence at anything which Sir Reginald might say, "that it's not often as bad as that."

CHAPTER XXVIII.

Mr. Jellipot Takes the Book

HAVING come to the privacy of their own room, the guilty pair faced one another, the three months' record of iniquity, and even the fact that the daily crime was still undone, being forgotten for the moment in the sudden shadow which had fallen upon them. They spoke almost at once, each voicing the strongest emotion which shook their minds.

"Oh, Fred, I am sorry! It was all my fault talking to you the way I did."

"Adeline, you've got to believe me. If someone doesn't, I think I shall go mad. I *know* I never hit the back of his head, and that stake wouldn't have cracked anyone's skull, unless it were a baby's of six months old."

Adeline's reply was at once obvious and profound: "Then, if you didn't, someone else did."

"Yes, they must have done it while I was running to you for help."

"It doesn't sound likely, does it?"

"It sounds mad. It's hardly more probable than that the doctors should find a crack when it isn't there. But it's a fact, all the same."

"Then it's our job to find out who really did it."

This reflection, obvious as it also was, reduced them to a worried silence. It might be their job, but how on earth was it to be done? Adeline was the first to break it with the hesitating query: "Fred, was the stick really so *very* rotten?"

"Well, it broke as it hit his head. The broken part looked rotten all through."

"Anyway, it wasn't a very thick stick." She urged her memory to recall just how it had looked as it had lain broken upon the ground. Certainly not very thick! "I suppose," she added, "it must be still there."

"Yes, unless the police have been smelling round."

"I don't see how they could have done that. To begin with, they wouldn't know where to look. Besides, who's said anything, and when? Percy hasn't been able to talk. No one knows what happened except the folk here. And it getting dark so soon after! No, the stick's sure to be lying there."

"I ought to go out early and get it. I ought to go as soon as it's light." Adeline frowned doubtfully over this proposition. She came near to speaking a fear in both their minds when she said: "We shouldn't want them to think you were trying to get away."

"I should have to take care that I shouldn't be seen. Not till I were coming back."

"I'd rather go with you, if you do."

"They'd be more likely to think we were making off if you did that."

"Still, I'd rather come. We've done everything together till now."

The remark reminded them both of the occupation of the last three months, which, perhaps by no proper logic, had led them to this. Were they to give it up now?

Fred said doubtfully: "It'll be all up, if we let tonight go."

Adeline answered sharply: "I can't bear to think of that now. It's been all my fault from the first."

"I don't see that it's been anyone's fault. Till I made a silly ass of myself today, we both thought it was rather fun."

She knew that to be true, but she knew also that Fred would never have attempted it but for her, and she had a miserable conviction that he would not have pursued his cousin with any weapon of chastisement three months earlier. Doubly, she told herself again, the fault was hers.

But Fred, neither blaming nor judging himself quite in the same way, stood in hesitation. He had felt an almost physical relief since he had made Adeline believe his protests about the weakness of that single, self-defensive blow. Suppose Percy should recover more easily than the doctors thought? Suppose nothing should happen to himself? Suppose that they should be kicking themselves in two days' time that they had lost their nerve, and so lost everything else, tonight?

Suddenly he recalled that Adeline had said that she kept one crime in reserve which he could always commit, even though they should be confined in an empty room.

"You said once that however we got cornered there was one crime I could always do."

"Oh, *that*? Yes. You can do that if you like. It was beating me."

"Beating you? You know I shouldn't do that.

"Yes, you would if you thought we should get ten thousand pounds, and it's what I should have asked you to do. But we're going to throw that up now."

"I'm not so sure that we are. I didn't give Percy any more than he well deserved, and I'm not going to throw everything up as though I've done something I didn't do."

"Well," she answered indifferently, "I've told you that you can. But you've got to play that game alone if you go on. I've had enough. Perhaps you'd better beat me for that."

As Fred made no response to this suggestion, she added, with a faint return of interest in her erudition as a student of English crime: "It used to be necessary to use a stick thicker than your little finger, or, at least, some man's little finger. It didn't seem to be clear whose, which must have been very confusing, because men's little fingers must vary in thickness more than a bit. But that trouble's over now. In the present state of the law, a man oughtn't to beat his wife at all. I don't consider that's quite fair considering how some women nag, but that's how the law is. The stick can be ever so thin—and quite rotten as well."

She broke off abruptly, conscious that she had said the wrong thing. He answered, with a dejection which her maladroit reference may have increased: "Well, I'm not going to try that, anyhow. If you chuck it up, I can see that I shall have to do the same. So if you really mean what you say, we'll just do nothing, and by midnight it will be too late to alter our minds. We shall just have a silly failure to look back on all our lives, ending up with a sickening mess."

She could not deny the essential truth of this summary of the position, but his allusion to the "sickening mess" reminded her that they were dealing with something which it might be impossible to put aside, to be looked back on in whatever mood. There might be a present battle to fight, perhaps, present and future misery to be endured.

She said: "There's one thing we've got to do. We've got to get rid of that book. If they're going to make any fuss about Percy's head, they're not going to be able to prove from that that you've been living a life of crime. They'd be sure to make out that we'd planned this, and that it hadn't worked out quite as we meant it should."

"I don't see how you can. Even if we had a fire, a book like that isn't easy to burn."

"There's only one way. Give it to someone to keep. Someone we can trust. Someone in whose things they won't look."

She had Evelyn in her mind as she said this. She felt Lady Crowe to be one who would not only be loyal to a trust she might undertake, but who had courage and wit for any emergency that might arise. She thought that she could persuade her to take the book, and that it would be safe and secret with her.

But at that moment she heard Mr. Jellipot coming up the stairs, the head of which was beside their own door. It could be no one but he. Only Inspector Combridge and he now slept in that wing, Mr. Kanwhistle being where he was, and the inspector had a brisker, louder tread. On a sudden impulse, she opened the door, and met Mr. Jellipot at the stairhead.

And then, as she faced him, meeting the kind but searching enquiry of his eyes, she realised that there was something of even more vital importance than that which she had come to say.

Impulsively she began: "Mr. Jellipot, will you do me a favour? Will you *try* to believe that Fred told the truth when he said that he only hit Mr. Kanwhistle once with that rotten stick? Will you say to yourself: *suppose* it's true, what *must* have happened to hurt him the way he was?"

The earnestness with which this appeal was made was sufficient to lead even Mr. Jellipot to disregard its rather difficult grammar. After a long moment of silent gravity he asked: "You believe that to be true?"

"Yes, I honestly do. I am quite sure."

"You know Mr. Corder better than we can possibly do. Yes, I will try to believe that."

It was, perhaps, more than she could have expected to hear, but she recognised that the assurance was without conviction. Even her own certainty could not lead him further than that he would "try" to believe a most improbable tale.

Still, she knew that the promise would be most literally kept, and that was much, for facts cannot conflict with possibility, and are usually discoverable to those who approach them with open minds.

Having succeeded in this appeal, her mind returned to its first purpose. "There's one thing I wanted to ask you. I've got a book I want someone to take charge of—someone I can trust. Would you mind doing this for me, as a matter private between ourselves?"

The question was met by a period of silence longer than before, and this time she saw that she had made a request which would not be so readily granted.

"A book?" Mr. Jellipot queried at last. "Presumably of financial value?"

"No, none at all. I just want to feel it's out of the way. I don't mind if it's destroyed. In fact, I should like that best, if it wouldn't be troubling you too far."

"You needn't consider that, Mrs. Corder. I will do anything I properly can to assist you in your present difficulty. But I must understand what I am asked—and, of course, why."

"I don't mind that at all. I just thought that you might prefer not to know."

"Possibly," Mr. Jellipot conceded to abstract truth, "you may have judged rightly on that point. There may be matters on which I should prefer to be uninformed. But I cannot undertake to be of assistance to you on such a basis. I must know what the book is, and why it is to be entrusted to me."

Among many theories which had already risen in an actively imaginative mind he had decided that the most probable was that he was to be entrusted with the manuscript of her current novel, which might contain an incident suggestive of what had actually occurred, the discovery of which would be prejudicial to her husband's defence. He saw that the secreting of this evidence might be an act of very doubtful propriety, which he could only judge by its perusal. There were other, widely different possibilities, but—no, he would certainly undertake nothing he did not understand fully.

"I don't mind you knowing in the least. It's about the way we've carried out what Fred was required to do under Miss Kanwhistle's will."

"You mean that it is a record of Mr. Corder's illegal actions?"

"Yes, we couldn't possibly have proved them if we hadn't entered them every day."

Mr. Jellipot pondered this. His curiosity was aroused. He saw that it was natural that the Corders should desire to get the book out of their hands, though it might not be evidence against them which could be used, the law not allowing a criminal charge to be prejudiced by the suggestion of other crimes. And yet, in such circumstances as these, might it not be considered admissible? Probably it would be allowed by a strong judge—and the point would go to the Criminal Appeal Court—and be dismissed there.

There was another consideration. He must do nothing which might appear to make him an accomplice in breaking the law, nothing which involved him in complicity with that confounded codicil.

"I'm afraid," he said, "that I can have nothing to do with that."

"Then what on earth am I to do with it? Do you mind telling me why you refuse?"

Faced by the distress in her eyes, Mr. Jellipot temporised weakly. "If you could assure me, Mrs. Corder, that your husband has abandoned that most foolish attempt—"

"Yes, we've just agreed about that. It can't go on after what's happened today." The wording of this reply raised a new doubt in his mind.

"I should require your assurance that the book contains no reference to today's unfortunate incident, or, if it did, I should hold myself free to act as justice might require me to do."

"There's nothing about it at all. I don't see how there could be."

But Mr. Jellipot still hesitated. "If you could go a little further than that, Mrs. Corder, and assure me that nothing which happened today had any relation to the terms of Miss Kanwhistle's will?"

It was Adeline's turn to show hesitation now. "I couldn't exactly say that. I don't suppose it would have happened at all but for that wretched will."

"Perhaps I put the point with less precision than it required. I should have said, if nothing done by Mr. Corder or yourself was with the object of fulfilling the terms of the codicil."

"Yes, I can say that. We weren't either of us thinking of doing anything wrong at all."

So on this final assurance Mr. Jellipot undertook the charge, though with a reluctance so evident that, in a less serious emergency, Adeline would have withdrawn her request. As it was, she had placed it in his charge, and closed her door only at the last second which secrecy required, for, as she did so, she heard the quick steps of Inspector Combridge mounting the stairs.

But she went to sleep with the feeling that something onerous had been ended, something essential done, and with a better hope of how the event was to terminate than was to be the experience of the coming days; and slept so well that she did not hear Fred as he rose before the first approach of the dawn, and descended silently through a silent house.

CHAPTER XXIX.

MR. JELLIPOT'S OPINIONS ONLY

IT was only about twenty minutes after Fred had succeeded in leaving the house unobserved by the side entrance that Inspector Combridge tapped on Mr. Jellipot's door, and that gentleman, who was normally an early riser, descended with him by the front stair-case, and left the house quietly enough, but in a more open manner, and after they had been served with coffee by the waiting butler.

Mr. Jellipot had had a short night. He had promised to destroy the incriminating volume at the first convenient opportunity, which was not likely to be until he had returned to his own home, and meanwhile there had been no bargain that he should not familiarise himself with its contents, which he had been curious to do.

The result had been to set his mind during the remaining hours of the night to serious consideration of the endless complexity and frequent triviality of England's legal enactments, among which her citizens move with a practised caution, upon which, rather than ex-act knowledge, they rely to avoid regulations which change continu-ally and multiply with the years.

He could see no prospect that these legislative enactments, with their retinue of vexatious or ruinous penalties, would diminish. Rather, they must continue to multiply, for the modern fashion of parliament was to sit for the major part of the year making new laws without end, restricted only by their available time for producing them. It did not appear to occur to anyone to ask whether England had, or ever could have, laws enough, or to suggest that it might be advantageous to give a regular proportion of parliamentary time to repealing some of those which our ancestors had inflicted upon us.

Yet, he asked himself, could it be fairly said that this ceaseless spate of restrictive enactments did more evil than good? Could it be supposed that they would be universally obeyed if no penalties were imposed upon those who should fail to do so? And if not, to what

criticism were they fairly open? What alternative could be preferred?

It was natural, such speculations having engaged his mind, and
the scandalous Kanwhistle codicil being so nearly connected with
the expedition on which they had set out together, that it should become a subject of conversation between Inspector Combridge and
himself, although he knew from past experiences that his companion's sympathies would be given more readily to the official and
conventional view of the "freedom" of modern life.

"When you talk like that," the inspector said, with some contro-
versial acuteness, "it sounds as though you think that if everyone
were allowed to do as they like it would make it a freer world. But if
you let one man do an annoying thing, you let another one be an-
noyed, and there's not overmuch freedom in that."

"It is a point," Mr. Jellipot replied, "to which I gave some
thought during the night, and it led me to the conclusion which you
have put more forcibly than I might have been able to do.

"The trouble does not, in the main, arise from restrictive laws,
or the penalties which are the almost inevitable condition of their
observance, although even that may be subject to some qualification,
in which connection I recollect that an American citizen whom I recently had the honour to meet told me that the difference between
London and New York which had most sharply impressed his mind
was that we put notices in our parks, 'Please keep off the grass,'
which are universally respected, whereas they prefer the curter ad-
monition, 'Keep off,' which is disregarded with an almost equal
unanimity."

"Do you mean," Inspector Combridge asked, with some excusable sarcasm, "that all the criminals in London would go out of
business if we said 'please' instead of running them in?"

"No," Mr. Jellipot replied, too seriously occupied by the subject
itself to resent, or perhaps even to observe, his companion's tone. "It
would be a result which could only be anticipated by an exceptionally sanguine mind. Although I was also told—and it may be more
applicable to the argument than would appear to a superficial
view—that there are notices in the Underground Railway Stations of
New York threatening that anyone who spits will be subjected to a
fine of five hundred dollars AND three months' imprisonment,
which cannot be said to err on the side of leniency, but which is as
little regarded as are the unmannerly admonitions to keep off the
grass—but I was not considering what may be called the professional criminal classes of London, but rather the general body of the

public, which is, so far as my observation goes, willing, and even nervously anxious, to keep the law."

"Well, if they do that—"

"But I was considering those many thousands who, surrounded by such numerous and complex regulations, inadvertently fail. Let me take an illustration from yesterday's newspaper reports. A lady was summoned—I did not observe by what authority—for allowing a small dog to run down the escalator of a tube station in London. Her defence was that she had had the animal in her arms, and that it had struggled free.

"It was not alleged that any harm had been done, nor am I aware that any critical danger to the public welfare is threatened by the presence of a small dog on the moving stairs. That may be because I have never examined the subject with the thoroughness which it may require. But, if I may judge from my own twice-daily observation, the regulation is well observed, and a dog running loose on an escalator is an object which I have never seen. Yet the lady was fined two pounds—or forty shillings in the phraseology which the courts prefer."

"You think that was a bit too much?"

"I think any fine would have been too much. I think it was a grave discourtesy from the community to the individual to require her to waste her morning attending the court at all. The position would have been amply met by reminding her of the regulation, and she doubtless would have held the animal, on a future occasion, in a firmer grip.

"I was led, by this incident, and by more cognate considerations, to conclude that it should be required of those who institute such prosecutions to show that the public interest requires an appeal to punitive legislation, which would otherwise remain dormant, to the general satisfaction of all concerned.

"I considered the setting up of some competent authority without whose leave no criminal legal process could be commenced, but I saw objections to this which I must not discuss, in view of the fact that our destination is very near.

"But I had what may have been a better thought. I considered that the nuisance might be controlled if all magistrates should have power to fine any official who should institute a vexatious prosecution, and that the onus should be on such a one to show that he did no more than public order required."

"That," Inspector Combridge said with emphasis, "would be a bit stiff."

"It would avert," Mr. Jellipot replied, with gentle obstinacy of voice, "an enormous amount of petty vexation, and the waste of time of magistrates and others who might be doing more useful work. A man who can start annoying one of his fellow citizens on such a pre-text as I have selected in casual illustration should be required to compensate her from his own pocket, or, under more serious cir-cumstances, should be sent to jail as a common pest."

"Well, I hope it won't come to that while I'm in the C.I.D."

"It won't ever come to that," Mr. Jellipot answered cheerfully. "The vested interests of my profession and yours, and still more of our admirable and very numerous bureaucracy, are too strong. And the idea itself, if I may say so without appearing to boast, is too sound. The English temperament is peculiarly averse from—"

But this peculiarity of the English temperament is something of which Chief-Inspector Combridge was never destined to hear. Mr. Jellipot interrupted himself to exclaim: "But who is that? Your eyes are much better than mine. I am almost certain I saw someone mak-ing off through the trees."

CHAPTER XXX.

BUT IT WAS NOT THERE

"THAT," Inspector Combridge answered, "is our young friend Frederick Corder, who has seen reason to visit the scene of the quarrel rather earlier than ourselves. He was starting to come back this way, but he may have heard us talking, and decided that it would be bad manners to interrupt."

"I am afraid," Mr. Jellipot answered apologetically, recognising the generosity of the plural pronoun, "that I am ill adapted by nature for investigations of this kind, and I have been looking forward to this little expedition with an added pleasure for the opportunity which it will give me of observing the methods by which you collect clues from the grass and leaves. But if you had observed Mr. Corder's presence earlier than I, I am a little surprised that you did not give him an immediate opportunity of explaining what he was doing here."

"I'm not going to find any clues," the inspector answered rather sourly, for he was a little doubtful of the simplicity of Mr. Jellipot's admiration. "I told you last night that we're leaving this bludgeoning row to the local police. I only came because you said you wanted to do some clue-hunting yourself before anyone else got about."

"I said," Mr. Jellipot replied with his usual equability, and his usual precision, "that I thought it desirable that the broken stick should be secured, in view of the conflicting evidence as to the nature of the wounds which it was said to have caused. I had no intention of searching for clues, for which I should have no ability. I should not know how to begin. It has always appeared to me to be a most peculiar characteristic of the criminal population that they persist in dropping buttons and other small articles about the scenes of their evil deeds."

Inspector Combridge made no answer to this, for they had now come to the scene of the tragedy. It was plain to see, in the growing light, how the car, after ploughing a broad, bough-breaking path to the spot, had backed and turned here, smashing the undergrowth down; and by the place where it had stood there were deep foot-marks of those who had been burdened with Mr. Kanwhistle's un-conscious weight.

They looked round, and could easily identify the tree trunk which had given its support to the injured man. The blood-soaked handkerchief still lay beside it.

"This," Mr. Jellipot remarked, "certainly supports Mr. Corder's tale."

"Yes," the inspector agreed, "but I don't see how that's any better for him."

"Perhaps you would explain."

"I mean that Kanwhistle didn't lean against that tree, and he certainly didn't get up from it and walk into the middle of the path, after he got that cracking blow on the skull. Corder must have come up behind him and brought the stick down, meaning to finish what he'd begun. It shows that it didn't happen in the fight at all."

"Why should he have done that?"

"He may have thought that he'd done so much harm already that it would be safer to finish him off."

"And immediately run for help?"

"That would be no more than revulsion from the horror of what he had done—and which he meant to deny. I don't see how he could have done anything which would have looked better for him. And, besides, men often do silly things when they get in a tight place."

"Well," Mr. Jellipot concluded, without disputing the frequent truth of this assertion, "we can judge better when we have found the stick."

"Which we shan't do. He was too quick for us this time."

They had both been searching the path, and the trampled brambles, as this conversation proceeded, and Mr. Jellipot was inclined to be of the same opinion, which further efforts only confirmed. Either to exhibit it in support of his own tale, or to remove evidence which would have destroyed it, Mr. Corder had come at this early hour to look for the broken stick.

Having come to agreement on this point, they walked back to the road together, where Inspector Combridge paused. "I think," he said, "I'll go round to the hospital on the way back, and see whether Kanwhistle's dead."

"Considering," Mr. Jellipot remarked, "that you said you would leave this affair entirely to the local police—"

"So I intend to do. But there's another matter about which I want a few words with Solomon, as he's here. "

"Then you won't need my company any further. I think I'll get back to breakfast."

Mr. Jellipot returned to Trees accordingly, and Inspector Combridge was met shortly afterwards in the lonely lane by Detective Riskall, a sallow youth, who appeared to be in a state of hardly suppressed excitement, either by his contact with so high an officer of the C.I.D., or the importance of the work on which he had been engaged.

"Well?" the inspector asked laconically.

"It was just as you said, sir. He came before it was properly light and picked up the pieces of stick, and went off with them."

"He didn't see you?"

"No, sir. I feel sure of that. I didn't interfere with him, as you said. I just followed him back."

"Quite right."

Inspector Combridge would have passed on without further words. He did not wish to delay talking to the young officer where they might be overseen, but Detective Riskall had more to say.

"Oh, sir, the superintendent told me, if I saw you, to ask whether the charge is to be manslaughter or wilful murder, if the gentleman dies. He said it might save him ringing up, which you might wish to avoid."

"Is he likely to die? What's the latest news that you have?"

"They say it's touch and go, and any minute might be the last."

"Then tell the superintendent to make the charge murder under such circumstances. It wasn't a blow struck in the heat of a quarrel. It was deliberately from behind."

"Very well, sir."

The two guardians of public order parted, and Inspector Combridge went on to interview Sergeant Solomon at the Cottage Hospital, but he could have learnt little from him, for Mr. Kanwhistle lay in a stupor which had not changed.

CHAPTER XXXI.

MR. JELLIPOT WOULD DECLINE

ADELINE waked only to the slight rustle of the window-curtains, as Janet drew them quietly apart, and to realise that the tea-tray was already beside her bed.

She looked across the room as the girl withdrew, and saw that Fred's bed was empty. His clothes were gone. She blamed herself that she had slept so soundly, for she had not meant him to go alone. She saw that her witness might add decisively to the weight of his unsupported word as to where and in what condition the stick would have been found. He had been foolish to go alone.

She blamed herself no less when he returned a few minutes later, and said that his expedition had been in vain, for the stick was not there. Someone—the police he supposed—must have taken it away.

He did not seem much perturbed about that. "Whoever's got it," he said, "will see that what I said must have been true."

Adeline was puzzled. "I don't see how anyone could, in the dark. No one knew where the place was, except Lady Crowe."

"Well, they did," he replied, with some irritation. "Anyhow, it wasn't there. "

Adeline put a doubt resolutely from her mind, yet the effort with which she did this was evidence of how strong and natural it was. If the stick had been stouter, less rotten, than he had said, would it not have been essential to make sure that it should not come under other eyes? And would not that have made it essential that he should dress quietly and go alone? But her own memory of the stick confirmed his contention. She thrust out a disloyal doubt, but showed her fear of how it might appear to others by her next words: "I hope no one saw you go."

"I couldn't say that. I rather think Combridge did. He and Jellipot followed me there, so that I had to scramble through the bushes, or we should have had a head-on collision."

"You're sure they hadn't been there before you?"

"Not unless they went twice, and the first time must have been in the dark, if so. It seems queer not to have anything to do today. I don't know whether I'm altogether sorry or glad—or should be, if there weren't this ghastly business about Percy hanging over our heads. By the way, there'll be those things we stole to send back. Fortunately, there weren't many of them. I suppose there's no way that the police can get on the track of them?"

"Not a chance. I don't mind telling you now. They're in a safe deposit in Pauline Everett's name, and she's got the key. Of course, she doesn't know what they are. I simply told her what I wanted her to do, and to say nothing. But you can trust Pauline."

Yes. Fred agreed that they could trust Pauline, a girl whose silence under all circumstances amounted almost to genius, and whose admiration for Adeline approached worship. There would be no difficulty about the cache.

"Shall you tell them you went out?" Adeline asked doubtfully.

"No, I don't think I shall. They might easily give it a wrong twist."

"Mr. Jellipot wouldn't try to. I don't know about the inspector. If you think they saw you, it might be the wiser way."

"Yes, perhaps so. We'll see what they say to us."

They went down to breakfast together, and found Mr. Jellipot alone in the room, seated before a plate of cold ham, which he was eating with the excellent appetite of those who take woodland walks at the break of dawn.

"I wonder whether it would be too early to ring up the hospital," Adeline said, "to see how Percy's getting on."

"Inspector Combridge has gone there to enquire already," Mr. Jellipot replied. "He may be here any moment now."

"I don't see," Fred answered, with apprehension and resentment about equally in his voice, "how he makes it out to be any business of his."

"As a matter of fact," Mr. Jellipot replied noncommittally, "Inspector Combridge is inclined to take the same view. He regards the matter as one which should be left to the local police. But I understood that he has some other business with the officer who is with Mr. Kanwhistle now."

Fred looked blankly at this. "Officer with…you can't mean they've arrested him? Or"—more sensibly—"that he's well enough to give his account of what happened?"

"I certainly don't mean anything more than I said, or, in fact, more than I know. It is customary in such cases for a policeman to sit by the bed of the injured man in readiness to question him if he should show signs of returning consciousness. It is a practice which is open to criticism, unless it be most discreetly and considerately performed. Sir Reginald thinks it to be indefensible. It certainly shows more care for what the police are accustomed to call the ends of justice than for the welfare of a wounded man. But the present case appears to me to be one which might be used as an almost ideal example in its defence. For if Mr. Kanwhistle were assaulted, or suffered from the effects of some accident difficult for us to imagine, while you were fetching help, it is of the utmost importance to you that he should be enabled to communicate the fact to a competent ear."

"We think the stick will go a long way toward proving that," Adeline interposed with an impulsive decision that Fred's visit to the scene of the quarrel should not be concealed, which she feared he was disposed to do, "and that seems to be in the hands of the police already, more likely than not. Anyway, Fred's been to look for it, and it isn't there."

Mr. Jellipot listened to this, but his eyes were upon Fred as he heard the announcement that he had been unable to find the stick. It was with an increased gravity that he answered: "I knew already that it is not there. I went myself with the same object, though a few minutes later than you, and Inspector Combridge was kind enough to come with me. We concluded that it must now be in your possession."

"No, it was gone before I got there."

Inspector Combridge entered the room in time to hear this last remark, the meaning of which was not hard to guess; but he bore out Mr. Jellipot's assurance of his aloofness, by receiving it with an expressionless face, and turning his attention to the steaming dishes the sideboard bore.

Judging that he had no intention of alluding to his visit to the hospital, and sympathising with the anxiety which the Corders must be feeling, Mr. Jellipot asked him: "Have you heard how Mr. Kanwhistle is getting on?"

"Yes, I'm sorry to say there's no sign of returning consciousness. The doctors seem to think he may continue in that condition for a good while."

As he spoke Evelyn entered, and the conversation naturally lapsed as she greeted her guests. Sir Reginald followed almost immediately. It was a business day for him, and his breakfast was a business-like meal. But his thoughts were on what he mentally called this damnable affair, and what he now considered to be his own culpable folly in asking the cousins together, and without informing them of whom they would have to meet. He had already telephoned the hospital, and learnt of the desperate condition of Percival Kanwhistle. He knew Danks well enough to gauge the exact meaning of what he said, and he judged that he had no more than the hope which the etiquette of his profession required. At any moment they might hear of the death of the injured man, and Corder might be arrested on a capital charge—or the police might not wait even for that.

He would have liked to ask the inspector one or two straight questions, arising from their conversation of the night before, but how could he do that with Mr. and Mrs. Corder hearing everything that was said? Evidently, breakfast must be cut short.

"Combridge," he said, "if you could spare a few minutes, I should like a word with you before I go."

Nothing had been said concerning the work which was the reason for Fred being there. It was as though it had been generally forgotten under the tragic shadow which had fallen upon them. But Adeline saw that he must work if they were to continue to accept Sir Reginald's hospitality—and, of course, providing that the police would leave him alone.

She saw also that Sir Reginald wished to discuss something with the inspector which their presence prevented. She curtailed her own breakfast to say: "Fred, if you've finished, I think we'd better be getting down to the house. You've got the inside sketches to do today, and you'll need the best of the light."

Fred, who had been eating with poorer appetite than those who had a less ominous future to face, got up at once, and next moment Adeline and he had left the room.

Mr. Jellipot, fixing upon the inspector a quiet but searching gaze, said at once, as though intending to clear the point before Sir Reginald should begin: "Mr. Corder says that he has not got the stick. When he got to the spot it had already gone. He supposes that it had been removed by the police."

"Oh, does he?" Inspector Combridge echoed sarcastically. "Then I can tell you we haven't done anything of the sort. I might go a bit further than that, but I've said that I don't want to interfere, and I meant just that. As a matter of fact, I think it will be best, if Sir

Reginald will excuse me, if I go back to town today, and then no one can think that I'm making any trouble that comes."

Mr. Jellipot began: "I am sure...."—and then paused, feeling that it was a matter on which his host or hostess should speak rather than he.

Sir Reginald said at once: "You know quite well, Combridge, no one wants you to do that. If you're not on this thing officially, you might give us advice or help that it would be very useful to have; and, if you are, we all know that you've got your duty to do."

"It's good of you to put it like that, but the fact is that they're wanting me back at the Yard rather urgently. Nothing to do with Corder, of course. He's not that important, as I suppose it's scarcely necessary to say."

"It's not necessary to give any explanation," Sir Reginald replied courteously, "if you feel that you ought to return to London. But I want you to understand that there's no reason on our side. No reason at all."

"Picker," Evelyn said, alluding to the under-gardener, "asked Soames to enquire whether his motor bicycle has come back, as he seems to have expected that it would yesterday."

Inspector Combridge looked as disconcerted by the interposition of this simple statement as Chief Inspectors of the C.I.D. are ever likely to allow themselves to do.

"It ought," he said, "to have been here yesterday. The fact is I sent it back by passenger train when I found how late I was liable to be."

Evelyn looked at him with an amused smile.

"You must have been rather worried lest you should miss the last train."

What could be the meaning of that? Confound the vagaries of these local lines!

Sir Reginald, with his eyes on the clock, and the knowledge that his car would be at the door within three minutes, interposed in explanation: "The fact is, Combridge, that the last train from Kettlewell that stops at this benighted hole leaves at six fifty-five, and it was rather late last night when you walked in. That's all that Lady Crowe meant. But it's no business of ours. And if you tell us that you're not concerned in this Kanwhistle affair, I needn't say we shall take your word.

"In that case, I shall phone the superintendent here as soon as I get to town—I haven't time now—and have a frank talk with him about it; and when I get back I shall have a try to get Corder to be frank with me—franker than I think he's been yet. But whatever he's done, I reckon it's more than half my fault, and I mean to see him through."

Inspector Combridge did not appear to object, or indeed to be particularly interested in that. "I thought," he said, "you might look at it in that way," and as he spoke Sir Reginald rose, gave him a hearty but hasty handshake of farewell, and went out, where Evelyn followed him for the usual ritual of goodbye in the hall.

Left alone with the inspector, Mr. Jellipot, with quiet pertinacity, held to the point on which he had been interrupted before. "Have I your permission," he asked, "to tell Mr. Corder definitely that the police have not got the stick?"

Inspector Combridge hesitated in his reply, but then said: "Oh, yes! You can make that as definite as you like. It's a fact. You can tell him he knows that stick a lot better than we do. But don't say you had that from me. I don't want to be in this at all." He paused, and asked sharply: "You're not thinking of undertaking Corder's defence?"

"No. Considering that I have not been asked, and that he has not been charged—"

"Well, he will be. There's nothing surer than that."

"I am sorry to hear it. Though I cannot say that I am greatly surprised."

"And it isn't much harder to guess that you'll be asked to undertake his defence."

"Which," Mr. Jellipot said with deliberate emphasis, "I should emphatically decline."

"I am glad to hear it. If Corder had been able to show us a rotten stick, as weak as he makes it out to have been, he might have had a dog's chance, but no more. But as he can't do that—"

"Yes. I am afraid he is in a very serious position. Even with Sir Reginald's very valuable support—"

"I don't care what Sir Reginald does, so long as you keep off the mat."

"As I most certainly shall."

"I dare say," the inspector went on, "he stands to benefit more by Kanwhistle's death even than if he'd been able to lay his hands on that ten thousand pounds. You'd find it hard to persuade any jury to let him kill his cousin, and walk off to enjoy a pile like that."

"But I can assure you that the question could not arise. Kanwhistle has a half-brother and some nephews and nieces, and there are some other cousins on that side of the family. I mean on his mother's side. Miss Kanwhistle was, of course, his father's sister."

"Well, that's interesting to know."

"And besides, we must not fail to observe that Mr. Kanwhistle is not dead."

"No, but he may be before the week's over."

There was something almost of satisfaction in the tone with which the inspector said this, which caught and surprised Mr. Jellipot's sensitive ear.

"You spoke," he said, "almost as though you would have been pleased to hear of his death."

Inspector Combridge looked disconcerted for a second time since he had risen from a table that was not yet cleared. "I couldn't have meant that," he said. "How could I? I've got nothing against Kanwhistle. Nothing at all."

He left the room rather abruptly, as though he preferred that the conversation should not be further prolonged. An hour later he left for London.

CHAPTER XXXII.

For Wilful Murder

IMMEDIATELY on his arrival at Leadenhall Street, Sir Reginald telephoned to the police headquarters at Kettlewell. He had no difficulty in being put through to Superintendent Chumley of the West Sussex Constabulary, an intelligent and friendly officer, whom he found to be already acquainted with the fact that Mr. Kanwhistle lay in a critical condition in the Cottage Hospital at Hither Dene.

The superintendent listened patiently to all that the wealthiest and in other ways the most important resident in the district which he controlled had to say on that subject, and he agreed that no man could be expected to remain in good-tempered quietude while his wife's clothing was being torn from her back.

"But," he asked, "are you sure, Sir Reginald, that that's all there was in it?" It appeared that he had heard of the peculiar provisions of the Kanwhistle will.

"Of course I know all about that," Sir Reginald answered, with some impatience, "but I don't see where it comes in at all. You can't blame Corder because his aunt made a lunatic will. But I'll tell you what I'll do. I haven't had a chance of talking it over with him yet— not without half a dozen other people being about. I'll get home early this afternoon, have it over with him thoroughly, and telephone you from Hither Dene. That ought to be good enough, even for the police. I suppose you don't *want* to make more trouble than there is now? It's quite certain he won't run away. And it isn't as though he's likely to go on breaking the head of everyone he happens to meet. Besides, I might get more out of him than he'd tell you, and save trouble all round."

Superintendent Chumley did not discuss the propriety of this method of investigating what, on the information he had received, appeared to be a case of most probable manslaughter, under circumstances of very doubtful extenuation (it isn't very convincing to pursue your enemy with a cudgel, and then say that you only struck him in self-defence—particularly when it was on the back of the head). He only said that he was sorry that it was too late to consider that course of procedure, as Sergeant Buller, from the Hither Dene station, already had the matter in hand. Did that mean that Corder was being arrested on no more than gossiping reports? Certainly not. He was being asked to visit the police station, where he would be invited to make a statement of what had occurred.

"Yes. I understand," Sir Reginald replied to this assurance. "Ever read the Bible, Chumley? *Go ye out into the highways and hedges and compel them to come in*. That's about what your invitations are. A man who could refuse them would manage to be absent from his own funeral. Well, if you're set to make trouble, you can have any bail you ask for from me, and I'll get Butcher on to the job."

The superintendent expressed satisfaction at hearing the name of that eminent criminal barrister. He said he always liked to see a man well defended. His private opinion was that these highly paid men made little difference, and it was certain that they ought to make none at all.

Sir Reginald rang off, and immediately refused to increase the overdraft of the Skellington Iron Works. "I ought," he said, "to have put a receiver in before now. You'd better phone Jellipot to issue the writ. Oh, but he won't be there! Well, his office will know what to do. Leave it till tomorrow. I'm in a bad temper today."

At midday he telephoned that he should be home for tea. Evelyn answered him. She said that Sergeant Buller had called at about ten o'clock, asking to see Mr. Corder, and on hearing that he had left for Maidcote Manor had followed him there. "I told him," she said, "that Mr. Corder hadn't done anything more than I should have expected you to do under similar circumstances, and he was very nice about it, but he said that the law was always a bit awkward about gentlemen breaking each other's heads. He said perhaps it wouldn't be very serious if Mr. Kanwhistle would have the sense to get well."

"Did Jellipot see him?"

"No. He said he'd much rather not."

Beyond that she had heard nothing.

Sir Reginald caught the 3:33 P.M. and was met by the limousine, in which he was surprised to see Evelyn sitting, though not in the driver's seat, for she rarely drove unless she were in her own car.

"I meant to come and meet you myself," she said, "but I decided it wouldn't do. That car looks worse now it's been cleaned than it did before. It's like a public announcement of the trouble in

Maidcote wood. Mrs. Corder came back an hour ago. They've got her husband at the police station. She tells me that she believes he's refused to make any statement until a solicitor's present. She put him up to that. He's not arrested at present. He's only 'detained.' She was going to get a local solicitor, but Mr. Jellipot advised her to do nothing till you had come."

"Quite right. I wonder why Jellipot's standing back. He always did dislike criminal cases, but in such circumstances as these—"

"He said that being connected as he was with the Kanwhistle will—"

"Yes, I see that. He may be right. We'll hear what he has to say."

"He's sorry for Mrs. Corder, but I don't think he really believes that her husband didn't find the stick there this morning."

"So am I. And so I don't either. I wish I'd had a few words with the young fool before the police got hold of him. But if he'll keep his mouth shut as his wife told him, he may come through yet well enough. I expect the stick was a bit heavier than he had made out. I thought at first that he might have done it with something else, but trying to make away with the stick settles that. I expect it was the first time he had done anything of the sort, and he didn't know how hard he could hit, or what a man's skull can be expected to stand.

"Yes, it does seem like that. But I still don't believe it. Somehow it doesn't sound right. He must have helped Mr. Kanwhistle try to stop the blood, and then, when he got up, hit him again from behind. Do you think he's the sort of man who would do that?"

"No, I should have said not. But I don't know him. And Kanwhistle may have said something that made him boil over again. Or he may have thought he'd injured him so much already that it would be safer to finish the job, and say it was someone else. It may have upset his plans when he saw you were there. We don't know what tale we should have heard from the two if they'd been alone. Probably that they heard Kanwhistle call out and drove his assailants off. But when he saw you were there, and didn't know what his wife had told you, he had to make the best of a bad job."

"I hadn't thought of that," Evelyn admitted. She saw that it was a more probable theory than any which she had been able to form. Yet she still held stubbornly to her own opinion. "Oh, well," she said, "I suppose the truth will come out at last."

"Not if Butcher can help it. He'll make the jury believe that Kanwhistle got out that pocket mirror that Corder saw, and cracked the back of his own head, if he really puts his heart into the job. But you'll find the police will sort it out before they go into court.

"They'll find that stick, for one thing, unless Corder's got the sense to tell them where it is. They'll do that if they have to turn over every leaf in the wood. They don't care, in a case like this, if they spend enough to put a penny on the rates for the next half year. It's our money that goes, and they get the credit for what they do. I'm going straight up to my own room."

The last words were said as the car stopped at the door. He added, as they went up the stairs together: "I'm going to phone Sergeant Buller before I come down to tea. I'll find out just how things are, and see what can be done before I meet Mrs. Corder. You can tell her I'm doing that."

It was a message which gave Adeline a better hope than she had had since she had parted with Fred at the police station at Hither Dene, but when Sir Reginald entered the lounge ten minutes later, he said: "I'm sorry I've no good news to give you. Mr. Kanwhistle died about an hour ago, without regaining consciousness, and your husband has been arrested for wilful murder."

"Then," Adeline said, "he's been arrested for something he didn't do."

CHAPTER XXXIII.

The Advice of Mr. Butcher, K.C.

THE next fortnight was a nightmare to Adeline, nor, it may be supposed, was it any better for Fred, condemned to a solitude of inaction with his thoughts continually upon the folly of what he had done, and the fear of what was still to be done to him.

Adeline stayed at Trees by Lady Crowe's invitation, so that she might be near her husband, and avoid returning to the loneliness of the Bloomsbury Street flat, or the callers who might have been more difficult to endure.

She had much kindness from these so-recent friends, and Sir Reginald kept his word in providing for the defence with no mention of the cost. The morning following Fred's arrest, when it was understood that the police would merely apply for a formal remand to enable them to complete their case, an eminent London solicitor was already present on his behalf. Next week Mr. Butcher, K.C., and two junior counsel of growing reputation represented the accused.

But Sir Reginald's prognostications were not fulfilled. How many leaves the police may have turned over, or at what cost to the patient ratepayers, was best known to themselves. But they did not discover the broken stick, nor did Fred admit that it had been found or hidden by him.

A private detective of international reputation, whom Sir Reginald instructed to find the actual murderer, on the assumption that Fred's protestations were to be believed, spent several days of diligent enquiry around Hither Dene, and reported an utter failure, though he did not call it by that name. He said that even an archangel could not find anything unless there were something to find, which sounded reasonable, but did nothing to assist the defence.

Adeline felt that she was failing Fred, it being her part, by all the canons of detective fiction, to discover the lurking murderer. But how was it to be done? She could think of nothing but wandering about the vicinity of the fatal encounter, as though the trees, which had seen all, would yield their secret to her restless prayers. Yet what could she hope to do, unless she should come upon that broken stake? And was she sure, *sure*, that that was what Fred would wish her to do?

So he still said. And so she must still try to believe.

She was not short of occupation, for the publishers were now clamouring for the manuscript of *More Jam for Jane*. If they could get it quickly through the press they did not doubt that they would reach phenomenal sales. She recognised that they asked no more than their due—actually overdue by the terms of her neglected contract. That was another consequence of the three months of continual—and now utterly abortive—crime. And a book which, on its own merits, would have sold fifteen hundred copies of its library edition might now run into six figures because she was the wife of a man charged with murder, and who had been invited to criminality by the Kanwhistle will.

For Mr. Saxton had put the interests of his paper before those of his friends, as she had always known that he would; and the *Morning News* had led the way in revelation, anecdote, and innuendo, in articles which only one who had lived in the flat below them would have been able to write, and which had yet skilfully evaded the law of libel on the one hand, and of contempt of court on the other, as a good journalist should be able to do.

And so she sat at times in the deserted garden of Maidcote Manor, struggling stubbornly to control herself to the light comedy spirit in which the concluding chapters of *More Jam for Jane* must be written, if she were to do justice to her own powers, and with the sombre thought of Fred in his cheerless cell continually, like a chilling wind, piercing the cloak of fancy in which she had wrapped her mind.

At the adjourned hearing on the eighth day, she had attended the little stuffy Kettlewell court, prepared for the ordeal of the witness box, and striving to find comfort in the formidable array of legal talent which Sir Reginald had thrown into the line of battle, but had heard only that the police asked for the adjournment to be continued for a further week, to which Fred's legal advisers had consented, with some demonstration of protest, and after a prolonged whispering among themselves. They disliked, with sound legal instinct, that which they did not understand, and there was no apparent reason for such delay. But with their own case in such deplorable form, and with the accused man pressing for the discovery of an alternative murderer, could they really be serving his interests by hurrying the proceedings on? More decisive than that had been the certainty that the magistrates would not refuse the application, whatever they might urge against it. They felt that they served their client's cause best by agreeing, with some ruffling of the feathers of indignation, and on obtaining a pledge that the case would be opened at the next hearing. The magistrates, considerate to the police, but sympathetic also to the legal fiction that all murderers are in haste to be tried, said that they would sit, on the next occasion, for two consecutive days if necessary, which, it was agreed, would be sufficient for the preliminary hearing. That Fred would be committed for trial was an assumption which even his own counsel felt it would be useless to challenge.

The second adjournment was to Thursday, June 2nd, and it was when Sir Reginald came home, rather later than usual, on the previous Monday evening that he said to Adeline: "We've had a consultation at Butcher's chambers today. He doesn't like the case as it stands, and wants to give your husband some advice, which he is anxious that you should support. I can't tell you anything more because I promised Butcher to leave it to him to put it in his own way. But he looks at it so seriously that, if his advice isn't taken, he is quite likely to return the brief."

"Well, we should still have two others," she answered, with an instinctive dislike to the idea that she should be used to persuade Fred to go against his own judgment, and in a way which, from the manner in which it was being put to her, appeared likely to be of an unattractive kind.

"I'm afraid that is hardly the customary sequel to such an action on the part of a leading counsel, and, in this case, I understand that there is absolute unanimity among the legal gentlemen concerned."

"Well, I suppose they ought to know best, if it's like that. I think I could get Fred to do anything in reason if I were convinced myself, but otherwise I should have a poor chance. What do you want me to do?"

"I want you to come into town tomorrow afternoon. You'd better come to Leadenhall Street first, and have tea with me at the bank, and we'll go to Butcher's chambers from there."

"Well, of course I'll come. I don't know how to thank you for all you're doing."

"I can't forget," Sir Reginald answered, "that the thing wouldn't have happened at all if I hadn't asked you here. But I can't say that anything I've done yet has been much good to your husband and you. It really depends on this conference tomorrow. Butcher has managed something which may be very important. And it is the sort of thing which is best understood without being put into plain words, so if he gives you a hint, you can understand that he means all he says, and a bit more."

"You mean that if Fred does as he says he knows of something that will get him off?"

"No, I'm sorry that I didn't mean that. Perhaps I've said too much already. But I want you to take Butcher's advice very seriously. By the way, I've asked Mr. Jellipot to be present. It seemed excusable, as he is acting in relation to the Kanwhistle will, from which all the trouble came."

"You mean Mr. Jellipot agrees, and he's to be there to help persuade me?"

"No, he knows nothing of Butcher's advice as yet. But I feel sure that he will approve, and it did occur to me that you might be influenced by that."

"Yes, I think I should."

Adeline thought again that it must be a distasteful pill if it were anticipated that so much effort would be required to induce her to swallow it, but she said no more, resolving that she would hear with an open mind.

Mr. Butcher's chambers were not in the older and more beautiful Temple buildings, but in a new block of offices which looked down on and across the river. His own room was lofty and spacious, which was fortunate on this occasion, for there are many chambers of equally famous barristers which would have failed to accommodate the assembly to which Sir Reginald and Adeline were introduced on this occasion, attracted both by the interest of the case itself and by the depth of Sir Reginald's purse, which assured the barristers and solicitors engaged upon it that, when it should be over, they would not be sent empty away.

Mr. Butcher was a ponderous man with a deep voice. Without his wig and gown he reminded Adeline of a wholesale fish merchant whom she had once met. Perhaps the resemblance (for the fish merchant had been an unattractive character) tended to prejudice her mind, but she forgot such feelings as the impact of a massive though unsympathetic intellect bore her down. She felt that Mr. Butcher, K.C., might care nothing for her or Fred, but he cared much for the briefs he took and the reputation he held.

As he shook hands with her he gave her one concentrated glance at which she felt as one who is weighed, measured, and put into her place in a problem of which all other factors have been already assessed.

She might have been even more intimidated by that formidable presence and the obsequious legal gentlemen who surrounded it, had it not been for the friendly company of Sir Reginald, who was not likely to be overawed by any assembly of mortal men, and the sight of Mr. Jellipot, seated unobtrusively at the farther side of the room. But she forgot herself in the realisation that they were all there in the interests of Fred's defence, and that there was something of vital moment to him which was to be said, and on which she was to decide. That was before Mr. Butcher began.

He addressed himself to her, not only by name, but with the steady gaze of his piercing eyes, as he might have done to a jury he had determined to win.

"We have asked you here, Mrs. Corder," he said, "because we are agreed that your husband is in a position the seriousness of which he does not entirely appreciate, and which can only be met, and its consequences mitigated, if he will take the advice of his experienced advocates, which we are very largely relying upon you to persuade him to do.

"The defence, as we have it now, the bald assertion that he did no more than strike one blow with a rotten stick, would, in any event, be of an almost hopeless character. But if that broken weapon could be produced—if it should appear to have been adequate to have inflicted the frontal, but not the more serious injury—then the absence of any more formidable weapon upon the scene of the encounter, and some other subordinate circumstances into which I need not enter, would have given us a faint chance. It would have depended upon whether we were faced by an intelligent jury, which, fortunately for those who are so accused, is not always the case. But in the absence of that stick—"

Adeline, thinking she knew what was coming, and conscious of its utter futility, found courage to interrupt.

"It's no use asking me to persuade him to say where the stick is. I'm certain he doesn't know."

"If you would kindly listen to me with a little further patience, Mrs. Corder! We are not asking you to do that. We are satisfied that he either does not know where it is, or that it is in his own interest that it should not be found.

"It may, of course, be discovered by others, in which case we must face an altered position, but the present is one which we shall not ourselves disturb.

"What I want you to put very seriously to your husband is the desirability of pleading guilty to the minor charge to the charge of manslaughter, which, Sir Reginald tells me, he is sure that the magistrates would accept. In that case the committal would be in time for the trial to come on at the Lewes Assize, before Mr. Justice Brightman, who is not of an unsympathetic temperament, in which event we are agreed"—he looked round the room as though he were announcing an opinion derived from the collective wisdom of the assembled lawyers—"we are agreed that the sentence would not be more than three years."

"You want him to plead guilty to manslaughter?" Adeline echoed blankly. "You mean he's to say he killed him, but he had some excuse? But he's sure he didn't. I couldn't possibly ask him to say that."

"Mrs. Corder, I am sorry to have to put it to you in this way, but have you thought what the alternative might be?"

Feeling as though these men around her were cruel judges rather than Fred's legal advocates, and that she was lonely in his defence, she answered desperately: "Yes, of course. The jury might believe the truth. They might acquit him of something he didn't do."

"In our considered judgment, Mrs. Corder, if he be tried for murder, he will almost certainly be found guilty. There is only one sentence for that. There might—there probably would—be a reprieve. The alternative to the capital sentence would be fifteen years."

He had spoken harshly, almost impatiently, of deliberate purpose, for he saw the stubborn unwillingness of Adeline's expression, and he was determined to bear it down, as he was clearly of opinion that it would be in his client's interest to do; besides that, it would relieve him from a line of defence in which he had no confidence, and which it would be no advantage to his own reputation to put before the court.

It was, in any event, an important advantage for the case to be heard before Mr. Justice Brightman. English judges are of high character and impartial equity, although there has usually been one of each generation notorious for the savagery of the sentences which he inflicts. But they have personal differences, which inevitably become known to those who plead before them. One is particularly hard upon robbery with violence. One will always pass severe sentences for long firm frauds. One regards the robbery of a church poor box with particular horror. There was one in quite recent years who condoned abortion, though it is fair to say that his mind was probably failing. Mr. Justice Brightman had an antipathy for those who molest women, and had been known to bind over their chastisers when another judge would probably have considered six or nine months in the second division a merciful sentence.

And, in this instance, Mr. Butcher was not merely guessing. He had lunched with Sir Richard Brightman and discussed the case with him in discreet but sufficient words. Such things are done, though they are not spoken abroad. In the absence of malice or bribery in its subtler forms, they may, on balance, do more good than harm. Mr. Butcher felt that he had done much for a difficult client in an unsatisfactory case. If he would not listen to reason now, his fate must be on his own head, and he must find another advocate to make a fool of himself with a lame tale.

"I want you to consider, Mrs. Corder," he went on, "that your husband's denial that he struck what was certainly the fatal blow will alienate sympathy from him if he should go into the witness box. It will also preclude him from giving an account of how that blow was struck, such as might put a better construction upon it than it will otherwise bear. It is a position which makes him an unsatisfactory witness, who ought to be kept out of the box if possible. Yet, if he plead not guilty, the position will be hopeless if he decline to give his own account of what occurred. A plea of guilty on the minor charge, if it should be accepted by the court, will avert this difficulty.

"You have to consider—it is a point of sinister legal importance which you may not have appreciated—that the encounter did not take place as a necessary and natural consequence of the assault which Kanwhistle made upon yourself. You had escaped from him. You were not seriously injured. Kanwhistle had gone. He was pursued by your husband, who had snatched up a weapon with which, it is not disputed, he struck a violent blow on the head of a weaponless man. When it is added that the man died from a second blow dealt from behind with murderous force, after he had been more or less incapacitated by the first, I think there can be no question that manslaughter is the most merciful verdict for which we can hope. By pleading guilty to that, we give away nothing—nothing at all—which we could otherwise hope to gain. But we may avoid a more serious verdict and a much heavier penalty."

Mr. Butcher had spoken the last sentence with impressive slowness. All eyes were now upon Adeline, waiting for her to reply.

Unwilling to be convinced, but with no adequate answer to the arguments she had heard, she said weakly: "Well, I will talk it over with Fred."

Mr. Caton-Merival, one of Mr. Butcher's juniors, a pleasant-voiced, pleasant-mannered young barrister, said: "We hope, Mrs. Corder, that you will do more than that. We understand that Mr. Corder is reluctant—naturally reluctant—to plead guilty, having the feeling that he was provoked, and that there was justification for what he did. But as a matter of law, we feel that we shall have done the utmost which is possible in his interests if the court can be induced to accept a plea of guilty to the minor charge. And we are relying upon you as the only one who can persuade him to save himself from what must otherwise be a long term of imprisonment."

There was an earnest sincerity in the quietly modulated voice which could not fail to impress her. Sir Reginald added, as though to encourage her to the words which were hard to speak: "You will be taking what we all agree to be the right course, Mrs. Corder, and by giving him that advice you will be rendering it much easier for him."

"I should like," she said, "to hear what Mr. Jellipot thinks."

"I have no doubt," Mr. Butcher was quick to say, "that Mr. Jellipot sees as we all do. It is a matter on which it is hardly possible for experienced legal opinion to differ."

"If Mr. Jellipot agrees that it's the best way—" she said, in evident inclination to yield, if she should find her last hope of support gone.

Mr. Jellipot was slow to reply to the appeal in her eyes. The room became silent, its attention concentrated upon him.

"The opinions which you have heard," he said diffidently, "are from those who are more experienced than I in the administration of the criminal law, and are of far more value than mine would be likely to be."

"You mean that you don't agree?"

"No." Mr. Jellipot spoke more firmly now. "That was not what I said, or meant. I have no doubt that the advice you have received is logically sound. And," he added, turning slightly to Mr. Butcher, "I am sure that the learned counsel concerned, in opening this avenue of escape from the worst consequences of a rash act, have done the utmost they could for the client who has put his interests in their hands."

Adeline frowned over this. "All the same," she said, "you don't think it's a right thing for me to persuade Fred to do."

"You must please, Mrs. Corder, not attribute opinions to me which I have not expressed."

"You haven't given me," she said stubbornly, "what I call a plain reply." Mr. Jellipot hesitated for a moment too brief for remark. He saw that if he should say frankly what was in his mind, it would be likely to influence her to refuse, and he was not sure of what the consequences might be. Quite probably that Frederick Corder would spend more than ten years in a felon's cell, while his lonely wife would curse herself for having listened to him.

175

He saw also that a decided refusal might result in Mr. Butcher throwing up the brief, less than forty-eight hours before the case would have its preliminary hearing.

"If you really place such a mistaken value upon my opinion," he said, "I must naturally be the more careful, and the more exact, in any advice which I may give. I would prefer, under such circumstances, to put it in writing, so that it remain on record, and beyond dispute."

"You will appreciate," Mr. Butcher said, with hardly controlled impatience, "that the matter is one of urgency."

"I am asked," Mr. Jellipot replied, with the increasing firmness which the actual crossing of verbal swords would commonly give to a deprecatory manner, "for an opinion which I have no wish to give, but which I feel I cannot refuse. I appreciate such urgency as the position has, and Mrs. Corder can be assured that she will hear from me without a moment of avoidable delay."

"Well, that's that," Sir Reginald said briskly, judging that there would be no advantage in further words. "I've no doubt that Mrs. Corder will think over all that has been said, and I feel sure that it will have the support which Mr. Jellipot has already expressed."

As he spoke, he rose, and Adeline rose at his side.

A feeling that she was showing an ungracious stubbornness to these gentlemen so much more competent to judge such an issue than she could be, and whose services were being given, if not freely, at least free of charge to her, caused her to look round, and say: "I'm sorry to seem awkward, but if you think what it means to me...!"

Mr. Butcher held out his hand. He said, with a ponderous benignity: "You have the sympathy of all of us, Mrs. Corder. And I am sure you will show the courage which the position requires."

That was one way of putting it. Was it really courage she lacked, she thought doubtfully, and, if so, for what?

As she left the room, Mr. Butcher looked round for Mr. Jellipot. He did not think, after what that diffident-mannered solicitor had said, that he would advise the woman to defy the opinion of all her regularly constituted legal advisers. But he was not sure. And he meant to have no doubt. A plain word that he would retire from the case if his advice were not taken should be sufficient. But Mr. Jellipot had withdrawn from the room.

CHAPTER XXXIV.

MR. BUTCHER WILL HAVE HIS WAY

Mr. Jellipot wrote:

Dear Mrs. Corder,

The unanimous opinion of your eminent counsel, and of the solicitors who instruct them, is one from which I should dissent, if at all, with extreme hesitation; but the question does not arise, as it is one with which I fundamentally agree.

Mr. Corder's denial that he struck the second and fatal blow is unsupported by any evidence, and is inherently improbable. Almost any jury would disbelieve it.

The alleged fragility of the stake with which he armed himself for the pursuit of Mr. Kanwhistle is supported to some extent by your observation and that of Lady Crowe, but the importance of this evidence is discounted by the fact that it cannot be produced, and that it is not necessary to conclude that the same weapon was used for the infliction of both blows, especially as one appears to have been struck slightly later, from a different position, and probably under different circumstances from the first.

It is less improbable that two weapons should have been used than that two separate assailants, unknown to each other, and actuated by no common object, should have been concerned in the attack. And whoever removed one weapon from the scene of the encounter could have removed two with approximately equal facility.

You will appreciate that, in stating these conclusions, I am not questioning the truth of Mr. Corder's assertion of his own innocence, but I am advising you that it is not likely to be believed.

I am also of opinion that it is a defence which will tend to alienate such sympathy as might be won by what would be considered to be a more truthful admission, and it would have other disadvantages.

You have, I think, been rightly advised that there would be a serious risk of a verdict of wilful murder being recorded, which, as you may know, allows less discretionary power to the court in the severity of the sentence which it pronounces than is the case with the alternative verdict of manslaughter, to which Mr. Corder is advised to plead guilty.

There remains, however, a quite separate question. If I were acting for Mr. Corder, and were as convinced of his innocence as you have stated yourself to be, I should hesitate to advise him to plead guilty to that which he had not done, even though I should expect that a much lighter sentence would result.

You, having so much at stake, may feel justified in persuading him to that course; or he may readily adopt it, if he be convinced of its expediency. But it appears to be a matter for your own decisions.

Very sincerely yours,

E. E. Jellipot

P.S. You will, of course, understand that there is no criticism of your legal advisers implied in the above penultimate paragraph, as their confidence in Mr. Corder's innocence may be less absolute than your own.

This letter, posted in London early on Wednesday morning, arrived by the late afternoon post. Adeline read it with no more satisfaction because it articulated the doubts which had distressed her own mind. She showed it to Lady Crowe—she had become Evelyn now—who said: "Mr. Jellipot means that, if he really did it, he would be wise to plead guilty to manslaughter. But if he's sure he didn't, he ought to stick to that, even though it means spending half his life in jail."

"Yes," Adeline agreed, "that's what I take it to mean. And he's right too." But there was no comfort in that.

"It's maddening," she went on, "that the days pass and we're doing nothing. I don't mean that anything could have been tried that hasn't. What I owe to Sir Reginald and you is more than I could ever repay. Money'd be no use at all"—It seemed that she was to have plenty of that; her publishers, being unable to bring out *More Jam for Jane* to satisfy the instant public demand, had revived *When Maud Went Home*, which faced her now in every bookshop window or bookstall at which she gazed—"But it's been like hammering on a blank wall. People won't look because they're sure there's nothing to find. I don't believe that private detective ever really tried. He just wandered round to make excuse enough for taking his cheque. And if someone else did it, as they certainly did, there must be *some* way of proving the truth. Well, I shall see what Fred says. I shan't persuade him one way or other. I shall just leave it to him."

Evelyn agreed that that was the best thing to do. She had the same feeling as Adeline that the detective's work had been of a too perfunctory kind—that the belief that Fred had struck that fatal blow from behind had been too general and too firmly held for any search for an alternative murderer to be seriously made. And though she might share Adeline's conviction, she knew that even Sir Reginald was disposed to attribute her opinion to sentimental bias.

Sir Reginald came home later, and read Mr. Jellipot's letter.

"Just," he said, "what I had expected he'd write. Sound, as he always is. And got the lawyers' vice of never saying a thing in two words if two hundred will do equally well, even worse than most of them have. But there's one thing he hasn't mentioned, for all that, though it oughtn't to be needed to tip the scale.

"If your husband gets out in three years—it will be less than that by a few months if he doesn't commit any breach of discipline such as poisoning the governor's soup—with nothing worse against him than having served a sentence for manslaughter for defending his wife—he won't find many will be against him for that, and he'll do as well at the book jacket trade as before. There are three firms of publishers who bank with the L. & N., and they've all got overdrafts swelling up like balloons, and I'd give him introductions to them that they'd be very foolish to disregard. Not that he'd need anything of the kind. And he'd have those sketches of Maidcote Manor to finish for me first. He wouldn't be too late for them. I know Jellipot thinks, at the price I'm asking, I shall be lucky if I sell it in twenty years."

"I can't understand why there should be any difficulty," Adeline said. "I think it's a lovely house."

"Well, there is. And I can't say that I don't see why. But what I'm trying to tell you is that if there's a verdict of murder, he won't be out for ten or twelve years, which is a big slice of a man's life to lose, and when he does—well, murder's got an uglier sound. He'll be welcome here, if I'm alive, as I hope to be. But he'll have more to live down.

"But as to having his own tale believed, and getting off free— well, I heard this from Butcher this morning. Those articles in the *Morning News* have been read where you'd expect, and, if he goes into the witness box, Cathcart"—Cathcart, K.C., was the prosecuting counsel whom the Crown had briefed in reply to the legal talent provided by Sir Reginald for the defence—"means to ask some questions about that codicil, and whether he tried to win the Kanwhistle stakes. I don't want to know what the answer will be to that. But it's just as well that he should know what he'll have to face, and be ready with the reply."

"Yes," Adeline said, even less cheerfully than before, "I'll tell him that. Thanks for letting me know."

She turned the conversation rather hurriedly from a subject concerning which she neither wished to be frank nor to lie.

In the morning she saw Fred under the conditions of grudged and imperfect privacy which are the particular disgrace of the English prison system in its treatment of accused persons, and she found that Sir Reginald had actually provided her with the final and decisive argument.

Fred was difficult, as she had expected. He said that nothing would induce him to plead guilty to what he was sure that he had not done. He appeared to find it hard to believe that the truth could be told in vain. He said that, even if he should be unjustly condemned, he would probably come out in less than three years, and he would be released without having disgraced himself by his own plea.

It was only when Adeline told him that he must expect to be questioned upon his three months' record of crime—"and it won't be any use denying it, Fred. They're sure to ask me too, and I certainly shouldn't"—that he wavered.

"I've been thinking," he said, "that they wouldn't be allowed to bring that in. And I'm sure I've heard that no one need give answers that incriminate himself."

"But Sir Reginald says that Mr. Butcher thinks there's a way they could. It's because of how the two things are all mixed up. And if you refuse to answer, because of incriminating yourself, it will be just the same as confessing, and they'll probably think you've done things a lot worse than you have."

"I could say just what they were, for that matter."

"And be arrested for some of them if you *did* get off on this charge, more likely than not."

"Yes, I see." With a gesture of weariness, he suddenly gave up the battle. "You win. You can tell Butcher that, if he sees no better hope when the prosecution have closed their case, he can withdraw the plea of not guilty, and offer to plead guilty to manslaughter, if that's what he wants me to do. Three years! Well, it's something to know the worst."

She went soon after that, unsure whether she had done well or ill, but yet with some feeling of relief that a decision had been made, and one which would spare Fred the ordeal of the witness box, and the telling of a tale which would be almost certainly disbelieved.

CHAPTER XXXV.

The Unexpected Happens

THERE could be no complaint of the manner in which Mr. Cathcart, K.C., opened his case. He explained the injuries from which Mr. Kanwhistle had died, on which the usual medical evidence would be called. He went into the peculiar relations between the two men—the one who was dead, and the one now in the dock—by the outrageous codicil which the late Miss Kanwhistle had appended to her will. Of course, neither of them was responsible for that. But so it was, by a convergence of circumstance with which the court might not find it necessary to concern itself at this stage of the proceedings, if at all, they met at the house of Sir Reginald Crowe. They—with Mrs. Corder, the wife of the accused—were alone together at Maidcote Manor on the afternoon of the tragedy. As to what happened there, they had a statement signed by the accused which admitted the main facts on which the prosecution relied, denying only that he had struck what must have been the fatal blow.

This statement would be confirmed in some vital particulars by the evidence of Lady Evelyn Crowe, certainly not an unfriendly witness, who would be called by the prosecution. Mrs. Corder had also been subpœnaed, although she could, of course, refuse to give evidence. Probably, however, she would prefer to give her account of the circumstances leading up to the tragedy, as it was the alleged conduct of the murdered man toward herself which was stated by the accused to have been the occasion of an affray which admittedly took place between the two men.

There was no witness of that. The truth must be inferred from the admissions of the accused, the observations of Lady Crowe, the nature of the injuries inflicted, and the reasonable deductions therefrom. So he went on.

To some of those who listened, it seemed that he spoke as one having no heart in what he did, as though he set out a case in which he did not even affect to believe. To others it seemed that this method was the deadlier in its colourless presentation of damning fact. But the absence of the dramatic element, and a certain prolixity which sometimes wandered into actual repetition, had a dulling effect, so that, in the small, crowded, ill-ventilated court, there were those who yawned.

Adeline and Lady Crowe did not hear this opening speech. They were shut away in the witness room. There they sat till the luncheon interval. Mr. Cathcart's speech had been followed by the medical evidence. Fred had no pleasure in hearing that. It is sometimes said in extenuation of such fatalities that the victim's skull was extremely thin, but it appeared that Percival Kanwhistle had had a particularly thick covering for his moderate brain. The blow he had received was one which few men would have survived for an hour. Could it have been inflicted with a wooden stick? Yes, if it were stout enough, and used with sufficient force by a man of average strength. Such as the man now in the dock? Yes, quite possibly.

Then came the luncheon adjournment. Fred was given a good lunch enough, which he ate with appetite. It was the irony of the situation that the evidence which was to convict him would come from no unfriendly lips—would indeed be in his favour, as giving some excuse of passion for what he did. And yet it must be fatal to him, when there was added to it that unbelievable, undeniable fracture of Percy's skull.

All the same, the fact that the witnesses *were* his friends, and that the prosecuting counsel had taken that almost perfunctory tone, reduced the temperature with which he reacted to this drama in which he was so greatly concerned. After all, it was all forecast. You might almost say it was all agreed. Three years! Well, he would live through that. It would be almost as hard for Adeline, waiting alone, as he did not doubt she would do.

After the luncheon interval, Evelyn was called into court. For the next half hour Adeline sat alone, rehearsing to herself what the facts—as far as she could remember them—were. She had not been clear as to how that momentous episode with Percival had begun, even a few hours afterwards. She was less so now. And she must avoid any reference to Fred's career of crime, or Percy's suspicions in that direction. She had not expected to be called by the prosecution. The summons for her attendance had only been served upon her last evening. But she must say what she could for Fred. It would do him no good to refuse. That was Mr. Butcher's opinion. She was to make Percy's conduct to her as bad as she fairly could. (Fairly had not been the learned counsel's word. He had said: "Tell her to lay it on as thick as she likes. They can't cross-examine, she being their witness. And she must make the most of her complaint to Corder. Not about him being called a worm. She'd better leave that out, if she can. But about Kanwhistle's conduct to her.") Well, she must do that, as far as she could without traducing a dead man. And the living surely had the first claim. Who was this coming now? Doubtless, the usher to call her. She must have all her wits for the next hour. To do what she could for Fred. Mr. Jellipot entered the room.

"You will be glad to know," he said, "that it will not be necessary for you to go into the witness box."

"Not necessary?" she echoed vaguely, less relieved by this information than by the tone in which it was said. "But I don't mind doing that, not if it will do Fred any good."

"But it is no longer necessary. The case has gone well enough without that."

"You mean he's pleaded guilty to manslaughter and there won't be anything worse than that?"

"No, I mean something much better. The prosecution have thrown up the case."

"You mean that it's all over? That Fred's *free*?" ("I mustn't faint," she said to herself, "I should look such a fool—such a fool—such an *utter fool*.")

Mr. Jellipot was pouring out a glass of water. "I'm afraid it won't be very palatable," he was saying in his quiet, casual voice. "It looks as though it's stood here for a week."

"It does taste rather stale," she said. "But I'm all right now. It was just at first. It was rather a shock. How did it happen? Where's Fred?"

"You are coming to meet him now. We are all going together to Trees. Inspector Combridge will explain. He has a confession to make. Something you may find rather hard to forgive. But there was some justification for what he did."

"I shouldn't find it hard to forgive anyone now."

"I'm glad to hear that. I am afraid some women would. But I must leave Combridge to explain." He led her as he spoke along the little corridor, out to a square vestibule which was now filled by a curious, chattering crowd that turned its eyes upon her, but was slow to open to let her through, and so to the outer door, before which Sir Reginald's limousine was drawn up. Fred was already in it, and Evelyn, and Inspector Combridge, and Sir Reginald at the wheel.

"Hullo, Fred," she said, "I knew you'd come through all right." She was scarcely aware of her own lie. They drove off through a cheering crowd.

CHAPTER XXXVI.

INSPECTOR COMBRIDGE EXPLAINS

"THE fact is," Inspector Combridge said, when they were all seated in the lounge, and Janet, an intent but disregarded listener, was handing round the tea, and the buttered scones, "I've known Mr. Corder was innocent, I won't say on the first night—I own I was doubtful then—but from very early on the following morning." He turned to Adeline as he said this, as though his apologies and explanations were specially due to her, rather than to the one who was most concerned.

"A few hours before Kanwhistle was killed," he went on, "he told me of an interview he had had in the village, the significance of which he couldn't guess, but which gave me a hope that he had put us on the track of a gang of drug traffickers who have been eluding us for the last two or three years.

"I didn't venture to telephone from here, lest there should be leakage from a crossed wire. I went into Kettlewell. I was called up to London from there, and when I came back, rather late in the evening, I brought a young officer, Detective Riskall, with me—a young man they wouldn't be likely to know—and part of his job was to be keeping an eye on Kanwhistle, because I couldn't be sure whether he had roused Cutmore's suspicions; if he had, we thought his life wouldn't be safe. So you'll understand that I wasn't much surprised when I got back and learned that he had been knocked on the head.

"But the tale, as I heard it first, seemed to point entirely to Mr. Corder, and I thought the two matters were separate, though I wasn't sure. I even had to consider whether he might not be one of the gang, especially as there had been some talk about that codicil having led him to take to a life of crime.

"And you will see that I hadn't anything against Cutmore that I could use. All I'd heard was from Kanwhistle, who couldn't speak.

Whether we should have had enough proof against him even now I'm not sure, if he hadn't made one mistake, in getting hold of the stick, and if I hadn't already set Riskall to watch him if he came out during the night.

"But it was a natural thing for him to do. He couldn't think at that time that there would be the faintest suspicion against himself, and he burnt the only evidence there was that Mr. Corder hadn't had a weapon suitable to cause the injury from which Kanwhistle died.

"Even Kanwhistle, if he had come round, might not have been able to tell who it was who had struck him from behind, if it happened in the most likely way.

"Our theory is that Cutmore was suspicious of Kanwhistle, though in doubt of how far he had given himself away to him. He went to Maidcote Manor that day to remove any trace there might be in the secret cellar of the use to which they put it at times, and—"

"Yes. That's true," Adeline interrupted, "Mr. Kanwhistle went down there, and saw or heard something he didn't like. He came up in a hurry and locked the door."

Inspector Combridge heard this with interest. "That," he said, "is a fresh bit, which fits in. I wonder you didn't mention it earlier."

"But how could I think it had anything to do with it? He said it was rats. It had gone out of my mind entirely, with what happened afterwards, till you made me think of it now."

"Well, perhaps that's natural enough. But it may have been whatever happened down there that made Cutmore resolve that Kanwhistle would be better dead. Though I don't say that it was a premeditated crime.

"What we think is that Cutmore was hiding near when Mr. Corder struck Kanwhistle down, and when he went off for help, and Kanwhistle, feeling a bit better, rose and began to stagger after him, Cutmore saw what he thought to be a chance too good to lose to finish him off, with the certainty that it would be put to Corder's account.

"Anyway, there's no doubt that's what happened. There was a fragment of wood in the wound—a splinter almost too small to see—which came off the bludgeon that Cutmore always carried about."

Inspector Combridge smiled at Mr. Jellipot as he said this: "You see, they always do leave a button or something behind!"

He went on: "From the moment I learnt that Cutmore had removed the stick during the night, I knew what had happened as well as though I had been there. But I'd no proof at all. Absolutely nothing except that Cutmore had picked up that stick, for which he might

187

have made a dozen excuses. No jury would have listened to it for a moment as evidence that he committed the crime.

"And I'd no motive to show, no evidence from any living man that the two had ever met. To show motive of any kind I had to prove Cutmore and his friends to be what they were, and the only chance of doing that was for them to feel sure that we had no suspicions of them, and had made up our minds that Mr. Corder had killed Kanwhistle.

"So I saw that the best thing I could do would be to clear out as quickly as possible.

"We couldn't stop you, Sir Reginald, bringing your own detective down here, but we told him confidentially how the matter stood, and he was careful to leave Cutmore and his wife, and that other old scoundrel Caldwell, alone. You'll find, now the whole thing's over, he'll return your cheque. We've paid him for what he did."

"I thought," Sir Reginald said, "he was rather dumb."

"Well, he did some good work for us while he was here, and it all helped to clear Mr. Corder, though it wasn't what he could report to you at the time.

"But what I've got to tell you is that we made seven arrests during the night and before noon today. We've got the heads of the gang at Eastbourne, as well as those here. They ran the stuff over by speedboat from France, and hid it here till they could unload it in London. We caught them with it, and there'll be six for gaol, and one for the rope.

"It's a queer thing that we hang a man for murder, but not for peddling dope, which is a lot worse. It was thinking of that that made me say to Mr. Jellipot once that I could almost wish that Kanwhistle would die. I meant so that Cutmore would get something more like what he deserves."

"Then I suppose," Evelyn said, "he wasn't a poacher at all?"

"No. It was just a blind to explain his sometimes being about during the night when they were bringing the stuff through. He used to make a habit of wandering round in the early hours, and of course they couldn't catch him at something he didn't do. I expect the game they used to make a show of came from the London market."

"There have been one or two occasions, Combridge," Mr. Jellipot said, "when we have been on different sides, and when, through no ability of my own, but the mere logic of facts, you have felt that—" He paused, as though in a difficulty, very unusual with him, of being unable to select the exact and yet inoffensive word which his thought required. Leaving the sentence unfinished he went on: "I trust you will get very full credit for the ability, discretion, and final

188

success with which you have handled a position of exceptional difficulty. I confess that it was one by which I was entirely baffled."

"Oh, I shall get that all right," Inspector Combridge answered, without enthusiasm. "There's no lack of that when you pull it off. It's when you do just as well, or better, and things go wrong, that you get kicks that you don't deserve. But for the chance of what Kanwhistle said to me, I might have come unstuck in this case as likely as not. And I don't like to think where Mr. Corder might have been then. As it is, he'll be able to claim some compensation from the H.O., and if he'll take a hint from me, which he mustn't repeat, he'll open his mouth wide."

"I suppose," Mr. Jellipot said reflectively, "that you won't want the public to know that you went on prosecuting an innocent man, however good the excuse may have seemed to you. Yes, I think he should."

"If Fred listens to me," Adeline spoke with decision, "he won't claim anything more than Sir Reginald has spent. I'm not at all sure that we got more than we deserved, and it's pleasant to think that it's done some good in the end."

Fred, who, in fact, had done nothing but listen up to that point, opened his mouth at last. He said that would be all right with him.

CHAPTER XXXVII.

MISS KANWHISTLE'S FINAL JOKE

IT was about fourteen months after Miss Kanwhistle's death that Mr. Jellipot received, among the morning letters which he had an obstinate habit of opening himself, however heavy the post became as his practice grew, a sealed foolscap envelope addressed to him in the handwriting of the deceased lady, and bearing the E.C.2 postmark.

It contained a will, properly signed and witnessed, and dated two days later than the objectionable codicil which she had appended to the one which Mr. Jellipot had drawn. The envelope contained no other communication, and though it was an easy guess that Miss Kanwhistle had entrusted it to someone before her death, with instructions that it should not be posted until she had been dead for the period mentioned, nothing was ever discovered on this point.

Mr. Jellipot read this document with care, while a pile of letters of various urgency and importance lay unopened before him. He then locked it in a drawer of his desk, and put it resolutely from his mind until the day's business was done.

At 4:00 P.M. he drew it out and examined the signature with care, even comparing it under a microscope with signatures of the deceased lady which were unquestionably genuine.

Satisfied on this point, he copied out the names and addresses of the two attesting witnesses, and instructed a clerk to seek them out and question them as to whether, and, if so, under what circumstances they recollected signing the document.

The following morning he learnt that they were both living, that they appeared to be reputable persons, and that, separately interviewed, they had given the same account of the occasion on which Miss Kanwhistle had asked them to witness her will.

Naturally, they had not read it, nor had it occurred to them that it was not the will which had been proved at her death. They both denied knowing anything of the document from the day on which they had attached their signatures at Miss Kanwhistle's request.

After receiving this report, Mr. Jellipot read the will again. It was written in a phraseology which was at times distressing to his legal mind, but the writer had evidently drawn freely upon the example of the previous one which he had prepared, and the most critical examination resulted in a half-reluctant decision that it was legally sound, and could not be ignored. The result was that he wrote to Mrs. Corder asking her to give him a call, if she could conveniently do so, on the following morning.

The Corders were still living in Bloomsbury Street, though Adeline, with over £2,000 in the bank as the profit of her last year's sales and a deposit on the signing of a new contract, had thought longingly of a cottage in such a setting as Hither Dene. But Bloomsbury Street was convenient for Fred, and she had enough sense to see that her royalties were not likely to rise again to the level of the last year. Reluctantly she had let the dream go.

She could not foresee that the novel on which she was now engaged, with the intriguing title of *She Cuts for Deal*, could hold by merit that which had been won in another way.

She did not hesitate, when she received Mr. Jellipot's letter, to put her work aside, and set out for the city, hoping audibly as she did so that there could be no more trouble over that wretched Kanwhistle affair. But how was that possible? And Mr. Jellipot was one whom it was always a pleasure to her to meet.

So she went in good spirits enough, and was pleasantly, though rather gravely, received.

When she was seated in the low and comfortable client's chair at the solicitor's left side, he told her with his usual lucidity, of the will which had come so singularly to his hand, and of the steps he had already taken to confirm its validity. "It is," he concluded, "a rather curious document."

As he paused upon this statement, she asked: "Is it any good, after this length of time? I should have thought—"

The tone of the unfinished sentence implied that, whatever its contents might be, she desired nothing more than to hear that it was a worthless document. It was a feeling with which he could very readily sympathise, but that understanding could not deflect the integrity of his reply.

"The mere fact," he said, "that a will is not discovered until twelve months after the death of the testator cannot adversely affect its validity, whether the delay be inadvertent or by deliberate malice. The position is rather peculiar in the present instance, because there is at least inferential internal evidence that it has been sent to me at this date by the deliberate plan of the testator herself.

"It is evident that if anyone were to plan that a succession of discordant wills should be disclosed at long intervals over a period of years after his death, an intolerable position would arise, and I suppose that an application to the Court for relief under such circumstances could be successfully made. It is a possibility to which I have given some thought during the last twenty-four hours, and I should be tedious if I were to tell you all the contingencies I have visualised, and the conclusions to which they led me.

"There is one difficulty which would often arise, but which fortunately does not in this instance. Mr. Kanwhistle, as you know, died intestate, and apart from certain sums too small to be relevant to the present issue, I had not yet felt that the moment had arrived at which I could properly make a final distribution of his estate.

"Fortunately also, he had, as you also know, substantial means apart from Miss Kanwhistle's money, with which alone we are now concerned.

"But I have not yet told you of the provisions of the will which is now before us. They are briefly these: 'In the event of Mr. Kanwhistle having paid over, or having given me instructions to pay over, a sum of ten thousand pounds to Mr. Frederick Corder, before this will came into my hands, it is to be of no effect'...."

"You mean that if Fred had done the year of crime, he was to have the ten thousand, but no more?"

"Yes. It appears to go beyond that. If Mr. Kanwhistle had made an unconditional payment of that sum, as you may recall that I proposed to him that he should do, the remainder of the inheritance would have been his. As it is, the whole estate is left without reservation to you."

"To *me*?"

"Yes. By a reasoning which I confess I am unable to follow as clearly as I should like to do, Miss Kanwhistle appears to have advised herself that the position as it now is will have demonstrated that neither of her nephews would be a worthy heir. She says also that she had read a book entitled *Pulling Barbara's Leg*, of which I conclude that you are the authoress—"

"Yes. It was the first book I wrote. It was a silly book."

"So she says. She implies that anyone who wrote such a book would need help. I am inclined to doubt whether everything from Miss Kanwhistle should be taken literally."

"I know what she said couldn't. Fred would have got on better with her if he'd been quicker to see that."

"So I can suppose."

"And you mean that this money is all mine?"

"Yes, I can say that with some confidence. The only risk you have is that Mr. Kanwhistle's heirs may dispute the will. I doubt that they could do it successfully, and from what I know of them, it is a contingency which I can advise you to disregard. They are not poor. They are numerous, so that their individual benefits would not be great. I should advise them that it would be a litigation which, at best, would dissipate the estate in costs, and, at the worst, involve them in heavy unprofitable expense. Incidentally, the amount you will receive will be much more than would come to them, as estate duty will not have to be paid for a second time."

"Well, I suppose I ought to be glad, but somehow anything connected with that wretched affair—"

As she frowned over the unfinished sentence Adeline looked most unlike the inheritrix of eighty thousand unexpected pounds. But then a look of questioning eagerness came suddenly to her eyes.

"I haven't heard anything about Maidcote Manor lately," she said. "Is it sold?"

"No. I believe not."

"Then I can buy it?"

"You wish me to put forward an offer on your behalf?"

"I want you to buy it for me. I'll leave all that to you."

"It is a position of trust which will oblige me to tell Sir Reginald that he is asking at least a thousand too much."

But Adeline scarcely heard, and cared nothing at all. In imagination she was already furnishing the dining room, and she knew where she could get just the rugs she would need for the great hall—

She went out to a smiling world.

ABOUT THE AUTHOR

SYDNEY FOWLER WRIGHT (1874-1965) penned over seventy volumes of science fiction, fantasy, classic mysteries, historical novels, poetry, and non-fiction, many of them being published by the Borgo Press Imprint of Wildside Press.

www.ingramcontent.com/pod-product-compliance
Lightning Source LLC
Chambersburg PA
CBHW032009240626
47153CB00003B/1181